PRAISE FOR
THE KEEPERS OF METSAN VALO

"Wendy Webb once again spins a magical web in *The Keepers of Metsan Valo*, weaving Nordic folklore, family legacy, and the bonds that unite us to each other and to the natural world. She is the sorceress of Lake Superior. Get ready to be ensnared!"

—Carol Goodman, two-time Mary Higgins Clark Award–winning author of *The Lake of Dead Languages* and *The Stranger Behind You*

"A novel taut with threats and secrets, family lore, and folktales. Who—or what—truly guards and keeps the magnificent house and grounds of Metsan Valo? That is the question that thrums through the novel. And who—or what—is threatening and haunting the family who calls it home? Dark, brooding, and mysterious, as all good gothics should be. Loved it."

—Kim Taylor Blakemore, author of *After Alice Fell* and *The Companion*

PRAISE FOR
THE HAUNTING OF BRYNN WILDER

"The action builds to a satisfying and uplifting ending . . . Webb consistently entertains."

—*Publishers Weekly*

"Endearing and greatly readable . . . [a] tale that is both warm and poignant."

—*Kirkus Reviews*

"Webb's chilling tale of a woman running from a tragic loss will put a spell on you."

—E! Online

"Prepare to lose yourself in Wendy Webb's lusciously written *The Haunting of Brynn Wilder*."

—POPSUGAR

"Enchanting."

—*The Nerd Daily*

"Wendy Webb weaves a searing gothic tale with elements of horror, mystery, and romance . . . It is incredibly absorbing and atmospheric."

—Bookreporter

"Wendy Webb is a rising voice in thrillers, and we can't wait to see what she does next."

—CrimeReads

"Suspenseful and engrossing, *The Haunting of Brynn Wilder* is a ghost story, a love story, and a chilling fireside tale in one. Readers will be drawn in from the first page, and they won't want to stop until they read the eerie conclusion, probably in the wee hours of the night."

—Simone St. James, *New York Times* bestselling author of *The Sun Down Motel*

"Evocative and beautifully haunting, Wendy Webb's latest transports you to a location you'll soon want to call home, in a story you won't want to put down. It's no exaggeration to call this the standout gothic novel of the year."

—Darcy Coates, *USA Today* bestselling author of *The Haunting of Ashburn House*

"A haunting tale of grief and loss that is beautifully layered with new beginnings and woven into a gothic ghost story both bone chilling and heartwarming."

—Melissa Payne, author of *The Secrets of Lost Stones*

PRAISE FOR
DAUGHTERS OF THE LAKE

"Simultaneously melancholy and sweet at its core."

—*Kirkus Reviews*

"Well-delineated characters and a suspenseful plot make this a winner."

—*Publishers Weekly*

"*Daughters of the Lake* has everything you could want in a spellbinding read: unexpected family secrets, ghosts, tragic love stories, intertwined fates."

—Refinery29

"Perfect for anyone who loves a good ghost story that bleeds into the present day."

—*Health*

"*Daughters of the Lake* is gothic to its core, a story of ghostly revenge, of wronged parties setting history right."

—*Star Tribune*

"*Daughters of the Lake* provides an immersive reading experience to those who love ghostly mysteries, time travel, and lovely descriptions."

—*New York Journal of Books*

"*Daughters of the Lake* is an alchemical blend of romance, intrigue, ancestry, and the supernatural."

—Bookreporter

"Eerie, atmospheric, and mesmerizing."

—*Novelgossip*

"Haunting and heartbreaking . . . A masterful work of suspense . . ."

—*Midwest Book Review*

"In Wendy Webb's entrancing *Daughters of the Lake*, dreams open a door between the dead and the living, a lake spirit calls to a family of gifted women, and a century-old murder is solved under the cover of fog. This northern gothic gem is everything that is delicious, spooky, and impossible to put down."

—Emily Carpenter, author of *Burying the Honeysuckle Girls*, *The Weight of Lies*, and *Every Single Secret*

"The tentacles of the past reach out to threaten Kate Granger in this atmospheric tale set on the shores of Lake Superior. Filled with all the intrigue of old houses and their long-buried secrets, this gothic tale will make you shiver."

—Elizabeth Hall, bestselling author of *Miramont's Ghost*

"Wendy Webb's deftly woven tale hits all the right notes. A lost legacy of lake spirits, restless ghostly figures, and a past shrouded in fog and regret blend in delicious harmony in *Daughters of the Lake*. The queen of northern gothic does it again with this quintessential ghost story [that's] every bit as compelling and evocative as her fans have come to expect."

—Eliza Maxwell, bestselling author of *The Unremembered Girl*

THE
STROKE
OF
WINTER

OTHER BOOKS BY WENDY WEBB

THE STROKE OF WINTER

A NOVEL

WENDY WEBB

Text copyright © 2022 by Wendy Webb

Published by Lake Union Publishing, Seattle

www.apub.com

Amazon, the Amazon logo, and Lake Union Publishing are trademarks of Amazon.com, Inc., or its affiliates.

ISBN-13: 9781542037600
ISBN-10: 1542037603

Cover design by Damon Freeman

Printed in the United States of America

To my lobster, Mary Gallegos.

PROLOGUE

The painter awakened, his head pounding. He was sprawled out on the floor of his studio, his clothes a damp tangle around him, a paintbrush still clutched in his hand.

He pushed himself up into a sitting position and rubbed his bleary eyes, the room coming into focus. A ray of hazy, dusty sunshine streamed in through the windowpanes. An empty bottle of wine lay on its side, a glass broken into shards next to it. The wooden floor was splotched with paint, the colors blending into a mosaic.

What in the world . . . ? He stared at the paintbrush in his hand, turning it around, slowly. Red, streaked with black. He dropped it as though it were on fire.

He scrambled to his feet and whirled around. What was this? How had he gotten here? Why was he here? He didn't remember coming into the studio. He wouldn't have. Not after what had happened. He was done with painting. He had made that clear to himself. Yet here he was.

He ran a hand through his hair, straining to reach back in his mind to piece together the previous day. There was lunch with his friend at the Boat Club in Salmon Bay. Yes. He remembered that. The drive back to Wharton. Yes. Twists and turns. Then what? He had read a book on the porch that afternoon, hadn't he? Opened a bottle of wine. Yes, it was coming back to him now. It had been a nice day.

But . . . what of dinner? What of the evening? It was all a blank. A great empty void.

He groaned as his head pounded. Aspirin. He needed aspirin. And his mouth felt and tasted like a hamster had died in there. He crossed the room to pour a glass of water from the tap in the bathroom, his hands shaking.

That was when he saw the canvases. Four of them. Or was it five? Could he possibly have painted all those in one night? It couldn't be. He squinted to get a better look. His stomach seized up into knots as he slowly walked closer, one short slow step after another. It felt like he was walking through quicksand.

When he focused on the paintings, his eyes grew wide as he realized what he was seeing. The horror of it hit him like a wave from the icy lake. What had he done?

Oh no. Dear God, no.

CHAPTER ONE

The snow came out of nowhere. Whiteout conditions bore down on Amethyst Bell as she drove from Salmon Bay back to Wharton on what had been a clear December day. The snow was coming down in sheets, the howling wind whipping it sideways with a fury. Amethyst couldn't see the hood of her car, let alone past it. Anything could be out there in her path. A deer. A dog. A person.

She silently cursed the holiday decorations she had driven to Salmon Bay to buy. Today of all days.

This stretch of roadway was precarious under normal conditions, with a steep, rocky cliff on the lakeside that had seen more than its fair share of accidents over the years. Local legends abounded about the area. People in Wharton said a shroud of evil hung in the air there, a menacing energy that lured motorists over the side with a treacherous siren song.

But Amethyst shrugged off those old tales. She had driven this road hundreds of times on her way to and from her family's vacation home in Wharton. She'd never been tempted to veer off the cliff, even if she always felt an uneasy tingling up her spine as she drove by it.

Strangeness in the air notwithstanding, she knew she was in a practical sort of danger then, not a haunted one. There were no gas stations, stores, wayside rests, or other places where she could safely stop the car, and she very much wanted—needed—to pull over. She couldn't see anything but white. But stopping too close to the roadway in whiteout conditions might mean someone wouldn't see her and could hit her from behind. Too far off it, and she could go over the cliff. With no better option, she inched along, using her memory as her eyes. A turn here, a straightaway there. She held on to the wheel so tightly her fingers ached.

After what seemed like an eternity, she took the familiar sharp right turn into Wharton and exhaled a breath she hadn't realized she'd been holding. A great wave of relief washed over her as she finally rounded the corner of her street. She pulled into her driveway, resting her forehead on the steering wheel as her heart raced. She had made it. She was okay.

She snapped her head up as she heard the yowl of a police siren and could make out the blue and red lights of a squad car disappearing into the whiteness. It was headed up the road toward the cliff. She shuddered, wondering if someone had gone over.

Amethyst grabbed her shopping bags and opened the car door, stepping out into the wind. Her feet sank into at least six inches of snow. Maybe more. Icy pellets punished the skin on her face as she hurried to her front door, closing her eyes against the fury of it.

A memory struck her just then. Amethyst had grown up hearing stories about legendary Lake Superior blizzards, of people losing their way in the blinding whiteness, becoming lost in their own yards, unable to get from their barns to the house and freezing out there. Thinking of them, those poor souls, she was grateful to be standing at her own side door.

Inside, she flipped the light switch. Nothing. She groaned and set her bags on the kitchen table. It wasn't surprising to find the electricity out in a storm this fierce. But she noticed that all her window shades on the main floor were open, and the bluish hue of the snow outside washed through the rooms of the house. It was never pitch dark in the winter here. The snow lit up the night.

Amethyst—or Tess, as she had been called much of her life because of her childhood inability to pronounce her own name: *Ama-tess*, she'd say—made her way into the living room and crossed to the fireplace. She had laid it with logs and kindling that morning, thinking she might enjoy a fire after dinner. Taking one of the long matches from the box on the mantel, she was grateful for her foresight. She lit the match and touched the flame to the dry twigs. They crackled and burned, spreading to the logs in moments. The fire settled into a slow burn, illuminating the room with a soft glow.

Tess walked through the main floor lighting candles, first around the living room, with its high ceilings, dark woodwork, and original hardwood floors. An overstuffed sofa and love seat sat positioned in front of the fireplace, a giant ottoman between them. Books were strewn here and there on end tables.

She wandered into the drawing room, which her parents had turned into a library and study years before, then on to the music room, where a Steinway grand piano was the focal point. She loved the grand dining room with its table that sat ten and a built-in buffet where Tess's grandparents' crystal glassware would sparkle in the afternoon sun, sending out prisms of light all over the room.

But the heart of the home was the kitchen, which still had its massive AGA stove, a fireplace with two well-used armchairs on either side of it, a scrubbed wooden table by the wall of windows, generations of beloved cookbooks, and copper pots hanging from wrought-iron hooks. There were modern updates, too, like the dishwasher, the enormous stainless-steel fridge, and a second oven and stovetop that came in handy when feeding a crowd.

Soon, the main floor was aglow. *This isn't so bad,* Tess thought. *It's pretty.*

What to do now? Tess grabbed an afghan and snuggled on the bench by the bay window in the living room that looked out onto the front porch and the yard beyond. She curled her legs underneath her and gazed out into the whiteness. It was snowing so hard and sideways that it was even accumulating on the porch. She'd have a long day of shoveling tomorrow, that was for sure.

The ringing of the phone startled her out of her thoughts. The old-school phone—a heavy base with a rotary dial and a handset—sat in a little alcove built into the hallway between the living room and kitchen for just that purpose. She unfolded herself from her perch on the bench to cross the room and answer it.

"Hello?"

"Hey, Tess. Jim here."

Jim Evans lived next door and owned the small grocery store a few blocks down the hill, one of a handful of businesses open in Wharton during the off-season. He and his wife, Jane, were well into their sixties, maybe even beyond that, but they both had a delightfully artsy bohemian style mixed with a lifetime of cross-country skiing that made them seem much closer to Tess's midforties. She hoped she would be as fit when she reached their age.

"Jim! How d'you like this snow?"

He chuckled. "Wish I had my skis instead of the car," he said. "I'd probably get home faster. I'm closing up the store and wondering if you need anything."

This warmed Tess from the inside out.

"Thanks so much, but I think I'm set," she said, remembering the leftovers in the fridge.

"Your power out?" he asked. "Jane said ours went out at the house about an hour ago. It seems like our whole side of town is all dark."

"Yep, mine is out, too," she said, nodding. "But I've got a fire going and a bunch of candles, so I'm fine."

"Okay," he said. "I'll be over in the morning to help you dig out. If you need anything in the meantime, just holler."

Tess thanked him and said goodbye. She put the handset back on the base of the phone and smiled down at it. This kind of neighborly concern was one of the nicest benefits of relocating to Wharton permanently. It made her think back to her family's history here. Her deep Wharton roots.

Tess had been coming to Wharton to visit her grandmother ever since she could remember, but her ancestors had built the home generations ago, when Wharton itself was new. Tess's father and uncle had grown up there, as had their father and grandfather.

After her grandmother's passing more than a decade prior, Tess and her parents had used the house as a vacation home. But Tess's parents had moved to Florida permanently a few years ago, after having been snowbirds there for years before retirement, so Tess and her son, Eli, who would turn twenty-two this year, were the only ones who used the house these days.

Built a century earlier, the house was a regal Queen Anne, with dusty-green siding, a wraparound front porch, a turret, and a deeply pitched roof. Tess had spent her childhood exploring its endless nooks and crannies.

The main part of the home had five bedrooms, seven fireplaces, and six baths. The house, known as La Belle Vie, or "beautiful life" in French, and a play on their last name, sat on the hill in Wharton, overlooking the harbor below.

Turning the place into a bed-and-breakfast seemed like a perfect fit. Tess had always loved her time in Wharton. She had also loved her career in hospitality, first as a server and then as a chef. And she loved hosting people for dinner or a weekend. Being an innkeeper in this home in Wharton would allow her to combine all those loves. She wondered why she hadn't thought of it earlier.

With her parents' enthusiastic blessing, Tess had packed up and moved to La Belle Vie as summer faded into fall. A new chapter. A new life.

The first order of business had been getting herself unpacked and deciding how to configure the house for guests. A large room had been shuttered generations ago—the door permanently bolted. The windows to the outside were shuttered in black. From the backyard, Tess could tell it was either one massive room or a cluster of rooms, but she had never seen the inside.

Tess wasn't sure why it had been closed off. It was just the way things were. Her grandmother had said something about the whole place being too expensive to heat in the winter, so that was why she shut up the back of the house. But that had never really made sense to Tess.

When Tess's parents inherited it after her grandparents had both passed away, heating the house in the winter wasn't an issue because they didn't live there year round. In any case, that wing had remained shuttered. Her plan was to open it up and handle whatever needed handling—rot, mold, rodents (*oh, please, no*), remodeling, whatever—and use that part of the house for herself when guests were in residence. An owner's suite.

Back on the bench in front of the bay window, she watched the snow and thought about a conversation she'd had months before with Simon Granger, her longtime friend who owned the most magnificent inn in Wharton, Harrison's House, just a few blocks away. Simon and Tess had grown up together, spending summers in their families' homes. He had turned Harrison House into an inn after his grandmother passed away more than a decade prior.

"It's about time," he had said when she told him about her plans for La Belle Vie. "You'll have the house to yourself in the winter, if you don't escape to Hawaii or Palm Springs like any other sane person. In the summer and fall, your guests will fund your life. You get to live in a place you love and make a living, too. Just like I do. It's perfect!"

She had agreed. It was perfect. As soon as she was ready for those guests who would be "funding her life," Simon would funnel them to her until she built up a following of her own. His inn was always at capacity, always turning people away. His recommendations would give Tess all the business she could accommodate, and then some.

In the fall, Simon and his husband, Jonathan, had taken Tess on an antiquing trip to replace her family's rather dated furniture with lovely and gracious pieces like bedroom sets and mirrors that would better reflect the period of the home. The main part of the house, where guests would stay, was all but finished, the bedrooms outfitted with gorgeous ornate bedroom sets from another time, interesting and delicate stained-glass lamps, and touches like silver hairbrush sets that women of the past would've used before bedtime.

Now it was time to tackle the shuttered part of the house, to create her sanctuary. Tess had figured winter would be the perfect time to do that.

And, as she settled back down onto the window seat and watched the snow accumulate outside, she knew the time had come to start that project. The first step was opening it up. But every time she thought about it, she noticed a gnarling in the pit of her stomach. Why didn't she want to do it?

CHAPTER TWO

Tess had heated a water bottle in front of the fire and taken it upstairs to the room she was using as her bedroom, for now. It was the most magnificent bedroom in the house and had been her grandmother's for as long as Tess could remember.

The bed had an ornate, heavy wooden headboard and footboard, carved with curlicues and swirls. The dresser had a pink marble top and a mirror that was cloudy with age. Two bedside tables had similar marble tops, and on each sat a lamp with a dusty-pink stained-glass shade. It really was lovely. Tess was trying to decide whether to move this furniture into the owner's suite she was getting ready to renovate for herself, or leave it in the room where it had always stood. She didn't have a good answer for that yet. She wanted it for herself, but moving it seemed like a violation, somehow.

Curling down into bed, warmed by the hot water bottle in that chilly room, she pulled the covers around her. It had been a long day. Sleep came quickly. But it would not stay the night.

Scrrr, scrrr, scrrr.

Tess woke with a start. There it was again. The scratching. She had first heard it a few weeks prior, and sporadically since then. Not every night, but always in the middle of the night. Never during the day. It was coming from behind the locked door that led to the back wing of the house.

She slipped out of bed and grabbed her phone, which still had some battery life, off the nightstand. It read 3:47 a.m. She groaned. She hadn't had enough sleep to feel ready for the day, but maybe just enough to keep her from falling back to sleep now. She switched on the flashlight feature on her phone to light up the room. She crept down the hallway toward the shuttered door, put her ear against it, and listened. *Scrrr, scrrrr, scrrr.*

"Get away!" Tess shouted, knocking on the door. "Go! Shoo!"

Scrrr, scrrr, scrrr.

Always in threes.

"This is my house!" Tess cried. "Get out!"

Scrrr, scrrr, scrrr.

It had to be some kind of infestation, she reasoned. A family of raccoons or squirrels. God forbid, rats. *Please, let it not be rats.* And she didn't even want to think about bats. She'd have heard more than just scratching if it were a bigger animal making the noise. Some little critters were making a nuisance of themselves.

She had been hoping it would just go away. That the animal or animals would scurry off when the workmen came to open up the door and the back part of the house saw the light of day for the first time in a few generations. But she now realized she had to do something about it before whatever was behind that door got into the main part of the house. That was all she needed.

Tess made a mental note to talk to Jim about it in the morning and went back to her room, curling under the covers. She closed her eyes and listened to the scratching, wondering what it might be and what it would take to get it out of her house.

Sleep came, eventually.

In her dream, Tess was walking through Wharton at night. But not the main streets. The alleyways, the lots behind buildings. Through backyards. She peered through windows into brightly lit homes where families gathered, blissfully unaware someone was lurking outside.

It was a foggy, chilly night. Tess could actually feel the chill of it in her dream and taste the fog on her lips. She heard her own breathing, loud, almost aggressive sounding.

On the streets now, she watched people gathering in front of restaurants and pubs, coming and going. *A night on the town! How nice for them.* She took care to stand in doorways and behind trees, anything that would conceal her from view.

She scanned the streets, the mosaic of faces watery and indistinct, until one face crystallized. A young woman, leaving one of the pubs. Tess followed her for a couple of blocks, getting closer and closer still until the woman met up with a companion. A man. They embraced, laughing. Tess chuckled, too.

They locked arms and crossed the street, leaving Tess standing where she was. She watched the lovely, lovely duo until they disappeared around a corner. Then she turned and headed down toward the water, the sound of her steps on the cobblestones ringing in her ears.

~❦~

Amethyst awoke to the sound of a snowblower. She opened her eyes and looked around her room in a vague sense of confusion until the previous night's dreams dissipated. She had been having the strangest dreams lately, but that one had to take the cake, she thought. It was almost as though she'd dreamed that she was an animal stalking the streets. A wolf. Or a mountain lion.

She stretched, slid out of bed, padded to the window, and pulled aside the curtains. The sky was the kind of crystal-bright blue that came only after a massive snowfall. Wharton was covered in a blanket of white. Snow was everywhere, piled on roofs, obliterating sidewalks, making the streets impassable. She saw her neighbor Jim, already outside in his parka, hat, and mitts, pushing a snowblower slowly up his driveway, leaving a cleared path behind him and sending snow flying high into the air to the side. She noticed people doing the same at houses up and down the street. The plows hadn't yet been by, having to come from Salmon Bay, which they were no doubt plowing out first.

Tess pulled on a pair of jeans and a sweater, popped into the bathroom to splash some water on her face and brush her teeth and hair, and made her way downstairs to the hall closet to hunt around for her boots. Absentmindedly, she flipped on the hallway light—it worked! The power must've come back on sometime while she was sleeping.

She fished her mukluks from the back of the closet and pulled on the boots, which were crafted out of moose hide with a technique perfected by the Ojibwe—the Indigenous peoples of the area—centuries ago and still used to this day. The boots were as comfortable as slippers and warmer than anything modern people could concoct. They were the boot of choice for most everyone in Wharton and along Lake Superior's North Shore, and could be found in any number of boutiques in the area. She shrugged on her parka and opened her front door.

Icy cold hit Tess square in the face, tingling and almost burning her skin, taking her breath away. She zipped up her parka, rooted around in the pockets for her mittens, and trudged through the snow on her front porch to where she knew the stairs were. There had to be two feet of new snow, and it had drifted all the way up onto the porch. She wasn't certain where the sidewalk to the driveway was, nor was she sure she even had a shovel in the garage. She stood there, looking around aimlessly, not knowing quite what to do.

Jim saw her and held up a hand in greeting. Switching off his blower, he met Tess at the end of her driveway. His face was red, and his eyelashes and brows were crusted with snow, but his expression was as exuberant as a child's. He was smiling from ear to frozen ear.

"I can't remember the last time we had this much snow!" he said. "I'm just glad the blower started up. We had heard rumors this winter might be harsh—something about the beavers and their thick coats—so I had this baby tuned up in November just in case. Good thing! Usually, I can handle the snow with just a shovel, but not today!"

Tess smiled at him. "You're loving this."

"Darn right!" Jim chirped. "It's got to be ten below zero out here. With the windchill, I'll bet it's thirty below. We never get this sort of weather in Wharton. Sort of makes you feel alive, doesn't it?"

"That's one way of putting it," Tess said, laughing as she noticed even her teeth were cold. She shot a look at her garage, where snow had drifted high against the door. "Jim, I don't think I've even got a shovel."

He shook his head. "Why would you? This has been a summer place for your family for so long, you wouldn't have needed one." He patted the handle of his snowblower. "Don't you fret. I'll get your driveway and sidewalk blown out. I saw a couple of teenagers—that Johnson boy, for one—walking up and down the street with shovels, doing people's porches and stairs. I'll call them over to get you shoveled out."

A wave of relief washed over Tess. What a thing, to have good neighbors. She knew how blessed she was.

"That sounds great, thank you," she said. "But I have one condition. I'll make up a big pot of my famous harvest stew. You and Jane come on over later. I've got salad fixings and wine and beer in the fridge, too."

Jim raised his eyebrows. "Famous harvest stew? You've got a deal! I brought home a couple of baguettes from the store last night, so we'll contribute those."

"Perfect," Tess said, turning to head back into the house. But then she had a thought that made her turn around again. "Oh! The store. Aren't you opening it today?"

Jim shook his head. "If anyone in town needs anything, they know to call me or Mavis," he said, referring to his store manager. "That's basically how it works in the winter. Bad weather hits, we close up, but not before making sure folks have what they need to ride it out. If they find themselves short of something necessary, Mavis or I can always zip down to the store to open it up for them."

As Jim happily returned to his snow blowing, Tess trudged her way back to her front porch. Inside, she pulled off her boots and left them, and her parka, in the entryway. As she walked through the house, she caught a chill. She touched the big radiator in the living room—ice cold.

Tess sighed but figured it wasn't surprising. This house hadn't been used in the winter very often during her lifetime, and who knew how long before that. And Wharton was famous for its unusually temperate winter months, so the heating system in La Belle Vie wasn't exactly top of mind for anyone. The boiler and radiators could probably use a tune-up. She made a mental note to call her parents to ask who, if anyone, had serviced it in recent years. Otherwise, Jim would know of someone who could come and take a look at it. Tess hoped it wouldn't need a complete overhaul or, worse yet, a new boiler. She hadn't been counting on that expense.

She lit fires in both the living and dining rooms and then headed back to the study—*her* study, she had to keep telling herself—and opened a notebook on the heavy antique desk. She had been keeping a running list of things she needed to take care of before the house was ready to open for guests.

Everything having to do with the main part of the house had been crossed off: Antique furniture, check. New linens, check. Oriental rugs, check. Fireplaces inspected, check. Plumbing inspected, check. She wrote *heat* and *animals* at the bottom of the list. There was a second list, "Owner's Suite." But it didn't have any items on it yet. Tess still didn't know what she'd find when she broke through the locked and, it seemed, heavily bolted door that led from one part of the house to the other.

She closed her notebook and was heading toward the kitchen to start her stew when the phone rang.

"Mom!" It was her son, Eli. Her heart jumped into her throat when she heard his voice.

"Hi, honey!" she said, as brightly as she could muster.

"I heard about the storm," he said. "Are you okay? Do you have heat? Lights? Is there a shovel there, at least? I hope you have wine, because if not, this will truly be a disaster of epic proportions."

Tess chuckled. "Yep, sweetie, I'm okay. Jim from next door is snow blowing the driveway, and some kids from town are going to come and shovel out the steps and porch. The heat's a little iffy, but I do have fireplaces in every room, so I'm not too worried about that right now."

"Make sure to start one in the kitchen right away," Eli advised, a serious tone in his voice. "You don't want the pipes to freeze or, worse, burst."

"Good idea," she said, not having thought of it herself. Ever the sensible kid. "I just came in from talking to Jim outside, so I'm making my way around to the fireplaces to get things blazing. Did you get any of this weather down in Minneapolis?"

"Just a dusting," Eli said. "And not any of the cold you're dealing with, either. What's going on? It's never that cold in Wharton."

"Tell me about it! This is really odd. Of course, it's the best day of Jim's life. I think he's going to blow out the entire town."

Eli chuckled. "Well. Okay. I just wanted to make sure you weren't frozen in a snowbank somewhere. Have you started the renovations in the back half of the house?"

Tess's stomach did a quick flip. Why did a sense of unease wash over her every time she thought about that project? "Not yet, honey. I've got the front half set. You should see all of the furniture Simon helped me find. It's really gorgeous."

"Well, when it's time to break open that door, let me know. I'll bring some friends up for a long weekend, and we can help with whatever you need. Painting. Plumbing. Demolition. Disposing of bodies. Whatever."

Tess laughed. "That sounds great. You know, I want this to be a family business, so you've got a stake in this, too."

"I know, Mom," Eli said, his voice softening. "I'm here for whatever you need. Be careful."

As they said their goodbyes, Tess hung up the handset and brushed tears from her eyes. But it was too late. The grief overtook her, the sadness she was still dealing with after almost losing the love of her life. Her son.

She had gotten the call at 4:17 p.m. on a Friday. That detail, for some reason, was seared into her mind. But she couldn't remember driving to the hospital, parking, or finding her way to his room in the ICU. The only thing she could remember was sitting at his bedside, holding his hand.

Her precious son had been hit by a car—a drunk driver, it turned out—as he crossed the street on his way home from work. Had he stayed talking with his coworkers for just a few moments longer, or left a split second earlier, or walked a bit slower or faster, he would not have been in that intersection at just the time the driver was careening through it. Had the driver gotten behind the wheel a moment later, or earlier, or not at all, he would not have driven through the intersection as Eli was walking through it. As it was, the driver was set on his course, Eli was set on his, and they collided with perfect, horrifying timing.

It did not seem random to Tess. She couldn't get over the symmetry of it all. A drunk driver getting behind the wheel. Her son getting off work. Eli walking down the sidewalk as the car came toward him. The two meeting at that precise split second.

Tess had felt a sort of frantic helplessness—the need to do something, anything to help Eli, but she could do nothing. The machines beeped. Nurses checked in.

This was her child. The boy who made her laugh every day, who taught her what real love was.

Oh, she loved her parents and her friends, but when Eli was born, she was completely knocked off her feet at the eternal vastness of the love she felt for this beautiful boy.

As she'd sat there next to her son, she'd drawn the phone out of her purse and called her ex-husband, Matt. She and Eli's father had been divorced for more than a decade. He lived in Las Vegas with his new wife, but he had been a wonderful coparent who loved Eli just as fiercely as she did.

When Matt answered and Tess heard his voice, her own seized up.

"Matt," was all she managed to say.

He was quiet for a moment. "What is it?" His voice was paper thin. Barely a whisper.

She struggled to get the words out. "Eli's in the hospital. He got hit by a car." She could not believe she had just said it. Spoken it aloud.

"How bad?" Matt whispered.

"He's in the ICU," Tess choked out.

"Okay," Matt said, clearing his throat, his take-charge attitude kicking in. It always did when he was afraid. "I'll be there as soon as I can get a flight."

CHAPTER THREE

During Eli's time in the hospital, Matt and Tess had quietly supported each other. Matt had set up his computer in the guest room and worked as much as he could, while Tess cooked to feed her soul as much as their bodies.

Matt coerced Tess out of the house for walks every day, as he had always done. She had forgotten how much he loved to walk and talk, getting his mind around an issue or problem as they rambled along. She had to admit, it helped. Had she been alone, she might have simply retreated into her terror and imagined the unimaginable. With Matt, she got out of the house every day, walking around her Minneapolis neighborhood, down to Minnehaha Creek, where they took a wooded path along the shoreline, watching the ducks float past. They'd even go for walks at night after dinner, spotting owls and woodpeckers and animals that came out during the cool of the evening.

Tess found that being together again with her ex-husband after such a long time was as natural as breathing. No old wounds surfaced; no lingering resentments came to light. So much time had passed. None of what had torn them apart held any shred of importance, not in the face of their beautiful boy lying in a hospital fighting for his life.

And then, after twenty-three days, Eli was ready to come home. Tess and Matt couldn't get to the hospital fast enough. Their boy was so thin, so frail. It was like he had lost half of himself, and in such a short time. His leg was in a cast, his arm in a sling. Broken ribs, a broken collarbone. A fractured leg and a massive concussion. Right away, Matt, who was also visibly shaken at the sight of their boy, announced he was going to stay awhile to help Eli get back on his feet.

Tess had to admit to herself that those weeks were pretty wonderful, the three of them playing at the family they might have been. Dinners together. Watching movies. Sharing sunny afternoons in the backyard. Eli bounced back slowly but steadily, gaining strength every day, working with a rehab therapist. Tess found herself enveloped in extreme gratitude for it all.

Was this the start of something? She tried to read Matt, eyeing him when he wasn't looking. Was he feeling it, too? Tess wanted to broach the subject many times, but something always stopped her words before she had a chance to say them.

It wasn't so crazy to believe it could happen. Yes, he was remarried and had a new life halfway across the country. Maybe this whole terrible situation could make her family whole again, make Matt realize what they all had lost when he left them all those years ago. She held on to that slim reed of possibility.

But it was not to be.

When Eli was nearly back on his feet, Matt announced it was time for him to return to his own life. It hit Tess like an icy wave. Her fantasy of embracing their shared life together again was over. For the second time. Deep inside, she had known it was coming. But she had held on to the possibility just the same.

And so Matt made his plans to leave. When he finally walked out the door for his flight home, she felt a little piece of herself retreat under a shroud, just as it had the first time he had left her. This—she, Matt, and Eli together as a family—was the life she wanted now; it was what she had always wanted, even during the decade when they were apart.

But it was not the life she was going to get. It knocked Tess over, the disappointment and grief of it all, even more than it had the first time.

But this time, it sank in as it hadn't before.

As she hugged her ex-husband goodbye, she did it with finality. He could have had this life, the life Tess wanted with all her heart, the three of them, together. But he didn't want it. It was as simple as that.

And when Eli felt strong enough to go back to his apartment and his life, Tess knew it was time to find her next chapter, too.

Eli's accident and Tess's final acceptance of her divorce had made her look at her own life with a critical eye. She had just been existing. Coasting along. But not really enjoying what she was doing. She had been working as a chef for a catering company but had been increasingly fed up with the demands of the job. She wanted something more. Something different. Something fulfilling.

That was when the idea of turning La Belle Vie into an inn hit her. She could still tap into her love of cooking and hospitality, but do it for herself.

The sensibleness of it all was what convinced her to do it. It made perfect sense to turn La Belle Vie into an inn. Didn't it?

❧

Later that afternoon, Tess stood in the kitchen at the massive butcher-block table, chopping meat and slicing veggies for her stew. A fire blazed in the fireplace, the Renaissance music channel played on her music app, and she was sipping a glass of cold chardonnay as she worked. Perfect. Very few things could be better than this for Tess. Nothing relaxed her more than cooking. Thinking of the perfect menu, shopping for the ingredients, and just the rhythmic act of chopping seemed to melt away all her anxiety and fears. The creative aspect of putting it all together, straying from recipes to concoct something new and her own, was lifegiving to her. It had been necessary during Eli's recovery.

These past few months, she had been compiling breakfast recipes with an eye toward making them for her future guests, along with snacks she would serve on the front porch before dinnertime as a sort of happy hour.

But tonight, it was all about making dinner for Jim and Jane. Her famous harvest stew. It was her own recipe, born one evening when she was making one of her all-time favorite dishes, French onion soup, and wondered what it would taste like with some steak thrown in. It had morphed and grown from there into what Eli called French onion soup on steroids.

She was using beef chuck, because that was what she had on hand, but any cut of beef would do. The stew had to simmer for two-plus hours so the meat would become fork tender.

She began by pouring a splash of olive oil into her favorite heavy dutch oven, along with some butter. As that melted, she added a bit of garlic and three large Vidalia onions she had sliced thin, along with chopped carrots and celery. She sautéed it all for a good thirty minutes until the onions started to caramelize.

Then came the meat, chopped into small, bite-size pieces that she had dredged by placing them and a scant quarter cup of flour into a plastic bag and shaking it. With the meat added to the pot, she sprinkled some thyme and sautéed the mixture for a couple of minutes until it made a sort of paste, then poured in a bottle of dark beer. Tess let that simmer for a bit and then added enough beef stock to cover the meat and veggies, put the cover on the pot, and turned down the heat. She checked the clock. Plenty of time for the stew to simmer into wonderfulness before Jim and Jane arrived.

She checked the fridge to make sure she had salad fixings and swiss cheese to round out the meal. Seeing that she was all set, she quickly washed her prep tools and cleaned up her work area—*Clean as you go in the kitchen*, her grandmother always used to say.

Tess topped off her glass and was about to head to her study to sit with her thoughts awhile and plan out her next moves on the back-of-the-house renovation when she heard a noise.

It was faint, at first. Was it really there? Tess turned off her music and listened closer. Yes, there it was—*scratch, scratch, scratch*—coming from the kitchen door. Not this again. Now something was scratching on another door, from the outside? Tess let out a groan. But it wasn't the same scratching she had heard during the night. This was different.

She looked out the window. The sun was low in the sky, casting a glow over the snowdrifts. She didn't see anything in the yard or the driveway, until she looked down. A white dog was huddled against the door, shivering. Its face was looking up at her, its eyes pleading.

It had to be ten degrees below zero out there. She wasn't in the habit of letting stray animals into her house, but . . . this dog would freeze to death if left to brave the elements.

Tess opened the door to a whoosh of cold. The dog just sat there, shivering, looking into her eyes.

"C'mon in," Tess said, with as much gentleness as she could muster. "You're welcome here, inside. Come in and get warm." Her tone was soothing.

The animal got to its feet and crept into the kitchen. Tess held her breath, not knowing how it might react—was it aggressive? But the dog noticed the fire in the fireplace and crept over to the hearth on shaky legs before lying down before it with a great sigh. It sounded like the groan of an old man whose limbs were sore and weary. Maybe that was exactly what it was.

Tess had grown up with dogs but hadn't lived with one since Eli was born—Matt was allergic, and after he left, it just never seemed the right time to add more responsibilities to her plate. But she loved animals and was, in her heart, a caretaker. Her heart swelled, thinking of this dog outside, braving the storm on its own. She found a bowl in the cabinet, filled it with water, and set it gently in front of the animal.

"You take a drink, now," she said. "You must be thirsty." But the dog didn't budge. It laid its great head on its paws and closed its eyes.

It probably needs to get warm, Tess thought. She eyed the animal. No collar. Its white fur wasn't terribly matted but could use a little love and care. She noticed a slight hint of auburn running along the length of its back. Its ears were pointy and pink inside, and its snout was long. It had the look of a malamute or white German shepherd or even a white wolf, but Tess couldn't be sure. She put it at about one hundred pounds. It wasn't malnourished but wasn't exactly carrying any extra weight, either.

What to do now? Tess headed into the hallway to the phone alcove and dialed Jim and Jane's number.

"Hi, Tess!" Jane chirped. "We were just listening to a program on public radio. Do you need anything for dinner? Still want us to come?"

"Yes, absolutely, I still want you to come! I've already got the stew on the stove. I'm calling about something else. I have a visitor. Maybe a houseguest."

"Oh?" Jane asked. "Someone from out of town?"

Tess smiled. "I'm not exactly sure. It's a dog that was scratching at my kitchen door. It was freezing cold and tired and is now curled up asleep in front of my fireplace in the kitchen."

"Smart doggie. Anyone would want to curl up in front of that massive fireplace," Jane said, and Tess could hear the smile in her voice.

"I'm just wondering if you or Jim know of anyone who has a dog like this one—stark white, about one hundred pounds. Sort of looks like a malamute or a shepherd."

"That's not ringing a bell with me, but let me ask Jim," Jane said. "Honey, do you know of anyone with a big white dog? Like a malamute or shepherd? A stray dog came to Tess's door."

"Wyatt Templeton has malamutes, but as far as I know, none are all white."

"You heard that?" Jane asked Tess.

"Yeah," Tess said. "And nobody else comes to mind?"

"Hi, Tess." It was Jim, apparently taking the phone from his wife. "So, you've got a lost soul on your hands?"

Tess glanced over at the sleeping dog. It was breathing deeply, seemingly thankful to be safe from the storm. "A beautiful dog, yes," she said. "He showed up at my kitchen door. So, you don't know of anyone who has a dog like this?"

Jim took a moment before he answered. "Not that I can think of," he said. "But when we come for dinner, I'll take a photo of him and put it on the message board in the store. If anyone's missing this dog, we'll hear about it."

"Great," Tess said. "Sounds like a plan."

"Hey, you'll need dog food," Jim continued. "I'll pop down to the store and grab a bag for you. A leash, too."

Dog food! She hadn't even thought of that. She wasn't sure how long she'd have this shaggy visitor in her household, but he'd need some food while he was with her. If she had a dog that was lost in a storm, she'd want whoever found him to treat him with the same kindness and love.

"You're an angel, Jim," Tess said. "Thank you so much. For everything."

"That's what neighbors are for. I was planning to go down to the store anyway to check on things. Make sure the pipes aren't frozen and all of that. It's no trouble to grab a bag of dog food. What time do you want us?"

Tess eyed the clock on the stove. The stew needed to simmer for at least another ninety minutes. "How about four? An early dinner."

"Perfect."

CHAPTER FOUR

For the rest of the afternoon, Tess sat in the kitchen jotting down ideas for her owner's suite renovations while the stew simmered, filling the room with a delicious aroma of onions, thyme, and beef broth. The dog slept deeply in front of the fire. Tess wondered how long he had been out in the storm, imagining the poor animal huddled under bushes or next to buildings for shelter from those punishing winds and icy shards. She hated to think of him out there.

Soon, four o'clock rolled around, and Tess heard Jim and Jane rapping on her side door. The dog woke and let out a couple of low barks, not aggressively, exactly, but in warning. He scrambled to his feet as Tess crossed the room to open the door, and before she knew it, he was in front of her, between her and the outside world.

"It's okay," she said to him. "It's just Jim and Jane." She opened the door, hoping he wouldn't continue barking or, worse yet, bite. But he just stood there, a silent protector.

"Come in, come in!" Tess said to her guests.

They trundled in, with choruses of "hellos" and hugs, Jim carrying the dog food and another bag, Jane carrying the baguettes and a bottle of wine. Both were wearing wool parkas with a Norwegian design decorating their edges, wool hats with ear flaps, and big woolen mitts. Quintessential northerners.

"You can hang your coats here," Tess said, gesturing to the hooks by the door, "and just leave your boots there."

While her guests were unwrapping from their outerwear, and the dog was circling around them happily, Tess opened the wine and poured glasses for them all.

"Well, look at this big fella," Jim said, petting the dog around the ears. The dog seemed to smile from ear to ear. "Where did you come from, huh?"

"Definitely not a stray," Jane said, running a hand along the fur on his back. "He's beautiful. And looks to be in pretty good condition, considering."

Jim set the bag of dog food on the counter. "Got a bowl?"

Tess retrieved a big stoneware bowl from the cabinet, poured a good amount of food into it, and set it down next to the water dish.

"Here's some nice dinner for you," she said to the dog, who sniffed at the food for a moment before taking a few bites.

Jim pulled his phone from his pocket and snapped a few photos as the dog ate his food. "I'll put these up in the store, but I'm sure I haven't seen this fella around town at all. So few of us left in the winter, you kind of get to know what's what with everyone and their pets."

"Especially you. With the store, you see all of us," Tess said, handing them both their glasses and then picking up her own and holding it aloft. "To good neighbors! Thank you so much for blowing the driveway, and to the boys for shoveling the porch and stairs."

The three clinked glasses. "Think nothing of it," Jim said. "Happy to help! That's what neighbors do."

Tess had assembled a selection of cheeses, crackers, figs, and grapes on a heavy wooden cutting board, which she had placed on the butcher-block table. People had always sort of gravitated to it, for some reason, standing around it during family gatherings while the cook busied him- or herself at the stove. That was where they all stood now, as the fire crackled in the fireplace and the AGA radiated its warmth. The dog turned in a circle a few times and curled up next to the fire with a contented sigh.

Tess looked at her neighbors and smiled. Jim was fit and wiry, his hair still a dusty blond. His blue eyes were full of emotion and kindness. He was definitely an adventure-apparel sort of dresser, always wearing something appropriate if a long walk in the wilderness suddenly came up, an ever-present Swiss Army knife on his belt. When tourists came to Wharton, you could always tell the newbies by their brand-spanking-new denim shirts, crisp jeans, and pristine hiking boots or water shoes they had purchased at an expensive outdoors store for the occasion. Jim was the real thing and lived the outdoors lifestyle to its fullest.

Jane was what Tess would describe as Northwoods chic, always wearing interesting dangly jewelry, mostly silver, clothes made from sustainable fibers—linen was her go-to in the summer, brushed cotton and smart-wool sweaters in the winter—in muted colors, flaxes and whites and deep blues. Her thick hair was cut in an asymmetrical bob and was completely white, which suited her to a T.

"The stew smells incredible," Jane said as she nibbled on a cracker topped with a decadent aged blue cheese.

The conversation turned to other things, then, the blizzard—who had dug out whom, whose pipes had burst. Many snowbirds made a practice of leaving house keys with neighbors who lived year-round in Wharton, and those neighbors had been checking on people's homes, just to make sure they didn't come home to a flood in the spring.

"I'm sorry if it's chilly in here," Tess said. "I guess my boiler went out." She turned to Jim. "Do you know of anyone who can fix it? Someone who could come soon? Like maybe tomorrow?"

"I do, actually," Jim said. "Wyatt Templeton. The guy with the malamutes. I'll give him a call and tell him to call you." Jim squinted at her. "Did you check the pilot light?"

Tess shook her head. "I wouldn't even know how to do that, so . . . no."

"I'll run down and check it real quick," Jim said. "It might be as simple as that."

Jim trotted down the back stairs. He was back in the kitchen a moment later, shaking his head. "Nope," he said, pulling his phone out of his pocket. He called his guy and arranged for him to be at the house in the morning.

Great, thought Tess. *One thing handled.*

Tess gave the stew a stir. "I think we're about ready," she said. She retrieved the salad from the fridge and set it on the table, along with plates, bowls, and silverware. "I thought we'd just eat in the kitchen instead of in the dining room. It's so cozy here with the fireplace and the AGA."

"Perfect," Jane said, clearing the cheese board. Jim put the baguettes on the cutting board and set it on the table, along with the wine.

Tess cut three pieces from the baguette and placed one in each bowl, ladled in the stew, and topped it with cubes of the swiss, which she stirred into the hot liquid.

"This looks absolutely incredible," Jim said, blowing on a cheesy spoonful before slipping it into his mouth. He closed his eyes. "Oh my."

Tess chuckled. It was nice, having friends in for dinner again. This was one of the first times in a very long time she had cooked for anyone except Matt and Eli.

After dinner, Tess suggested they take their drinks into the living room, where she had already started the fire. As they followed her down the chilly hallway, Jane said, "I haven't been in this part of the house before."

"Really? That surprises me, you two living next door and all," Tess said, but upon thinking about it for a moment, it made sense. Jim and Jane had moved to Wharton a little more than a decade prior, and after her grandmother died, her family vacations had sort of petered out. Eli had been getting to the age where he wanted to spend more time with his friends, and her parents had been spending more time at their place in Florida and were only in Wharton sporadically during those years.

Jane took in an audible breath as they entered the living room, the fire glowing in the fireplace and illuminating all the woodwork. "This is gorgeous," she cooed, running her hand along the fireplace mantel.

The house really did have some beautiful features, including its original woodwork, like the ornately carved mantel. Tess saw it anew as she watched Jane admire it. Tess had spent a good bit of time polishing the woodwork throughout the house until it gleamed like new, dusting off the years, coaxing it back to its deep, rich beauty. Seeing it through someone else's eyes made her heart swell with pride. It was all too easy to take a thing for granted, even something beautiful, when you lived with it every day, she thought. The extraordinary faded into ordinary, even mundane.

"That painting above the fireplace," Jane said, squinting and taking a few steps nearer to it. "That's one of your grandfather's, isn't it? I'd know a Sebastian Bell anywhere. Is that your father, as a boy?"

"It is," Tess said. "My uncle and grandmother, too."

Jane was right; Tess's grandfather's style was distinctive. He painted scenes of life in Wharton—the lake, the cliffs, the ferries, the beaches, the wildlife, the people—his watercolors and oils blurring the lines of familiar images into his own personal dreamscape. Northern Impressionism, an art critic had once dubbed Sebastian's style, and it had stuck.

This painting, *Picnic at Mermaid Cove*, depicted the family relaxing on a beach, not a care in the world, the vastness of the lake shimmering like diamonds before them. Her father, Indigo, and her uncle, Grey, were small, playing in the sand with pails and shovels, the beginnings of a sandcastle rising up between them. Their mother, Serena, sat on a beach blanket next to a picnic basket. She was wearing a white cotton dress, her feet bare, her wavy brown hair cascading down her back and blowing slightly in an unseen breeze.

But there was something sinister underlying the idyllic scene, as there was in many of her grandfather's paintings. In this one, the water seemed almost alive. Faces gazed out of the waves—malevolent faces—watery tentacles curling up onto rocks on the shore in a way that almost surrounded the unsuspecting family, as though, in an instant, the lake could send a massive wave to engulf them all on a whim.

That was how all his paintings were—an otherwise utterly normal moment, with otherworldly danger lurking just out of view. Tess had never known her grandfather, but she couldn't help but wonder what kind of man he was if that was how he saw the world.

The art gallery in town, WhartonScapes, featured prints and framed fine-art reproductions of his works, but the originals hung in museums all over the country, and indeed the world. The previous year, one of his more famous paintings, *Angry Inland Sea*, which captured the lake in all its fury on an especially stormy night, had fetched more than $7 million at auction.

Only part of that money came to the family. Tess's grandmother had established the Sebastian Bell Foundation for the Arts, which provided arts scholarships to aspiring young (or any age) painters, some years after Sebastian had passed away. For the past year or so, Eli had been working with Tess's father in administering the foundation and would take over one day soon after Indigo finally relinquished the reins and retired. He had taught his grandson well. Eli was up to the job and enthusiastic about it.

Indigo, who had inherited his parents' fortune after his brother, Grey, disappeared after Wharton's annual Fourth of July celebration decades earlier, had put part of the proceeds of that massive sale, and others over the years, into the foundation, and the rest into a trust for Tess and, when her son was born, for Eli, accessible only if they worked for a living. Some of it went into a retirement account that Tess couldn't access until she was sixty-five.

Tess looked upon it as a cushion that she would dip into only when necessary. It allowed her and Eli, as it had allowed Indigo, to pursue careers they really enjoyed, rather than having to work at a job they didn't like in order to simply live. Tess knew how fortunate she was, and she made sure Eli knew it, too.

That was what was paying for Tess's renovations to La Belle Vie, which, she reasoned, would've pleased Sebastian Bell a great deal. She liked to think so, anyway.

"It's amazing to see this up close," Jane mused, studying the painting. "The brushstrokes. Do you have others?"

Tess shook her head. "This one came with the house. It's always been here. Apparently, my grandfather loved it a great deal and never wanted to sell it. My parents have another one in their home in Florida, but that's it. We don't keep many of his works lying around."

"No, they're lying around in MoMA," Jim piped up, gazing at the painting. "He really was remarkable, wasn't he?"

"I wish I had inherited some of his talent," Tess said. "But, alas."

"Oh, I don't know about that," Jim said. "The dinner you just served us was a work of art in itself."

This warmed Tess from the inside out. *How nice of him to say that.* And, she had to admit, he was right, in a way. Cooking was creative. Finding just the right dish to serve at the right time, taking care to select foods that she knew her guests would love, preparing them in her own way. Making sure everyone was happy. Hospitality was an art. Her canvas was a table. She guessed it wasn't so different, after all.

Jane turned to her, pulling her out of her own thoughts. "Do you have some sort of security system? I mean, for when you open the house up to guests. You don't want one of them walking away with this masterpiece."

Tess nodded. "Since nobody was living here full time when my parents moved to Florida a couple of years back, my dad put in the same kind of security system that museums use. The frame is bolted to the wall, so it's not going anywhere easily. But if anyone touches it, or even gets too close, an alarm goes off, and the police are called immediately."

That painting had hung above the fireplace at La Belle Vie for as long as Tess could remember. But, security or no security, she'd talk to her father about moving it before the first guest arrived.

CHAPTER FIVE

After Jane and Jim had gone, Tess bundled up to take the dog outside for a walk. At first, he was reluctant to step through the doorway, thinking perhaps that he wouldn't be allowed back inside. But Tess coaxed him, tugged a bit on the leash that Jim had brought with him, and soon the dog gingerly stepped across the threshold and into the night.

At first, he pulled and tugged at the leash, but then he settled into the rhythm of the walk, trotting at Tess's side. They walked through the snowy streets, which by that time had all been plowed. Snowbanks were piled high on the curbs. She had never seen Wharton blanketed like this. It looked like a winter wonderland, a totally different town. Lights burned brightly from many of the houses, and Tess could see families around their own dinner tables or in their living rooms. It was a cozy feeling, watching the domestic tableaux through their windows.

It was still bone-chilling cold, but Tess was wearing her warmest jacket and boots. The cold nipping at her cheeks invigorated her, at least for the moment. As she turned the corner toward home, the dog began pulling her toward the door, visibly relieved to be going back inside.

In the kitchen, Tess peeled off her parka, pulled off her boots, and grabbed a towel to wipe the dog's snowy feet. He complied, politely lifting each paw in turn.

"I can't just keep calling you 'the dog,'" she said to him, his sweet face smiling. She petted his chilly fur. "When you came to me, you were nearly frozen. But that's not a good name for a dog. How about Snowstorm?"

He wagged his tail. "Snowstorm," she said again, scratching behind his ears. "Good boy, Snowstorm. Or, how about just Storm?" She smiled at him. "Yes, that suits you. Storm."

She knew Jim would post photos of the dog in the store, on the store's website, and on the town's website. And if this dog had a family fretting about his safety, Tess hoped they'd see those photos. But deep down, she hoped he had found where he belonged.

As the night wore on, it was getting chilly in the house. One more cold night to get through—the furnace guy Jim had recommended was coming in the morning. Tess turned on the water, just to a trickle, in the kitchen and bathroom sinks to keep those pipes, which were on exterior walls, from freezing overnight. She opened the cabinet doors beneath both sinks and switched on the battery-powered space heaters, which she had fetched from the basement earlier in the day. They wouldn't provide a lot of heat, but just enough, and were much safer than the electric variety, which always scared Tess as being a fire hazard.

She had to do what she could: frozen or burst pipes were no joke, and she didn't want to be dealing with that in the morning or, worse yet, in the middle of the night.

Then she gathered some firewood from the woodpile out back into the canvas log carrier and lugged it upstairs to her bedroom, Storm close behind.

"All of this fuss just to keep warm. I feel like a pioneer woman," she said to the dog. "Maybe I'll make soap next. Start canning food." She chuckled at her own weak attempt at humor.

In her bedroom, Tess started a fire in the fireplace, and the warm glow lit up the darkness. After changing into her pajamas, she snuggled under the covers and settled in to watch the news. She had turned on her heating blanket before Jim and Jane arrived, so her bed was toasty, even if the air in her room was still ice cold.

As she reached for the remote, Storm jumped up onto the bed and, after turning in a circle a few times, curled into a ball and put his fluffy tail over his nose.

"I guess it's a one-dog night around here," Tess said, referring to the expression that people sometimes used to denote how cold it would be outside: one-dog, two-dog, or three-dog night. She reached for the remote and flipped on the television.

Halfway through the weather segment—*More cold and snow on the way, awesome!* Tess groaned—the dog's head popped up, his ears on high alert. He let out a low growl and a few soft barks.

He must have heard it, Tess thought. *The scratching.* So, she wasn't the only one.

He jumped off the bed and stood at the closed door, growling low in his throat.

"Do you want to go check it out?" she asked him as she slipped out of bed.

Tess turned on the light and opened the door. The dog hurried through it. She followed close behind. Sure enough, Storm stopped at the shuttered door at the end of the hallway and began barking loud and long, scratching at the door. Tess wasn't sure what to do, but she knew one thing. There really was something behind that door. She hadn't been imagining it. There was no other explanation for why Storm was barking. She hoped it wasn't a raccoon.

But then, the commotion stopped as quickly as it had started. Storm fell silent, cocked his head, and listened at the door. He stayed that way, on high alert, listening carefully for several minutes. Then he looked up at Tess, as if to say, *It's gone.* With that, he turned and began trotting down the hallway toward the bedroom, but Tess noticed he didn't go all the way inside. He turned back toward Tess and waited for her.

"I'm coming," she said, shivering in her nightgown in the chilly hall.

Back in her room, she added a couple of logs to the fire, and it crackled to life. Storm was already back on his perch on the bed, curled up but watching her intently. She closed the bedroom door against the chill of the hallway and, just thinking of it, headed to the en suite bathroom and rolled up a towel to place under the door. She wanted to keep the heat from her fireplace in her room and keep whatever was behind that closed door out there.

⁓✥⁓

Another night of strange, disturbing dreams. It had begun to be a pattern and was always the same—Tess walking through the streets of Wharton. Prowling. Peering into windows. Following people down dark alleyways. Lingering by the lake, watching the angry water roil and crash into the rocky shore. In this dream, it was almost as though she took flight, on dark wings.

She woke with a start, tangled in her sheets, her hair wet against her head, her nightgown damp from sweat. She reached for the water glass on her nightstand and, propping herself up on an elbow, took a gulp. Glancing at the clock, she saw it wasn't yet four o'clock. *Not this again, too.* She groaned and snuggled back down under the covers, too exhausted to put another log on the fire.

The next morning, Tess had just taken her first sip of coffee when the phone rang. She had already been out with Storm and given him his breakfast, and she had just sat down at the kitchen table and was about to flip on the morning news. She pushed herself up from the table to answer the phone.

"Hi, is this Tess?"

"It is. Who's this?"

"I'm Wyatt Templeton. Jim Evans let me know you've got a boiler that's not working. I'm the guy coming over this morning to look at it, and I was wondering if about nine o'clock was a good time."

Tess glanced at the clock—it was nearly that now.

"Sure," she said, taking a sip of her coffee. "I'm here. Jim mentioned you might be able to come today. Come on by whenever it's convenient. Feel free to use the side door just off the driveway. Most people come and go that way."

"Will do," said Wyatt. "See you soon." And then he rang off. Tess hoped this repair wouldn't be too costly, but if Jim was recommending this guy, she felt like she could trust him. Both to do the job honestly and to come into her home.

She settled back down at the table and thought about what she had to do that day. After the heat, the main things were, right away, contacting somebody about the animals living in the back part of the house—she had forgotten to mention that to Jim the night before—and getting in touch with some demolition people who could open that door and let her see what, exactly, she was dealing with. She had been putting that part of the project off, for reasons she didn't quite understand, but now was the time she had to deal with it. Maybe this Wyatt would know someone around town who could help with those things.

In a few minutes, Storm roused himself from his place by the fire in the kitchen. He jumped up and was at the door before Tess heard the knocking. She could see a male shape through the curtains that hung on the door windows and knew it had to be the furnace guy.

She crossed the room to open the door, Storm standing firmly between her and Wyatt on the other side. Another whoosh of cold blew in as she opened it.

"Hey," she said to the man, ushering him inside. "Thanks for coming so quickly."

"Glad to help out," he said, shrugging out of his parka. "I'm Wyatt."

Storm circled him, sniffing. Wyatt leaned down and ruffled the fur on the dog's back with one hand, setting down the tool kit he was carrying in the other.

"You must smell my dogs," he said, as Storm wiggled around him. Wyatt turned his gaze to Tess. "Jim mentioned last night this fella came calling," he said, motioning to the dog. "Asked if he belonged to me or anyone I know, and now that I've seen him, I can tell you the answer's no. I've never seen this dog around town before." He hung his parka on one of the hooks and started to pull off his boots, but she held up a hand to stop him.

"You'll want to leave those on," she said. "We'll be going down into the basement, and it's pretty dirty down there."

"Got it," he said, wiping the soles carefully on the mat before stepping onto the kitchen floor.

"Would you like some coffee?" Tess asked. "I just made a fresh pot."

"Sounds great," Wyatt said, leaning against the butcher block. As Tess poured his coffee, she got a better look at the man. He was wearing jeans and a black-and-white checked flannel shirt over a gray T-shirt, all very well lived in. His hair was jet black and cropped short, his eyes an unsettling gray-green. Tess wasn't sure she had ever seen eyes that color. He was about her age, give or take a few years.

She handed him the cup and topped off her own.

"So, what are we dealing with, boiler-wise?" he asked her and took a sip from his steaming cup.

"I'm not sure," she said. "My grandma put in a new one about twenty years ago, that's all I know. The weather was so warm before the blizzard, I hadn't turned it on yet."

Wyatt smiled. "I don't think anyone had their heat on yet. I know a guy who won't turn his on until the first overnight freeze. So, yours isn't working at all?"

"No," she said. "The radiators are stone cold. Jim checked the pilot light, but that's not the problem."

"They might have to be bled—that may be all this is," he said.

He must've seen the confused look on Tess's face because he went on. "You need to sort of flush the radiators out every now and then.

Every few years. It's a buildup of air pressure that you have to release. Do you know if that's been done?"

Tess shook her head. "I'd bet against it."

Wyatt finished his cup and set it on the butcher block with finality. "Okay. Let's see what we're dealing with." He picked up his tool kit and looked around. "Where's the basement door?"

Tess wasn't all too thrilled to be heading down into the basement, which had always creeped her out as a child. But she couldn't send this man down there to root around on his own.

She turned on the light at the top of the old wooden staircase. It was the kind that consisted of just stairs, with no boards between them, so you could easily catch your foot on the way up and trip—as she had, many times, as a kid.

"Be careful on these rickety stairs," she cautioned.

He nodded. "No worries. I know my way around these old Wharton houses."

As they descended the stairs, Storm following behind, Tess noticed how dank and musty it smelled. Generations of dust hung in the air, along with a hint of malevolence that she always felt whenever she came down here.

Rows of metal shelves contained all manner of junk—old paint cans, gardening things, tools. A spade. A shovel. A pair of big loppers, all well worn and covered in dust. Her grandmother had been an avid gardener, but it seemed that nobody had set foot down here in years. Certainly she herself hadn't, not since her grandmother had passed away.

"This basement is actually in pretty good shape," Wyatt said.

"Really?" Tess wrinkled her nose at the gloom.

"Sure, it could use a good cleaning, but everything looks sound to me." Wyatt spotted the furnace. "Here we are," he said, nodding toward the behemoth.

"You're familiar with these?" Tess asked.

"Intimately," he said with a chuckle. "You don't have to stay down here while I tinker around if you aren't completely fascinated by old heating units."

Tess smiled, relieved. "I'll be in the kitchen if you need anything," she said and headed back up the stairs.

She brewed another pot of coffee, just in case Wyatt wanted a second cup after he worked. Then, she sank down on one of the kitchen chairs and waited.

Tess's thoughts floated here and there. As she considered this man, she thought about the fact that, over the years, she had observed a few types of people in Wharton and on Ile de Colette, the island a twenty-minute ferry ride away.

Like many tourist communities, there were the summer people who had vacation homes in the area. Many, including her own family, had rather upscale tastes, which was why Jim's grocery store always stocked fine cheeses from England, France, and Italy; charcuterie; organic produce; fresh pasta. If you needed the odd can of marinated artichoke hearts, pomegranate seeds, or a baby eggplant for a recipe, you could always pick it up there, along with locally grown veggies and other things like jams and pies made by people in the area. Many of the shops, too, catered to summer people, both homeowners and tourists, stocking expensive, trendy clothes, locally made jewelry, pottery.

And then there were the year-round residents of a few different ilks. Some were artisans, writers, musicians, painters, chefs, and other creative types who had somehow found their way to the area and stayed because of the artistic vibe. Others, like her friend Simon, ran businesses that catered to the tourist trade. Still others had grown up in Wharton or on Colette and were the people who kept the place running. Regular working folk who plowed the streets and ran the ferries and fixed what went wrong in the fancy houses, cobbling together a living as the backbone of the community. Tess figured Wyatt was in that camp. If he didn't know how to do something, fix it, or handle it, he'd know someone who did. Together, they made Wharton.

Soon, she heard him climbing up the stairs. He came through the doorway with a smile on his face.

"All set," he said. "Like I figured, I'm going to bleed your radiators. I think that's going to do the trick."

"Oh?" Tess said. "Is that a big process, or . . . ?"

Wyatt shook his head. "Easy. It's just a matter of turning a valve on each radiator to relieve the air pressure and let that air escape. It's common in houses with hot-water heat."

"Great!" Tess said. "Can you do it now? Do you have time?"

"You bet," Wyatt said, fishing inside his tool kit and coming up with a small key. He smiled an infectious smile as he held it up to show her. "This is all I need." He looked around. "I'm going to start at the other end of the house and work my way toward the kitchen," he explained. "Do you want heat in every room? We can turn some of them off, if you'd like. Why heat the whole house if you're not using it, right?"

Tess hadn't thought of that. She turned it over in her mind. "I think we'll heat the whole main floor," she began, "but upstairs, maybe just my bedroom and bathroom?"

"Sounds like a plan," Wyatt said.

"Can we turn on the heat pretty easily if I have people coming to stay?" Tess asked. "My son is coming for the holidays, and maybe earlier than that."

"No problem," Wyatt said. "You'll be surprised how fast a room heats up."

Tess smiled at him. "Okay. Let's do it!"

Wyatt set off, and within an hour or so, he was back in the kitchen, bleeding the radiator there. It really was a simple process, Tess noticed. "Let's go upstairs next," he said. "You can show me which room is yours, and which you might want to heat for your boy."

Tess pushed her chair back from the table and led Wyatt up the back stairs to her bedroom, silently grateful for the advice her grandmother had given her long ago, when she was just a child.

"Honey, always make your bed first thing in the morning," Grandma Serena would say. "That way, you'll start the day accomplishing something. One small thing. Then you'll build on that."

It wouldn't do to let this stranger see her bed rumpled and unmade. Tess didn't know quite why, but the sight of it would have felt too intimate, too personal. As it was, her bed was as tidy as any would be in the B&B she intended to turn this house into.

After her room and bathroom were handled and Tess could hear the heat hissing in the radiators, she thought it was a good time to talk about her other to-dos with this man.

"So . . . I have a couple of other projects that I need done sooner rather than later, and I'm wondering—can I show you what they are? Maybe you can take them on, or if not, maybe you know someone who can?"

Wyatt smiled, leaned against the doorframe, and ran a hand through his hair. "Sure," he said. "What kinds of projects?"

She stepped through the doorway. "I'll show you."

They made their way down the hall to the shuttered door.

CHAPTER SIX

"This door leads to the back part of the second floor," she said, as they stood in front of it. "I had the idea of renovating it into an owner's suite, for me to live in when I open this place up to guests."

"Oh? You're making it into a B&B?"

Tess nodded. "That's the idea," she said. "I'm hoping to have it ready for summer, but I really don't know what the renovation is going to entail."

"So, you don't know what condition it's in?"

She shook her head. "I've never been back there," she said. "It's been closed off as long as I can remember. My grandmother had said something about it being too expensive to heat or maintain or something, and when my parents inherited the house, they just never bothered with it. We used it as a vacation home, so there was really no need."

Wyatt ran his hand along the wooden door. "No knob, even," he said. "It's completely shuttered, then, not just locked." He glanced back at her. "We could break it down, but that would be a shame, this beautiful old door." He touched the doorframe and the hinges. "We could take this off entirely. Or—is there a back way in? Windows?"

She nodded. "There's one room that looks like it was a sunroom or even a greenhouse. It juts out and has big windows on three sides. But they've been shuttered, too."

"Hmm," Wyatt said, still staring at the door. "Now that I think about it, those windows would have one-hundred-year-old glass, if I'm estimating the age of this house correctly. Maybe older. You don't want to break that, either. Easiest way in will probably be through this door."

"Ideally, what I'd like in the end, when all the renovations are complete, is to be able to lock this door when I have guests in the house," Tess said. "Not that they'd . . ." Her words trailed off.

"Oh, no, I get that," Wyatt said. "You need your privacy and protection from people who are, really, strangers under your roof."

The two of them walked down the back stairs together, into the kitchen.

"Another cup of coffee?" Tess offered. "Or water? I've got some sparkling."

"Water would be great, actually," Wyatt said.

"Please, take a seat." Tess motioned to the kitchen table as she opened the fridge and pulled out two cans of sparkling water. She handed one to Wyatt and joined him at the table.

"I can get the door opened up for you," he said, taking a sip, considering it. "Not a problem. I have a crew of guys who can help with the renovation, too, depending on what you need. That is, if you want me to do it."

"Are you sure it's not too much?" she said. "I was hoping you might have time, but . . ."

"Absolutely," he said, smiling. "Things slow way down in Wharton in the winter, so I've got plenty of time. And I'm sort of anxious to see what's behind that door, too, now that I know you've never been back there."

Tess winced, knowing what she was about to say next. "There's something else you need to know, before we open the door," she said. "It's the other project I need help with. I meant to mention it to you earlier."

"Oh? What's that?"

She took a deep breath. "I think there's an animal living back there," she said with another wince.

His eyes grew wide. "An animal? What makes you say that?"

Tess glanced at Storm. "I've been hearing scratching noises at night," she said. "And last night, Storm was very upset and stood at that door, growling."

"Oh yeah," Wyatt said, nodding. "Dogs know. No doubt. You've got a critter. Maybe a few. What does it sound like? Mice? If so, that's an easy fix."

Tess shook her head. "I'm not sure, but I think whatever it is, it's bigger than a mouse. Or mice. I'm thinking, like, a squirrel or, God forbid, a raccoon."

"How long have you been hearing it? The scratching."

"Since winter fell," she said. "I moved here in September and didn't hear anything until, I don't know, late November, maybe. So just a couple of weeks. But not every night."

"Only at night?"

She nodded. "I figured it was some kind of reaction to me opening up the house and starting renovations. I was hoping it would just go away, but . . ."

"Sometimes animals that get in leave on their own, back the way they came," Wyatt said. "Especially now because there's a dog in the house. Animals can smell dogs and won't stick around. But—" He paused before continuing.

"But what?"

"If it's a raccoon, or even if it's a couple of squirrels, they can do a lot of damage in a very short time," he said. "We should get that door open today and see what we're dealing with. Tomorrow at the latest."

Tess's eyes grew wide. "Today?" she squeaked. There it was again, the gnarling feeling in her stomach every time she thought about opening that door. "Isn't that a little sudden?"

Wyatt shook his head. "No," he said. "You could have major damage back there because of that animal." He slid his chair back from the table and pushed himself up to his feet. "Let me get going and make a couple of calls. I know a guy in Salmon Bay who specializes in getting animals out of houses—raccoons, squirrels, even a bear once, I heard. He traps them humanely and moves them into the woods."

"You don't think it's a bear . . . ?"

"No, no. I highly doubt a bear would be hibernating in your house." He chuckled. "But if it's a raccoon, that's sort of your worst-case scenario. They can and will fight if cornered, especially by a dog. And can carry rabies. You don't want this guy"—he nodded toward Storm—"anywhere near that. You'll need somebody who's trained to get it out. I'll call my guy in Sammy. Once we get the thing trapped and out of here, then we can see what we're dealing with in terms of how it got in."

Tess stood up to see him out. "So, you think it'll be today?"

Wyatt nodded, pulling on his parka. "Depending on what my guy has going. But like I said, things quiet down in the winter, so I wouldn't be surprised if he can make it happen today."

Tess closed the door behind him and watched him climb into his well-worn truck, tossing the tool kit into the back. *Okay,* she said to herself. *This is happening.*

❧

Tess snapped on Storm's leash and bundled up. She felt like taking a long walk, despite the cold. After wandering around town, Storm sniffing here and there, her waving to Jim through the window as she passed the grocery store and to Beth St. John, who owned Wharton's independent bookstore, Just Read It, she circled back and started up toward home.

From her vantage point, a couple of blocks away from the house, she could see that back room on La Belle Vie, with its windows that had been boarded shut for generations.

Except, now, one wasn't.

Tess could see the glass reflecting the sun, as clear as day, while the others were dark. She hadn't noticed it before. When was the last time she had been around to the back of the house? She couldn't recall.

All at once, she saw a shadow in the window. Movement, a dark thing. She held her breath. There it was again. A shape.

So, it was true. Something was in there. Or was it a trick of the light?

She quickened her step, hurrying up the street toward the back of the house where she saw it. Sure enough. One of the boards on the windows had been taken down.

Tess just stood there, looking up at it, wondering, the tightness growing in her stomach. Could a raccoon do that? She had heard of raccoons taking covers off chimneys, pulling away flashing, and even peeling off roof shingles to get inside. She squinted up at the window. It wasn't broken that she could see. But whatever it was might have found itself trapped inside and somehow pried off the shutters in an effort to get out. She needed to call Wyatt. He was right. It had to be today. She didn't want to spend another night without this being taken care of.

It was dangerous not only for her and Storm but also for the animal that was trapped inside without food or water. She hadn't thought of that before. Delaying would mean a slow death for whatever was in there, and Tess couldn't stomach that.

She hurried back inside and snapped off Storm's leash. She crossed the kitchen to the hallway alcove to call Wyatt, but before she had a chance to reach the phone, it started to ring.

It was him. "Hey, Tess. My guy from Salmon Bay can be at the house by about two o'clock. Is that too soon?"

"No!" she said, louder than she had intended. "I was just out for a walk and noticed one of the shutters is off one of the back windows."

He was quiet for a moment. "It wasn't like that before, I'm assuming?"

"Not that I noticed. Ever since I can remember, those windows have been shuttered, dark."

"Got it," he said. "I'll bring another hand to help me get that door off, and we'll see what we're dealing with. My guy from Sammy is going to bring some traps and other gear. We'll get this handled for you."

"Thank you," she said.

Tess glanced at the clock on the wall. A couple of hours to wait.

She had been planning this renovation for months, but always made some excuse to delay the project. And, now, she remembered the reason why.

When she thought back on her childhood of growing up in this house on summer vacations and holidays, she realized she had always felt a sense of unease about that door. She'd hurry by it if she was going down the back stairway or, better yet, avoid it altogether by using the main stairs. There was always something vaguely malevolent about it to her. She could feel it, but her grandmother, and later, her parents, would always pooh-pooh it away as nothing but a child's imagination.

It wasn't just that door, she realized. She had remembered, earlier that day, feeling uneasy in the basement, too. But wasn't that normal in very old houses? The basements weren't exactly inviting. They were usually unfinished, dank, smelly, and filled with things that would scare young children: old trunks, ancient toys, mementoes from another time. History hung in the air in those types of basements. No matter how much spit and polish you used to renovate them, they still clung to the past. And whatever demons that past might contain.

But at the same time, Tess realized that, as the years passed, those childhood fears had faded, as childhood fears do. The boogeyman didn't live under beds. Mirrors weren't gateways to the unknown and didn't harbor specters that would appear if you chanted their names three times. Monsters didn't lurk in closets. Things that went bump in the night were just old radiators, and the groans of an aging house were just its bones settling down for a nap. Sure, they bubbled to the surface now, but Tess figured that was the memory of the past rekindling, as it did with other memories of her lifetime growing up in the house. Board games in the drawing room. Music after dinner. Playing in the backyard.

There was nothing so scary about that door or what lay beyond it.

CHAPTER SEVEN

The time it took for Wyatt and his crew to arrive seemed to drag on forever. Would they never come? Storm curled up at Tess's feet in the living room as she tried to immerse herself in a book, the hissing radiators taking the chill out of the air.

Finally, the dog raised his head, ears perked, and growled. He glanced at Tess as he jumped to his feet and made his way into the kitchen. She followed. The knock came a few moments later.

Tess opened the door and ushered in Wyatt and two other men, red faced from the cold, all laden with toolboxes. One was carrying a metal trap that had been folded up, and the other was toting a step stool.

"Thank you for coming so quickly," she said, closing the door behind them.

"Tess, meet Grant and Hunter," Wyatt said, motioning to the other men. "Grant does a little bit of everything around Wharton, and Hunter's our guy from Salmon Bay who can handle that critter invasion problem for you."

"Hunter?" she said, grinning at the burly man with thick reddish-brown hair. "Well, that's appropriate."

He let out a loud laugh, his eyes twinkling. "Don't I know it? I guess my line of work was meant to be, now wasn't it?" A slight brogue added music to his words. Tess couldn't tell if it was Scottish or Irish, but whatever it was, it suited him. Tess warmed to him immediately. She wondered what had brought him to Wharton, but figured it was probably the same story as so many others: came as a tourist and stayed.

"We'll get whatever has taken up residence out of here and back into the wild," he went on, smiling broadly. "Don't you worry about that."

The man loved his work, that was clear, Tess thought.

The other man, Grant, was quieter, much more reserved. Older. He seemed uneasy. Almost uncomfortable. His hair was sort of that non-color between blond, brown, and gray—maybe a mixture of all three, and he was thin and wiry. This man worked physically for a living, there was no doubt. His face was deeply lined, as though he had lived hard at some time in his life. But his eyes were a deep brown and held a kindness and depth that Tess could see right away. *Still waters run deep*, she heard her grandmother whisper in her ear.

As they hung up their coats, Wyatt was chattering.

"Okay!" he said, clapping his hands together. "First thing is getting the door off. I think all it's going to take is removing those hinges, but we'll see when we get into it."

Hunter held up his hand. "Before that's done, we need to make sure all of the doors of the other rooms upstairs are closed. And"—he turned to Tess—"is there a door at the bottom or top of the stairway? The last thing we need is that critter to run from the back room once we get that door off and find its way into the main part of the house."

Tess had to think about that for a minute. "There's a door from the second floor to the back stairway, so we can close that. But the front stairs are wide open, I'm afraid."

Hunter squinted. "Okay, we'll deal with that. It might mean moving a couple of boxes or pieces of furniture in front of the stairway, to block the animal's hasty retreat, if it comes to that. They don't usually get by me, but there's always a chance." He winked at her.

Tess couldn't help laughing. Then she thought of the old steamer trunks she had bought on a recent antiquing trip with Simon. "I know just the thing. In the third bedroom down the hall, there are some antique trunks. That should do the trick."

The crew gathered up their various tools and were about to climb the back stairs, Tess and Storm following behind, when Wyatt turned around and stopped her.

"You might want to stay down here with him," Wyatt said, scratching Storm on the top of the head. "We'll get the door off and assess the situation. Hunter will do whatever he does to discern if an animal is living back there, and if so, what kind of animal. He'll find where it goes in and out. It's best that you keep Storm down here in a room where you can shut the doors. The last thing you want is this dog to be on the scene when an angry, scared raccoon bolts out of there. He's a tough guy, but I've seen raccoons fighting, and it's not a pretty situation."

Good point, Tess thought, imagining the chaos that would occur if Storm started chasing, or much worse, cornered, a raccoon. "Okay," she said. "I can stay right here with him in the kitchen. I'll wait until you tell me it's safe to come upstairs."

He smiled at her and raised his eyebrows. "Are you anxious to see what's behind the door?"

She nodded. "Weirdly, yes. I mean, I can do without a full-on animal infestation, but I'm very curious to find out what's back there."

"I'll do my best not to damage the door in any way," he said. "I know you want to be able to close and lock it."

"Godspeed," she said, chuckling. He might need it.

Tess closed the stairway door behind Wyatt, and she heard them tromping their way down the hall, toolboxes, animal trap, and all. She crossed the room and closed the door into the dining room, too, just to be safe.

And now, more waiting. Tess sank into a chair with a sigh. Storm seemed to sigh, too, perhaps wishing he were part of the action. But his ears were alert, listening to what was happening just one flight away.

For the next hour or so, Tess could hear banging and muffled voices. Her stomach was in a tight knot as she wondered what was happening up there. *Did they get the door off? Did they find an animal?*

Storm, who had been lying in front of the fire, got to his feet, ears perked. He began to pace around the kitchen, patrolling from door to door to door.

A loud bang from upstairs reverberated through the house, and Storm stopped in his tracks. The fur on his back stood up. His lip curled to expose his fangs. The dog was staring at the back stairs, snarling like a wolf. A serious, deadly warning.

There it was again. *Bang, bang, bang.*

Tess pushed her chair back from the table and stood up, too, slowly, watching Storm all the while. His intensity took her breath away. He was on point to attack. She realized she didn't know this dog, not really. He had been with her for only a couple of days. Would he turn on her? But as soon as the thought went through her mind, she dismissed it. Somehow, some way, she knew he was protecting her. She felt it, deep inside.

"What is it?" she managed to squeak out.

It seemed obvious that Hunter must have found whatever it was that had been scratching. Tess hoped he had it trapped by now. She also hoped the animal hadn't done too much damage. She could only imagine the level of cleaning she'd have to do if it had been trapped in there for any length of time. Her stomach tightened. Then, footsteps on the stairs. Someone hurrying down.

The door opened and Wyatt came through it just as Storm blew by him, barking furiously as he raced up the stairs.

"Whoa!" Wyatt said, nearly bowled over by the dog.

Tess gasped and locked eyes with Wyatt for a moment before she hurried up the stairs after the dog, Wyatt following close behind.

They ran down the hallway toward the door, which Tess could now see was open. Storm roared through it, barking deep and low.

"Hey, big fella. Easy now." It was Hunter, talking to Storm. Tess stopped in the doorway to see the dog respond to the man, take it down a notch, and scan the room.

"Did you trap the animal that was in here?" she asked, wincing. "Or is it still on the loose?" As she said it, she caught a glimpse of the trap. It was empty. Her stomach dropped.

"Storm," she called into the darkness. And sure enough, the dog appeared, trotting to her side. But his ears were perked, the fur on his back standing straight up. *He may not be stalking anything right now, but he's ready,* Tess thought.

"There's no animal," Hunter said. "I've checked all throughout the room. There's no way anything could've gotten in or out. Come and take a look for yourself. I'll show you."

Tess exchanged a glance with Wyatt. He nodded, as if to say, *It's okay.*

She took in a deep breath and walked over the threshold of the door that had been closed to her for her whole life.

"As you can see," Hunter began, shining a flashlight into the corners and onto the ceiling, "there is no entranceway . . ."

He continued his explanation, but Tess wasn't really listening. She was entranced by what she was seeing for the first time.

It was one big room, spacious, uncluttered, surrounded by windows on three sides, all but one window shuttered. Tess noticed what seemed to be an added room or an alcove of some kind, in one corner—a bathroom, perhaps? A dressing room?

A shaft of dusty light streamed in from the one exposed window, but the rest of the room was dark and gray. Shapes stood here and there, but Tess couldn't quite tell what they were.

Sure enough, there was the one open window. Tess saw the shutter, a wood panel the size of the window it had covered, placed neatly on the floor beneath it. How in the world had it gotten there? Who had opened that shutter? It certainly hadn't been pulled off by a raccoon.

Maybe she had been mistaken, she thought. Maybe it had been open all the while.

Her footsteps echoed, and she rubbed her arms against the chill.

She flipped a light switch. Nothing. "Can we get any more light in here?" she asked nobody in particular. "I'm assuming the electricity has been turned off, but what about the windows? Can we get those shutters off?" The day was bright and blue, and the sun would light up this room instantly. She desperately wanted to see the secrets this room held.

Grant gave her a quick nod. "We can remove these pretty easily," he said, tapping on one of the shutters. "They're just attached by a hook at the top of the sash." He grabbed the step stool he had brought with him and moved it under one of the windows, climbed up on it, and began to pry one of the hooks open. He tugged at the shutter for a moment until he was able to lift it off. Wyatt took it from him and set it onto the floor. They did the same with a few of the other windows, and soon the sunlight was streaming in.

What Tess had seen as dark, inky shapes came into view as the sun lit up the room. A long wooden table, well worn and covered in paint splatters, tubes, and small tubs, along with a few cloths. Brushes were strewn here and there. An easel lay on the floor by a window—was it broken? A sagging sofa and an armchair sat against one wall. Chairs were overturned. A coffee table lay on its side.

On the floor, more tubes and paint cans, some having spilled onto the hardwood and dried long ago. Shards of glass glinted in the sun.

Empty bottles of wine lay here and there, and one dusty bottle still stood, uncorked, on the table, next to a wineglass.

All at once, it hit her. Of course—this was the studio of Sebastian Bell. This was where her grandfather had painted his priceless works of art.

She could just imagine him, sitting at the easel, brush in hand, putting the final strokes on the paintings that hung in galleries all over the world. This was where the magic, the artistry that had captivated so many, had happened. This very spot.

It amazed Tess that, during all her growing-up years, all the lazy summer days and cool nights she had spent in this house, she had never thought twice about her grandfather's studio being here. Her grandmother had never mentioned it. Tess had always just assumed he had a studio in town. In the gallery, perhaps, or in one of the old buildings by the waterfront. He had always been inspired by the water, so it made sense to her he would have had an artist's studio or loft there.

Why wouldn't she have known about the studio being right here, under this roof? But, as Tess thought more about it, as she looked around this room, she realized it wasn't all that surprising. She didn't know much about Sebastian Bell at all. Not where his studio was. Not the kind of person he was. Even though she was his only grandchild, she didn't have a peek behind the curtain. She had no idea what he had been like as a man, a husband, a father. Certainly not as a grandfather—he had died long before she was born. She saw what the public saw, an artist with an incredible talent. A man who was inspired by the greatest of great lakes. A man who saw beauty in the lake's fury, and suspicion in the lake's calmness. That was what his paintings conveyed, anyway.

Grandma Serena and Tess's dad didn't often talk about Sebastian Bell, but when they did, it was in the way one might talk about a famous person in history, in the context of him being a great artist whom the world admired. And more than that, a great man. A beloved son of Wharton. A patron of the arts. He was known to frequent art classes at the Wharton schools, showing up with a flourish, giving pointers to aspiring young painters.

There was a tangible cloak of pride wrapped around her family because of him, a feeling of reverence, admiration. Yes, he was a member of the family, but so out of reach, so untouchable, that the idea of him painting here, in the studio in this house that Tess had grown up in, seemed like discovering a buried treasure.

But, as Tess turned it over and over in her mind, she realized the whole thing was more of a disconnect. It was too personal to think of the great man here. This was the house where she had played with her dolls, written in her diary, lain on her bed fretting about boys she had met during her summer vacations. To think of him putting his greatest inspirations down on canvas just steps away from her bedroom? It didn't quite seem real. It was like discovering Picasso had spent time painting in your basement.

". . . so that's how I know you haven't had an animal." Hunter had been yammering this whole time.

How long had she been standing there? A few seconds? Minutes? A lifetime? Tess wasn't sure, but his words drew her out of her entrancement. She blinked her eyes a few times and shook her head.

"You're telling me there's no way an animal could've gotten in or out?" she said, finally.

"No," he said, drawing out the word. "I'm not saying definitively a mouse couldn't have found its way in here. All old houses have mice. That's just something we all live with. I'd need to look more carefully in the light, but right now, I'm not seeing any holes or cracks or any way anything bigger than that could've gotten in."

He walked over to the fireplace, bent down, and shone his flashlight up into the chimney. "The flue is closed," he said. "Even if a squirrel or another animal managed to get in, it's not like they're closing it up behind them. To my eyes, this flue is the only way into this room, and it's shut up tight."

"Are you sure?" Tess asked him. "All of these nooks and crannies? Nothing could've gotten in or out? I've been hearing something behind this door. Did Wyatt tell you about that? Scratching. At night. There was definitely something in here."

Hunter shrugged. "I don't know what to tell you," he said. "I'll take a more careful look around, for sure, but you can see for yourself that this room hasn't really been disturbed. Yes, things are in a bit of . . ."— he chose his words carefully—"disarray. But I'm telling you, if a squirrel or raccoon were in here, there would be a lot more damage. These sheets would be torn up, to make nests, for one thing. There would be an access point. A hole that we could readily see."

"What about bats?" Tess said, cringing.

Hunter shook his head. "We don't have a lot of bats in Wharton, and those that are here hibernate during the winter. If you had bats hibernating in the house, there wouldn't be just one, but a lot of them. And we'd have seen them right away. And smelled them."

She cringed at the thought of it. She and Hunter locked eyes for a moment, and her imaginings of her grandfather fell to the ground in a heap. She had other things, more real and tangible, to worry about. The look on this man's face said it all.

A tingling worked its way up Tess's spine. If that were true, if there had been nothing in this room all this time, what had been doing the scratching?

CHAPTER EIGHT

All at once, Tess wanted everyone out of this part of the house. She didn't want to talk about animal intruders. She didn't want to talk about the scratching, much less think about what she—and Storm—had heard.

In addition to that, Tess was overtaken by the uneasy feeling that these men, these strangers, were standing in *Sebastian Bell's* studio. Hallowed ground for most of the art world. Her stomach gnarled at the haphazard way it had been left. Paints open, spills long since dried up. Easel on its side. Wine bottles everywhere. It wasn't as though her grandmother had cleaned it up after Sebastian had died. It seemed to Tess that it was just the opposite. The room had been shut up quickly. To not even take the wine bottles to the trash? To not have tidied up just the least little bit before closing the door forever? Why?

"I'll bet you guys could use a beer right about now," she said, her voice shaky. She walked toward the doorway, trying to get on more stable footing. "Let's reconvene in the kitchen."

With that, she made her way into the hall and toward the back stairs, her heart beating in her throat.

In the kitchen, she crossed the room to the fridge, grabbed a bottle, and held it aloft. "Any takers?"

"Twist my arm," Grant said, with the first smile she had seen from him since he had gotten there.

"Just to be sociable," Hunter chuckled, pulling a chair out from the table and sinking down into it.

"I can't let them drink alone," Wyatt said, joining Hunter at the table. "That's just not right."

Tess handed beers all around and poured a glass of wine for herself. She took a sip with shaking hands.

"Thanks for all of the help, guys," she said, glancing from one to the other.

Wyatt took a sip of his beer, considering the job's postmortem. "It really wasn't too much trouble getting the door open," he said. "Once we got the hinges off, a couple of good bangs did the trick."

Grant eyed Hunter and gave him a small smile. "It was this guy who was responsible for all of the theatrics, with his heavy gloves and his trap—"

"He was ready for a tiger to pounce out of there," Wyatt said.

"And if one had, you'd have been mighty glad I was prepared, smart guy," Hunter said, laughter in his voice.

Tess couldn't help but smile, even as a tendril of dread was working its way up her spine. All the laughter and good feelings at the table seemed to fade into the background as one thought centered itself in the forefront of her mind.

What was making the scratching noises? And would she be safe from it tonight, with the door open? She imagined herself huddled under the covers, the scratching ringing through the dark house.

"What are your feelings on next steps?"

Wyatt's question brought her back into the room. Tess shook her head. "I'm not sure. Cleaning, I guess, is at the top of the list. Then I'll be able to see what I'm dealing with."

"Tess is thinking of turning the space into an owner's suite, for when guests arrive," Wyatt explained to the others. "I hope I'm not speaking out of turn here."

Tess waved away his concern. "No, that's the plan. It's no secret that I'm opening an inn. Intending to, anyway. And I'll need help getting that suite in shape, that's for sure. If you guys are available—"

Wyatt nodded. "My life is so very rich and full that I have absolutely nothing going on. So, weirdly, I'm available."

Tess chuckled. She liked this man. He seemed familiar to her, somehow.

"Wharton gets so sleepy during this time of year," Hunter added. "I don't want to use the term *ghost town*, but . . . all of us who work in the tourist trade cobble together this and that in the winter."

"And not much of this, and very little of that," Grant said, surprising Tess with his humor. Laughter all around.

"I guess you've got yourself a crew, for better or worse," Wyatt said with a grin.

"A motley one, but a crew," Hunter piped up.

"Now that you've seen the space, what are you thinking?" Wyatt asked.

Tess hadn't thought that far ahead, but his question set her imagination whirring. It was one big room, with an added smaller room that Tess thought might be a bathroom. She hoped it was, because then the plumbing would already be there. The pipes may need to be replaced, but it would not have to be plumbed from scratch. That was a big plus. Maybe there would be room to add a deep claw-foot tub or a jacuzzi.

In her mind, she saw a sort of studio apartment for herself, with a sleeping area in one corner (near the fireplace?) and a living area in the other, with an overstuffed sofa and a chair-and-a-half with an ottoman. Bookshelves could line the one wall without windows. A television, somewhere. Maybe a small fridge and a hutch for a few dishes.

She searched her mind, thinking back to what she had seen in the room—had there been a closet? If not, she'd have to build one. Wouldn't be too difficult, she figured.

What of the floors? Tess hadn't really noticed them but assumed they'd be the same hardwood as the rest of the house. They might need refinishing, which was also easy enough to do.

In her mind, she saw colors. Indigo and amethyst, accented with gray, for Sebastian Bell's children and grandchild. The colors could be in the rugs and on the walls, in accent pillows and the bedspread.

It came together so easily. In an instant.

She smiled up at Wyatt. "I think I know exactly what I want to do in there," she said. "But a closer look will tell us more."

Grant finished his beer and placed the bottle on the table with finality. He pushed his chair back from the table and got to his feet. "I hate to break up the party, but Susan is expecting me," he said. "We're having dinner with the kids on Zoom." He rolled his eyes as he elongated the word.

Tess glanced at the clock. Nearly five. She hadn't realized it was so late, but as she looked out the window, she saw the twilight illuminating the snow. Her favorite time of day.

"I'd better run, too," Hunter said, taking a last sip. "Don't want to make that drive back to Salmon Bay in the dark."

Tess nodded. She knew that road well.

"So, listen," Wyatt began. "I'll huddle with Tess to talk about next steps. Then I'll get back with you two—"

Tess held up a hand to stop him. "We haven't talked about money yet. We should get that straight before—"

Wyatt shook his head. "Of course. We'll get all that worked out, but don't expect this to cost anything close to a fortune."

"We're cheap labor!" Hunter piped up. "Especially for a neighbor who's opening a business in the area. We pitch in to help our own around here."

"Yes, indeed," Grant said. "It'll keep me off the streets."

Tess looked around the room and smiled. This was one of the treasures of Wharton, the community spirit of neighbor-helping-neighbor that most everyone seemed to embody. But she had no intention of letting them do the work for subpar rates, or worse, for free. As they said, all of them had to cobble together a living during the winter months. She'd definitely pay them.

"I'll keep the fridge stocked with beer and feed you, too," Tess said.

Wyatt raised his eyebrows. "I've been told you're quite the chef," he said. "Jim hasn't stopped talking about the dinner you served last night."

Tess smiled. "It was fun to cook for people. I haven't done that in a long time."

After a round of goodbyes and seeing Hunter and Grant off, Tess said, "It's about time for me to walk Storm."

"I could join you on the walk?" Wyatt asked. "I love this time of day in the winter."

What a wonderful idea, Tess thought, and the two of them pulled on coats, boots, and hats, and hitched up Storm, who was already wiggling with excitement. The three of them stepped out into the cold as Tess closed the door behind them.

Winter twilight in Wharton was a magical time. The sunset cast purple and pink hues across the sky, illuminating the snow with a bluish cast. The lake, with its deep, dark coldness, looked black in comparison, but it was still as glass against the frozen shoreline. Snow decorated the pines. It looked like a scene from an enchanted fairy tale.

They walked through town on the way down to the lake. Many of the houses were dark—homes of summer people, no doubt—but others were brightly lit. Tess could see families inside through their windows. Some were preparing for dinner, others were lounging in front of the television or reading. Many of the businesses in town were already closed for the night, but the lights of the Flamingo were on. It was one of the only restaurants open in the winter, along with the Frittata, which specialized in breakfast and lunch but also served dinner in the winters to locals.

LuAnn's boarding house and diner were closed up tight, as it always was during LuAnn's Hawaiian winter getaways, but up the hill, the lights in Harrison's House were blazing. As they passed Just Read It, the town's bookstore, its owner, Beth St. John, caught sight of them through the window and waved. Tess saw the coffee shop was still open, too.

As they reached the lakeshore, Tess marveled at the fact that it had frozen solid. The lake had so many forms, so many moods, so many colors. On the famous beach on Ile de Colette, the water was crystal clear. Some days, when storms were on the horizon, it was an ominous gray green. Other days, with the sun glinting on the water like diamonds, it was a deep blue.

With the northern lights sending shafts of greens and blues and purples into the sky on winter's nights, the purple sunset on the horizon at twilight, and the different colors of the lake, no wonder her grandfather had been inspired by this place. It was an artist's canvas.

"You grew up in the Twin Cities, right?" Wyatt said, breaking the silence.

Tess nodded. "I did. But I came to Wharton to visit my grandmother during the summers."

"Serena Bell," Wyatt said. "What a great lady."

Tess raised her eyebrows. "You knew her?"

Wyatt nodded. "I grew up here in Wharton," he said, looking out over the frozen lake. "My dad was a wilderness guide. He took people on kayaking trips throughout the Redemption Islands. I guess that's how I caught the bug to do it myself."

"Oh, that's what you do for a living? A guide? When you're not helping people turn on their heat?"

He chuckled at this. "In the summers, yes," he said. "I usually take three or four trips every summer, leading people from island to island, just like my dad did."

A wilderness guide. It seemed to suit him. But she had the feeling there was more to the story. With people in Wharton, it seemed there was always more to the story.

"So, how did you know my grandma?"

"I'd known of her around town, of course, but we really got to know each other when I was helping out on one of my dad's trips," he said, his eyes shining. "I was just out of high school at the time, so that's how long ago it was. She organized it. A group of senior women." He laughed, remembering. "We camped for four nights. It was a hoot. I would've pitied the bear who might have wandered into their campsite. Thank goodness the bears had the wisdom to stay away."

Tess looked at this man with new eyes.

"I had no idea," she said. "My grandma knew how to kayak?"

"She was a champ."

It made Tess wonder what else she didn't know about Serena.

They turned from the lake, then, and headed back up toward the house. "Feel like dinner?" Tess asked, without even thinking about it. "I could throw together a pasta dish with what I have on hand . . . ?"

All at once, Tess felt her face redden. Why had she blurted that out? What was she thinking? The man probably had someone to go home to. Obviously he did. Why had she been so forward? She winced a bit at what she thought might have been an awkward gaffe. The last thing she wanted was uncomfortable feelings between her and someone who was helping her with the house.

"I'm sorry—" she started.

"Pasta sounds great," he said, dispelling her fears in an instant. "I'd love that."

Tess smiled to herself. So it wasn't so inappropriate after all.

As they walked back up the hill toward the house, Tess eyed the man at her side. What did she know about him, really? Jim had recommended him to fix her heat, so there was that. He was handy around old houses. He had a dog, or dogs, she remembered, and was good with Storm. And now she learned he was a wilderness guide in the summers and, she assumed, an expert kayaker. You'd have to be to take groups into Lake Superior's unpredictable open water. And, he knew her grandmother. That was enough to have dinner with a man, wasn't it?

She wondered what else she might discover about Wyatt. And all at once, she realized she was eager to find out.

CHAPTER NINE

Back in her warm kitchen, Tess grabbed some pasta out of the cabinet and peered into the fridge to see what she had on hand. A couple of chicken breasts, Parmesan cheese, coconut milk. A half-full pack of bacon. Some fresh basil. Spinach in the crisper. Onions and tomatoes on the countertop.

"How about CBST pasta?" she asked.

"CBST?" Wyatt asked.

"Chicken, bacon, spinach, and tomato," Tess said, smiling.

It was one of Tess's go-to dishes, a fun twist on fettuccini Alfredo, without the heavy cream. After setting the pasta water on to boil, Tess cooked the bacon in the bottom of a heavy Dutch oven until it was crispy, and put it aside, reserving some of the drippings in the pot. To that, she added onion and garlic and, after sautéing for a few minutes, the chicken. After the chicken was nearly done, it was time for the tomatoes and spinach.

In that same pot, she scooched all the items to the side, added some olive oil and butter, and a bit more garlic. Once that was hot, she sprinkled in three tablespoons of flour. She stirred it around until it made a thick roux, and added a few cups of coconut milk, stirring until it all thickened up, scooping the chicken mixture into the fray. She finished it with the Parmesan, which melted around everything and created a cheesy goodness.

After she added the cooked pasta to the mix, she crumbled the bacon on top.

While Tess was busy at the stove, Wyatt put another couple of logs on the kitchen fire and poured drinks.

She served up the pasta, and they settled down at the table. Tess couldn't remember the last time she had cooked dinner for a man other than her ex-husband. She couldn't remember the last time she had been on a date. Was this a date? Was that what this was? No, she concluded. It wasn't a date. Tess eyed Wyatt across the table.

"This looks awesome," Wyatt said, oblivious to her wonderings.

During dinner, they chatted about Wharton in the winter, which businesses were open, which families typically stayed on. Tess asked about Grant and Hunter, both of whom Wyatt had known and worked with for many years. Grant was a father of three grown kids, she learned, all of whom lived out of state. Hunter was married to a teacher in the Salmon Bay schools.

As interesting as it was to learn more about her "crew," Tess's thoughts drifted back to the room upstairs, what they had found, and what they hadn't. She was anxious to go back in there and get a better look.

"Do you think it would be a major hassle to get the electricity turned on in the back room?" she asked as they were finishing up their pasta.

He shook his head. "I noticed a breaker down in the basement," he said. "Should be just a matter of flipping the switch. I'm sure Serena killed the power when she closed up the room, but I can't imagine she would've done anything more permanent than that, like cut the lines."

"Would you mind going downstairs with me now to find out?"

Wyatt pushed his chair back from the table, grabbed both of their plates and silverware, and set them in the sink. "Let's do it," he said.

Tess turned on the basement light, and they headed down the rickety stairs. Wyatt went right for the back wall, and Tess noticed the breaker box was there. She wasn't sure she had ever seen it before. Good thing to know about, she thought, shaking her head at herself.

She really should have learned everything there was to know about this house before starting to renovate it into an inn. She had a tendency to do that—jump into something without thinking about all the variables.

Wyatt opened up the box, and after a moment or two of studying it, he flipped a couple of switches.

"That should do the trick," he said, looking over his shoulder at Tess. "Should we go up and check it out?"

A moment later, they were climbing the back stairs to the second floor. Sure enough, Tess could see light blazing into the hallway from under the closed door. She remembered trying the switch earlier in the day. She must've left it on.

"You put the door back on its hinges," she said to him, smiling.

"We did," Wyatt said. "It didn't take any time at all. There's no knob, so it just pushes open and closed, but I figured you'd want it in its place until we get to putting a knob back on."

Tess pushed open the door. She was, at once, relieved to see that getting the electricity on in the room had been just a simple matter of flipping switches in the basement, but her stomach dropped as she took in the room's disarray once again. She was chagrined that Wyatt was seeing it, too.

She opened up her arms. "Why would my grandmother have left it like this?" she asked, not expecting an answer.

Wyatt winced and shrugged. "To tell you the truth, I was wondering the same thing earlier today when we opened it up. I didn't know your grandmother too terribly well, but it really doesn't seem like something she'd do."

Tess nodded. "I know. It doesn't. I mean—to not even do so much as throw the wine bottles into the trash before shutting the room up for good? I just don't get that."

"Did you ever ask her about it? Why she closed off the room?"

"No," Tess said, shaking her head. "Other than her explanation that it was too expensive to heat all winter, which doesn't make a whole lot of sense because, for the last several years she was alive, she went to Florida with my parents during the winters."

Tess thought back to all the summers she had spent at the house. She'd never given the closed door much thought, other than feeling a bit weird about it as she passed by on her way down the hall. Why hadn't she been the least bit curious?

"I can tell it's bothering you."

"Yeah," Tess said. "It really is. I just don't understand myself. Not even asking her about it. My dad never said anything about it, either. And the other thing . . ." Her words trailed off as she gazed around the room.

"The noises."

"Hunter said there were no animals in here, but I'm telling you, I've been hearing scratching sounds at night. And Storm heard them, too. I wasn't the only one."

"I believe you," Wyatt said. "It's nuts. But Hunter is right. If an animal had been in here, we'd see evidence of it. Not to be indelicate about it, but there would be poop everywhere."

"That's right! And he checked the whole area, right? Even this little room?" She pointed to the small room in one corner and began to walk toward it.

"Yes, he checked everywhere," Wyatt said. "I'm sure he was in there, too."

The door was closed. She tried the knob, and sure enough, it clicked. But she hesitated before pushing it open. A sense of dread soaked into her skin, through her pores. It was as though the very air in the room were warning her away.

She glanced back over her shoulder at Wyatt. "I feel really . . ."

He nodded. "I know. So do I, weirdly. But you should just open it. You're going to need to see what's in there eventually. It might as well be now."

When I've got someone here with me, Tess thought.

Tess pushed the door, slowly, gingerly, to reveal a bathroom, which seemed bigger on the inside than it looked from the outside. The room was dark—it had no windows—but she saw a claw-foot tub on one wall. A large sink and countertop across from it. Painting supplies were strewn all over the countertop. Pots of paints on the floor. Towels and brushes everywhere. Presumably painting rags. This must've been where Sebastian washed his brushes.

She flipped the light switch and gasped aloud as the overhead light illuminated the room. Everything was stained with a grayish rust-colored hue. The floor, the countertops, the sink, the tub. The towels and rags. *What in the world?*

Tess turned to Wyatt, who looked similarly confused.

"Paint, obviously, right?"

She shrugged. "I guess."

Only then did Tess notice the items that were leaned against the wall, behind the tub. Canvases. Several of them, stacked together, turned toward the wall. She couldn't see if they were empty canvases, or . . . could they be . . . ? She took a quick breath in. Were those canvases undiscovered paintings by Sebastian Bell? There had to be four or five of them, or more. They would be worth a fortune.

She shot a look at Wyatt—he was glancing down at the pots on the countertop and the towels and rags on the floor. She didn't think he had noticed the canvases. All at once, she very much wanted to be out of the room.

"Well, I guess Hunter was right," she said brightly, flipping off the light and ushering Wyatt out of the room. "No animals in here, either."

She gave the room a last look and pulled the bathroom door shut behind them. Her entire body was sizzling with the thought of what she might have just found. She was already imagining what she'd do next. When Wyatt left for the night, she would head back into the room to discover what, if anything, was on those canvases. If it was as she suspected—unknown works by Sebastian Bell—she'd call her father right away.

Wyatt had walked ahead of her, across the room and to the door, which they had swung half-closed behind them when they came in. The look on his face was quizzical . . . bordering on fear.

He glanced up toward her. "Tess," he said.

She stood, frozen to the spot where she stood in the middle of the floor. She shook her head, trying to stop the revelation that, somehow, she knew was coming.

He swung the door closed so she could see what he was seeing.

Scratch marks. Three long scratch marks.

CHAPTER TEN

Tess and Wyatt just stood there, staring at the door, mouths agape. Tess couldn't quite believe what she was seeing. And yet there it was.

"What is this?" Tess whispered, finally. She crept toward the door to get a closer look and ran her hands along the scratches that were clearly there, digging her own fingernails into the marks.

So, she hadn't imagined it.

"Are these new?" she asked, looking up at Wyatt. "I mean, fresh? Is this the scratching I heard?"

He shook his head. "I'm not sure." He pointed to the wood next to the scratch marks and winced. "And I'm not sure what this is, either."

A stain. A dark stain, different than the grain of the wood. Wyatt touched it and looked at his fingers. Nothing.

Was it paint? It looked the same as the stain in the bathroom.

Tess took a breath in, and all at once, the room seemed to fade into the distance. It became deathly silent, and Tess could see herself, there, in hazy detail, with Wyatt, observing the scratch marks on the door. It was as though she were above herself and Wyatt, looking down, floating on the ceiling of the room. A dark shadow was beside her.

Just as suddenly as it happened, she was back in her body with a thud. Tess blinked at Wyatt a few times and then very much wanted to be out of that room.

"Come on," she said, pushing him out the door and closing it, hard, behind him.

"Tess," he said, but she was already hurrying into the room next door.

"Help me with this," she said, pushing an antique armoire, but not getting anywhere with it.

Wyatt came through the doorway and stopped. "What are you doing?"

"I need to push this in front of the door to the studio," she said, grunting as she moved the massive piece of furniture less than an inch.

"Wait a minute, now," Wyatt said, holding up his hand and slowly walking toward her. "It's okay. Let's take a breath."

Tess looked at him, and it seemed like he was trying to calm a wild animal. Her? Was she the wild animal? What *was* she doing? She took a couple of deep breaths.

"I don't know," she said, shaking her head. "I just thought . . ." Her words evaporated into the fog that seemed to have settled in around her. Or in her mind.

"Tess, there is nothing in that room," Wyatt said, finally. "It really didn't look like those scratches were fresh."

"But I heard . . ." She didn't know what else to say. She'd heard what?

She tried again. "I just got a really bad feeling in there," she said, the words coming out slowly, carefully. "I don't know if I'll be able to sleep if that door is open."

Wyatt's expression was one of confusion. Furrowed brow. Narrowed eyes.

She understood the disconnect he seemed to be feeling. First, she couldn't wait to get the door open to see what the room contained. Now she said she wouldn't be able to sleep if it wasn't closed. And blocked.

Just then, Tess wished she had never done it.

Pandora's box.

Wyatt glanced around the room. "This armoire isn't going anywhere, not unless I get Grant and Hunter back over here to help us," he said. "But you and I can probably move the old steamer trunk in front of the door. If you're sure you want it there."

Tess nodded. "I'm sure."

Together, they shoved the trunk in front of the door, and Tess sat down on top of it with a sigh. "I know it's silly. If something is in that room, it might be able to open the door—which we can't lock yet—and crawl over this trunk."

Wyatt squinted at the trunk.

"Let's put some stuff on top of it. Pots and pans. A lamp. Something that would make noise if an animal does try to crawl over it."

Tess smiled at him. "That's a very good idea," she said.

They went from room to room and collected "noisemakers"—a couple of newer lamps that Tess could live without if they got broken, a silver bowl and pitcher, a wrought-iron candelabra. They stacked them on the trunk.

"Perfect," Tess said. She could almost feel her blood pressure dropping, her stomach untangling at the sight of it. There was no way an animal—or anything—could get out of the room and past that barricade without something falling to the floor and waking her up. And not just her. Storm would hear it immediately if anything made its way out of that room.

She looked around. Where was Storm? She realized she hadn't seen him since they went down into the basement to check the electricity.

And then, she caught sight of him. He was crouched at the end of the hallway, trained on the back stairs. The fur on his back was standing straight up, his ears at attention. He was growling, a low and menacing sound.

Tess shared a quick glance with Wyatt. He shrugged.

"Hey, boy," Wyatt said, a little too brightly. "What's up?"

Wyatt walked toward the dog until Storm turned and gave him a quick bark. *Stay back.* Wyatt stopped in his tracks.

Tess and Wyatt watched as Storm growled at someone, or something, on the back stairs. Tess's body vibrated with dread. And then Storm shot off, barking and snarling, running down the stairs at full speed.

Tess wasn't altogether sure she wanted to follow.

"Come on," Wyatt said, taking her arm. "We need to see what he's going after."

What was happening? Had opening the door let something loose into the house? That was the only thing Tess could think of to explain the dog's odd behavior. The guys had opened the door and then, perhaps, didn't realize that an animal—the thing that had been doing the scratching—had slipped by them and gotten into the main house. It was what Hunter feared might happen, after all. And apparently, it had.

But even as the possibility was turning over and over in Tess's mind, she knew it wasn't right. There was no animal in this house. Storm would've smelled it, heard it, found it hours ago.

So, what was he barking at now? What was he chasing?

Down in the kitchen, Tess saw Storm standing at the back door, growling.

"What's out there, boy?" she whispered, gingerly walking up to him. She looked out of the window into the whiteness beyond. She didn't see anything. Or anyone. She glanced back at Wyatt and shrugged.

"I'm going to check it out," Wyatt said, pulling on his coat. As he reached for the doorknob, Storm began growling again. Fiercer, this time.

As soon as Wyatt opened the door, Storm ran through it.

Wyatt followed, and Tess did, too, with no time to grab her coat. The cold pricked her face and arms and blasted through her sweater. But she didn't care. She was just watching Storm, who was walking down the driveway, sniffing.

Wyatt was close behind. He turned to Tess. "I don't see anything," he said. "Nothing unusual, anyway."

"Let's look for tracks in the snow," she said, walking along the sidewalk leading from the driveway to the front porch. Nothing out of the ordinary. Tess's own footprints from earlier in the day. Tracks left by Grant and Hunter and Wyatt. There were so many tracks, she couldn't be sure which, if any, were new.

Tess noticed Jim at the window of his house. He waved. A moment later, he appeared through his side door.

"Everything okay?" he called out.

"C'mon over," Tess called back. "I have a question for you."

Jim didn't bother with a coat, and as he crossed his sidewalk and onto her driveway, Tess could see he was wearing slippers. This brought a smile to her face. It was below zero. A true northerner.

By that time, Storm was satisfied that the threat—if there had been a threat at all—was gone. He was once again his old friendly self, standing at Wyatt's side. But Tess had noticed that the dog had patrolled the driveway and sidewalk, sniffing carefully, before coming back up to the house.

What had he been looking for?

Tess ushered Jim, Wyatt, and Storm back into the kitchen and shut the door behind them.

"What's up?" Jim said, scratching behind Storm's ears. "This fella was barking like the house was on fire."

"That's what I wanted to ask you," Tess said, and then told Jim the story of how the crew had opened the sealed door earlier in the day.

"Considering the scratching I heard, and Storm's reaction, I thought maybe an animal had slipped out of the room unnoticed and somehow gotten out of the house or . . ." Her words dissipated into the miasma of unreality that surrounded them. She didn't think that at all. But she was hoping Jim would corroborate it all the same. Maybe he had seen something that would make sense of all this.

But he shook his head. "I haven't seen anything, or anyone, around the house at all," Jim said. "Although, I trust dogs' reactions to things, and this guy was alerting you something wasn't right."

"Exactly my thought," Wyatt said. "We just don't know what that 'something' is."

Tess sighed. But then, she had a thought. "Jim, do you have a security camera?"

He shook his head. "I have them all around the store, but here at the house? No. We've never needed one."

Tess made a mental note to get cameras for her front and side doors.

The three of them chatted for a bit about other things, then, but Tess wasn't really listening. She wasn't sure what, exactly, had happened. Her mind was going in so many directions at once, and she didn't like any of them.

The only thing she knew for sure was that she wanted to get back into the room. Despite all this strangeness—the scratching, Storm's reactions—she was more concerned with something all too real. She had to know if those canvases were undiscovered paintings by her grandfather.

But at the same time, her stomach knotted at the idea of exploring the room by herself, at night. Even with Storm here, that room held too many strange and unsettling vibes for her to feel comfortable going back in there alone.

As she looked from Wyatt to Jim, she wondered whom she would trust to go into that room with her, given the very real possibility there would be artwork worth multiple millions stacked haphazardly there. She didn't know these men, not really. They were friendly strangers, who, she hoped, would become true friends. But she wasn't about to risk trusting either of them with a fortune. There was only one person to trust with the notion there could be undiscovered Sebastian Bells lying around, she concluded, and that was Eli. And he wasn't here with her. She would have to go back into that room alone. But during the light of day.

"Well, I think I'll head back home," Jim said, touching Tess's arm. "You call me if you get the feeling something's not right. Anytime. Jane and I are just a few steps away."

Tess pulled him into a hug. "Thank you," she said.

He shook his head. "Think nothing of it. Dinner at our place next week?"

"I'd love that," she said.

And then he was off, scuffing across the snowy driveway in his slippers.

"Okay, so that was a whole lot of nothing," Wyatt said, pulling out a kitchen chair and sinking down into it. "We don't have any answers, do we?"

"No," Tess said, shrugging. "So much is running through my mind right now, I can barely form a coherent thought."

"I get that," Wyatt said. "The scratches. The stains. Storm's weird behavior."

"All of that," she said. "Plus, I've always felt a little weird about that door. That room behind it. Now we've opened it, and it's given us nothing but more questions."

Wyatt glanced at the clock. "I hate to say this, but I really need to get going," he said. "The dogs are going to be wondering about their supper."

Of course, Tess thought. Wyatt had other things to do. But she felt a pang in the pit of her stomach at the thought of him going away. She wished he would stay.

"Jim mentioned you had dogs," Tess said, by way of making conversation as Wyatt pulled on his coat, which he'd taken off as they talked. "What kind? I think he said malamutes?"

Wyatt smiled. "That's right. One is black and white. One red and white. Luna and Maya. They're good girls. I got them as a rescued pair about five years ago."

"Bring them over sometime," Tess said. "I'd love to see them."

"I'll do that," he said, smiling. But Tess watched as that smile faded as quickly as it had appeared. "Will you be okay here by yourself tonight?" he asked. "You seemed pretty spooked."

Tess wasn't quite sure how to answer that question. She desperately wished for someone else to be with her, after the strangeness of the day. But she couldn't very well say it out loud to Wyatt. Instead, she managed a smile.

"Of course," she said. "I've got my bodyguard here to protect me." She glanced at Storm, who had calmed down and was curled into a ball in front of the fire.

"Okay," Wyatt said, holding her gaze for a bit longer than usual.

Something was happening between them, Tess thought. A moment. The air itself seemed to buzz around her like fireflies.

"Thanks for dinner," he said, finally. "It was delicious. I can't believe I neglected to brag to Jim about it. He's been talking up your cooking to the whole town."

Tess chuckled. "Anytime. My kitchen is always open."

Wyatt leaned against the doorframe. "I really don't want to go. Is that bad to say? Should I not be saying that at this juncture? I'm really out of practice at this. Whatever this is. Is this something? Or not? Am I presuming too much?" He chuckled. "Well, for sure I'm talking too much."

Tess crossed the room and put her arms around his shoulders. She gave him a quick kiss on the cheek, their faces touching for an electric moment.

"I'm out of practice, too. At whatever this is. Or isn't. Maybe we can just muddle through it together."

Wyatt smiled. "I could call you tomorrow."

"Yes, you could."

"Or later tonight."

"That, too."

"Okay, then," he said and pulled open the door. He started to walk through it but turned back over his shoulder. "If anything happens—not that it's going to—but if it does, call me. No matter what time it is. I don't want you in here battling with a raccoon on your own."

And then he was gone. Tess shut and locked the door behind him and watched through the window as he climbed into his truck. He started it and let it run for a moment before backing down the driveway and disappearing down the dark street.

She didn't quite know what to make of the man. Whatever "this" was, he was certainly honest and up-front about it. *What a concept,* she thought. *A man who doesn't play games.*

Tess turned to the empty kitchen, which seemed even more empty without the hustle and bustle of the day.

She poured herself a glass of wine and settled down in the armchair next to the fire, eyeing the back stairs. What a strange day. First, the realization that the room had been her grandfather's studio. The confusion about why it had been left in such disarray. The little bathroom and the canvases. The stains everywhere. And then, those ghastly scratches. Like whatever was in there had been desperate to get out.

But there had been nothing in the room.

Tess turned it over and over in her mind and wondered if her curiosity about what those canvases contained would get the better of her that night.

CHAPTER ELEVEN

After watching a couple of episodes of a favorite old sitcom to take her mind off things, Tess turned out the lights in the living room and kitchen and started up to bed, Storm at her heels. Even though she had turned off all the lights downstairs, she flipped all of them on upstairs. Stairway, hallway, and every room she passed.

It might be silly and wasteful, she thought as she switched on the light in her bedroom, *but if that's what it takes for me to get to sleep tonight, that's what I'm going to do.*

She stood on the threshold of her bedroom and stared down the hall toward the room they had opened that day. The curiosity seemed to be eating at her from the inside out. But getting any more answers would have to wait until morning. She had no desire to venture in alone at night. That was silly, too, she knew.

After she had changed into her pajamas and brushed her teeth, Tess settled into bed, where Storm was already stretched out, occupying at least half of the mattress space. She smiled at the dog. "Please, make yourself at home," she said.

She propped the pillows behind her and picked up the phone to call her parents. She wanted to talk to her dad about what, if anything, he knew about that back room. Had it ever been opened, that he knew of? She might not get anything from him, she thought she probably wouldn't, but that, in a way, would give her some answers. If he knew nothing about it, had never been in the room since Serena had shut it up, that meant those really could be undiscovered paintings by Sebastian Bell. There was no way her dad would've let millions of dollars languish all those years.

But just as she was about to make the call, she glanced at the clock. It was an hour later at their condo in Florida. They were probably in bed.

Phone in hand, she very much wanted to talk with someone. Should she call Wyatt? Hearing his voice would be nice, but . . . it was too soon in whatever "this" was, she thought. He had just left a few hours earlier.

Instead, she dialed Eli.

"Hi, Mom," he said. "What's up?"

Just hearing her son's voice brought a smile to her face. "I got a dog." "What?"

She turned the phone toward Storm, snapped a photo, and sent it to Eli.

"He looks great! But how did this happen? You're not allowed to get any pets without consulting me. Or new cars. Or houseplants. I thought that was clear."

Tess laughed. "He showed up at my back door during the blizzard. Jim—you remember, the guy next door who owns the store?—has the dog's photo up on the bulletin board looking for his owner, but . . . I think he's mine now."

"Well, good," Eli said. "I never liked the idea of you being in that creepy house all alone."

This took Tess off guard. "Creepy? Why do you say that?"

"Oh, I don't know," Eli said. "Maybe it's the constant moaning of the undead during the night. The rattling of chains, although, sure, that's totally cliché, but nobody told the ghosts. The odd disembodied head floating around from time to time."

Tess laughed out loud. "You goofball. There's no moaning. Or heads."

Eli chuckled, too. "Yeah, I know. It's just that the house is so old. Like, one hundred years, right? And it looks like the kind of house that would be haunted. Plus, there's that door."

"The door," Tess said. "We opened it today!"

Eli went silent for a moment. "You opened it? How? And, who is 'we'?"

"Jim recommended a guy from town, Wyatt, to come over and fix the heat," Tess said.

"What was wrong with the heat?"

Tess realized she hadn't been communicating with her son as well as she might have over the past few weeks. All at once, she remembered what it felt like when Eli was away at school and she was in the dark about what he was doing, with whom, and when.

She thought, not for the first time, that somewhere along the line, Eli had turned from her dependent into her protector. Their roles hadn't reversed—yet—but, as with her own parents, Tess saw how that nearly always happened.

By the time Eli had gotten to high school, he had become very protective of his single mother. As though he felt that he was the "man of the family," to use a rather archaic and outdated phrase. But that was sort of what it had seemed like to Tess. He had started mowing the lawn and shoveling the driveway. He did his own laundry and helped with cleaning up the house. He wanted to know where she was going on the rare occasions she had gone out at night, and he waited up until she got home. It was usually a book club with friends or a dinner out that wrapped up by about eight o'clock. She chuckled to herself. The wild and crazy life she had led.

His concern made her eyes sting with tears. "Oh, honey, I guess I haven't kept you up to date on the happenings in La Belle Vie," Tess said, as brightly as she could.

"Ya think?"

"Okay. So, the heat was out, but it was a really easy fix. When Wyatt—the heat guy—was here, I asked about the possibility of him opening the door. *The* door. He called a couple of his friends. One is an animal guy—"

"Animal guy? Do I even want to know what that is?"

Tess laughed. "He's an animal wrangler," she said, almost unable to get the words out because of her laughter. She imagined Eli's horrified face and couldn't stop it from bubbling up. "And his name is Hunter," she squeaked out.

She heard her son laugh loud and long. "No," he said finally. "You are making that up."

Tess wiped her eyes with a tissue. "Honest to God," she said. "Wyatt wanted him here when they got the door open because I had been hearing . . ." Her words trailed off.

"If you say *moans*, I'm ending this call right now," Eli said.

"Not moans," Tess said, wincing slightly at the thought of telling him the truth. "Scratching sounds. Like there was a squirrel or raccoon or something behind the door."

"Oh crap," Eli said, a grave tone in his voice. "What a mess. Was there?"

"No," Tess said. "They got the door open, but nothing was in there. No animal. No disembodied heads."

Eli was quiet for a moment. "So?"

"So, what?"

"So, what was behind the door?"

Tess took a deep breath in. "Sebastian Bell's studio."

She heard Eli gasp. "What . . . ?"

"Yeah," Tess said. "That's what I thought when I saw it."

She wasn't sure how much to tell her son. Should she mention the disarray? The stains? She quickly decided to leave out those details. He would only worry.

"You're telling me random people got a look inside Sebastian Bell's studio? The animal guy?"

"Well," Tess said, fidgeting in her bed, "I guess that's true. They had to open the door. So, they saw what was inside."

"Okay," Eli said, elongating the word. Tess could tell he was turning the matter over in his mind. "So what?"

Tess smiled, getting the reference. She had taught Eli this exercise when he was a child. It was the act of saying, or thinking, "So what?" when there was a problem or a crisis, a way to work toward a solution. It had started when four-year-old Eli had dropped his favorite stuffed elephant into the mud. Tess had found him crying. Completely destroyed by the sad turn of events.

"Oh!" she had said to him. "Mr. Tusk fell in the mud."

He nodded and sniffed in response.

"So what?"

Eli had looked at her with a furrowed brow. "So what?"

"Yes," Tess had said. "Mr. Tusk fell in the mud. So what? Think of what will happen next because he's in the mud."

Eli pursed his lips. All at once, the tears and frustration were gone. "He'll get dirty."

"He *is* dirty. So what?"

Eli looked up at her. "You'll probably give him a bath."

Tess smiled. "I will give him a bath. Just like you get every night. So what?"

Eli smiled. "And then he'll be clean again."

"Why don't you scoop up Mr. Tusk, and we'll give him a bath together," Tess said, leading her son and his muddy elephant to the house.

Back in the moment, Tess realized she hadn't been taking her own advice about cognitive reasoning. She could've used a lot of "so whats?" that day.

Tess thought for a moment before she responded to Eli's question. "So, there's something else."

Eli was silent, waiting for her to go on.

"I'm not sure about this, Eli, but I think I might have found canvases. Well, I know there are canvases, but they were stacked together and turned toward the wall so I didn't see what, if anything, was on the front of them."

"You're not saying—"

"I might be saying."

"Oh, wow," Eli said, taking a breath in. "Did the animal wrangler et al. see them?"

"No," Tess said. "Not that I know of. The canvases were in a little bathroom off the main room, and I think I was the first one in there. When I realized what they might be, I ushered everyone out of there."

"Good. Please keep it that way. Have you called Grandpa?"

"Not yet," Tess said. "I'm planning to call them in the morning."

"Mom, this goes without saying, right?"

She knew just what he meant. "Yes. It goes without saying, but I'll say it. Nobody is getting a look at those canvases but me. And you, if you want to come up."

"I can be there this weekend," Eli said. "Is that soon enough?"

"Sure," Tess said. "In the meantime, I'm going to find out what, if anything, they are. I'll do that tomorrow morning. I didn't really want to go back into that room at night by myself."

"Worried about disembodied heads?"

"Something like that."

After they said their goodbyes, Tess snuggled down in bed. She reached over to turn off the lamp on her nightstand but then thought better of it. The light stayed on. If anything was planning to creep out of that room in the middle of the night to bother her, she wanted to be able to see it.

Tess slipped into a hazy dream, images coming one after another, like a slideshow. She was wandering through Wharton at night, the streets wet with rain. She could feel the dampness seeping through her clothes, into her skin.

Then she was outside a house, peering through the windows at the family inside. A woman was at the stove in the kitchen, her husband relaxing in an armchair in the living room. But her eyes turned back to the woman. A butcher knife glinted in her hand.

Next, she was on the wooded cliff outside of town, looking down toward the rocks below. The moon was reflecting on the deep, dark water in a long shaft, and the sky was filled with stars. A rumpled heap lay on the rocks, waves lapping at it.

Next, she was inside the studio. But it didn't look anything like it had the day before. Paints were on the table, an easel set up by the window. Everything was orderly—not neat as a pin, exactly, but not the haphazard chaos they had found when they opened the door. A young woman came out of the bathroom wearing a silk robe with a paisley pattern and walked toward a settee that was positioned in the middle of the room. She reclined on the settee and pushed her hair back from her face. Somehow, her neck seemed to be throbbing with life. And then, a tiny trickle of blood appeared there, growing wider and deeper until it was a red gash.

CHAPTER TWELVE

Tess's eyes shot open. She was confused for a moment, her dreams still hanging in the air, swirling around her. She was damp with sweat, and her comforter and sheets were tangled around her legs, as if she had been thrashing around in the night.

She pushed herself up and reached over to the glass of water on her nightstand. She took it with shaking hands and drank a big gulp, the cool water slipping down her throat, calming her. It was just a strange and upsetting dream. That was all. Nothing more. She was in her own house.

Then she noticed Storm. He was staring intently at her bedroom door, which was closed. A deep, low growl rumbled in his throat. And then she heard what he was growling at.

Scrrrr, scrrrr, scrrrr.

Not again, she thought. Was this how it was going to be now? Every night? They had opened that door and found nothing that could have been scratching. Not one shred of evidence that an animal had been trapped in there. If not an animal . . . what was it?

Fear sizzled through her body. She slipped out from under the covers and stepped out into the hallway.

All was dark, except for a shaft of light seeping out around the studio door. The light seemed to radiate, vibrate with life. But . . . hadn't she turned on all the lights before going to bed?

And the scratching was unbearably loud. As though it came from the house itself. Or inside her own head. She had to make it stop.

"Stop it!" Tess shouted. "Stop that scratching! Stop it right now! I mean it!"

The scratching noise went silent. Storm went silent. Tess held her breath.

All at once, she was a woman on a mission. She disassembled the "noisemaker alarm" that she and Wyatt had set up earlier that evening. Lamps went on the floor, candelabra beside them, along with all the other items. That done, she shoved the steamer trunk out of the way and opened the door.

The room was buzzing with energy. Or maybe, Tess thought, it was she who was buzzing. She didn't remember leaving the light on, but it was blazing. The studio was bright as day.

"Whoever is making that noise, you really need to stop it," Tess said, in a loud voice, turning in a circle and getting a good look all the way around the room. "It's disturbing me, night after night. That's unkind. I am the owner of this house, and I demand that you stop it."

Nothing. Maybe it was a futile attempt, but she tried.

Something compelled Tess to move across the room. She stepped carefully, slowly, with Storm at her heels, to the little bathroom in the corner. She opened the door and peered inside. Canvases, just as she had last seen them. Stacked together, turned against the wall.

She took a deep breath and took hold of one of them, lifting it up and turning it around.

And there it was, just as she knew, somewhere deep in her soul, it would be. An undiscovered painting by Sebastian Bell. She had been right. She carried it out into the main room and laid it on the table to get a better look.

The painting depicted a woodland scene, high on a hill overlooking the water. An image much darker than the lakescapes he was best known for painting, both in color and in tone. It was the view through the trees at night, tall jack pines with gnarled trunks. Fireflies dotted the dark spaces between them. The inky lake lay at the bottom of a cliff, the moon creating a pool of light on its black surface. Tess thought she knew the area he was depicting. It was the cliff outside of town, the treacherous stretch of road on the way to Salmon Bay.

And then she saw the faces in the trees and on the ground and even in the water. Wild, terrified eyes. Open mouths as if they were screaming. Or moaning.

The hairs on the back of Tess's neck began to tingle. The image was beautiful, a true Sebastian Bell, but what it depicted made her stomach tighten.

Anguished souls.

It was familiar to her. She had seen that image before. But she didn't quite know where. Or how.

She left the painting where it was and hurried back into the bathroom to get a look at the others. She flipped through them, as though looking at prints stacked together in a gallery.

Tess gasped when she realized it. These were all finished paintings.

She counted four. With the first one out in the main studio, five. She had no idea what they all might be worth at auction, but it would be in the millions. If not more. She stood there for a moment, wishing the hour weren't so late—or, to be more exact, so early—so she could call her dad. She couldn't wait to tell him about this.

Tess carried the canvases out into the studio, two by two, and turned them over on the table beside the first one. When the table was full, she carefully placed the rest on the floor side by side. Her heart was beating wildly as she drank in the images.

The colors were mostly dark—deep greens, blues, and blacks. A splash of red and white here and there.

They were not typical Sebastian Bell paintings, although his style was unmistakable. It was the subject matter that seemed different somehow. Whereas he usually depicted scenes that took place outside near the wild, unpredictable inland sea of Wharton, these were images of the city, the woods, the surrounding area. The lake was in the background of some of them, but certainly not the main focus.

As Tess looked closer, she realized some were scenes of Wharton at night. Wet streetscapes. Views of homes, as if looking in through the windows from the outside. A woman making dinner in the kitchen as her husband sat with a drink in the living room, staring off with a stony expression on his face. His mouth was a straight line. Anger seemed to radiate from him. The drink, which seemed to be a glass of scotch, was nearly empty. In the kitchen, the woman was leaning over the stove, her head in her hands. She seemed to be crying.

A family around the table, with a teen girl sullenly staring at her plate. Tense expressions on her parents' faces. Certainly not a happy family. A sense of shame heated up Tess's cheeks. It felt as though she shouldn't be seeing these images. She shouldn't be intruding on this family's moment of pain.

Still another. In this one, a fire blazed in the living room fireplace, but the lights were low. On the second floor, a woman was reaching up to draw the curtains on her bedroom window, her husband holding her from behind.

Another painting depicted a woman, walking down the street, away from whoever was observing her. The hem of her dress blew in the breeze. It felt as though Tess, and anyone who observed this painting, were following the woman, unbeknownst to her.

These were voyeuristic images. Snippets of other people's lives, observed in secret, with them not knowing it. Tess's stomach turned over. This wasn't right.

Then her eyes were drawn back to the first painting she had seen, the scene on the cliff, a vision through the pines at the moonlight shimmering on the water. The anguished souls crying out in the ether beyond. It held a horrifying beauty, a sense of tragedy in the landscape and the water, as though the very land and lake held the memories of all who had ever perished there.

Tess turned to another of the paintings. It was a woman, wearing a paisley robe, reclining on the settee in the studio. She was smiling, but her eyes didn't smile with her. Tess detected a look of fear there, an anxiety behind the forced smile. This painting, unlike all the others, featured the subject looking at the painter. And the subject, this woman, was afraid, but trying not to show it. Her eyes held a depth that Tess hadn't seen in her grandfather's other works—her full face was depicted, that was the first thing. He tended to paint his other subjects from the back or the side, rarely looking straight at him. A red gash, a brushstroke, was on the wall behind her.

All the works looked so familiar to her, as though she had seen them before. Tess's skin began to crawl when she realized why.

Her dreams.

These were scenes from the dreams she'd been having over the past several nights. Walking down the dark streets of Wharton.

Could it be? Tess ran a hand through her hair and shook her head. It couldn't be. That was silly. She looked closer and thought back to the images that had run through her mind on previous nights.

There was the house where she had looked into the window. There was the woman she had followed. There was the cliff she had peered over. The crumpled mass she had seen in the dream was not in the painting, but she was certain it was the same location.

In her dream of the woman in the paisley robe, she hadn't seemed afraid. Not then. But in the painting, it was clear. She was not a willing subject for the artist.

What was this? What was happening?

All at once she felt cold. It was as though the temperature in the room dropped in an instant. She breathed out and could see her breath wafting through the air.

Tess called for Storm, and the two of them bolted out of the studio. She slammed the door behind them and shoved the steamer trunk across the threshold. She stacked her "alarm items" on top of it and stood there for a moment, trying to quiet her racing heart.

The light in the studio went dark.

Tess hurried down the hallway to her room, Storm at her heels. She shut the door behind her and pushed her dresser in front of it for good measure.

She took a sip of water and slipped under the covers. Storm didn't hop up on the bed with her. Instead, he curled up in front of the door. Tess glanced at the clock on her nightstand. Four thirty. There would be no more sleep, that was for sure. She grabbed the television remote and turned to a local channel for the early morning news. Anything to get her mind off what had just happened—or hadn't happened—in the studio.

CHAPTER THIRTEEN

Tess opened her eyes. Light was streaming in around the blinds in her bedroom, and a game show was on the TV. She rubbed her eyes and looked at the clock. Almost eight thirty. Somehow, she had fallen back to sleep, and Storm was curled up at her feet.

She reached down and scratched Storm around the ears. "Is it time to go out?" He jumped off the bed and stood at the door in response.

Tess pulled on jeans, a sweater, and socks and slipped into her bathroom to run a brush through her hair. She splashed some water on her face and held the towel to it for a long minute, shaking her head.

What had happened last night?

Tess shoved the dresser away from her door and opened it, following the dog toward the back stairs. She looked over her shoulder at the door to the studio. Her makeshift alarm was still intact. She needed to get somebody here today to put a lock on that door.

After a brisk walk with Storm—the temperature was creeping up from below zero—she filled his food and water bowls and brewed herself a pot of coffee. She poured a steaming mug and added a splash of cream, sank into the armchair by the kitchen fireplace, picked up her phone, and dialed.

"Honey!" her mother said. "How's everything in Wharton?"

"Good, Mom," Tess said, her voice catching in her throat. How she wished her parents were here with her now. No matter how old she got, she would still be their daughter. At this moment, she needed the sense of parental protection that she was lucky enough to have felt all her life. "Is Dad around? I have a couple of questions about the house."

"Indy!" Tess heard her mother call out. "It's Amethyst. For you."

A moment passed. And then: "Sweetheart!"

"Hi, Dad," Tess said, all at once melting into his little girl again. Tears pricked at the backs of her eyes.

"Your mom and I have been out walking on the beach this morning," her father said. "I'm sorry about that. I hear you're still in the deep freeze in Wharton."

Tess chuckled. "I just got back from a walk myself, and yes, we're still below zero," she said. "But it felt good. Especially after the night I had last night."

She winced. There it was. No going back now, but she was unsure of how to broach this subject with her father. What did one say? She wished he were here to view the paintings for himself.

Indigo Bell was silent for a moment, reading his daughter's tone more than her words, as he had always done. "What's the matter, honey? Did something happen?"

Tess took a sip of her coffee. "Dad, I had the door to the back room opened yesterday," she said, slowly.

She heard him take a breath in. "You did?"

"I'd been talking to Mom about opening it up and making that back room into an owner's suite, for when guests start coming. A place for me to retreat so I'm out of their hair and they're out of mine."

"Oh?" he said. "You've been talking to your mother about this?"

Tess furrowed her brow. "Yeah," she said. "Didn't she tell you?"

"She didn't," Indigo said, slowly. "I wonder why. Your grandma wanted it to stay closed off."

"I know. Is that why you didn't open it up?" Tess asked. "After she died, I mean?"

Indigo let out a long sigh. "I guess so, honey," he said. "It wasn't an issue when she was alive. Those were her wishes, and I never even thought about going against them. Now you know, it was Dad's inner sanctum. His studio. But after she passed, I know I could've opened it back up, but I just . . ." His words seemed to evaporate. "I guess it was easier to keep that door—that chapter—closed. Sleeping dogs, and all of that."

Guilt seemed to seep out of the floorboards and wrap itself tightly around Tess. Had she done the wrong thing?

"I'm sorry, Dad," Tess said. "I—"

"Oh, sweetie, don't be sorry," Indigo said. "It's your house now. You make the rules. You didn't even know the man."

"The renovation wasn't the only reason I needed to open it up," Tess said, her words coming out in one long stream. "That could've waited awhile, but things became more urgent because I heard sounds coming from in there. Scratching. Behind the door. At night. I thought an animal might have gotten in."

"Oh no," Indigo said, taking an audible breath in. "Was there much damage?"

"No, Dad," Tess said. "That's what was so odd about it. I definitely heard all of these noises, but when we got the door open, there was nothing."

"Nothing?"

"No evidence to suggest any animal had been in there."

Her father was silent for a moment.

"Tess," he said, his voice soft and low. "What are you calling to tell me?"

This caught Tess off guard. *What an odd thing to say,* she thought. It was as though . . . Did he know what was in the studio? Had he known all along?

"Dad," she said, choosing her words carefully. "Did you know that room pretty well?"

"Of course," he said. "I was rarely allowed in there when I was a boy—that was the artist's private lair—but I knew that was where he painted. He spent most of the day, and night, in that studio when he was working on a new painting. I didn't agree with your grandmother, you know. About closing it up. What she said about the heat—we all knew that was silly. I personally think it was just too painful for her to see it, after he died. Too many memories. That studio was his heart and soul, where he created his masterpieces."

"I found five of them."

It was as though the air had been sucked from the room.

"What?" he said, his voice dropping to a whisper.

"Five paintings," Tess said. "They were in the little bathroom off the main room, stacked together, facing the wall."

Tess heard her father gasp.

"Honey," Indigo called to his wife, his voice harsh, "Tess found five of Dad's paintings."

"Whaaaaat?" Tess heard her mother say.

"The room was in complete disarray," Tess went on. "Wine bottles everywhere. Papers. Glasses. Nothing had been cleaned up. It was as though Grandma had just—"

"Honey," he said, breaking into her words. "I'm going to stop you there. Did anyone else see them? The paintings, I mean. I imagine you had workmen there to get the door open."

"Yes, I had workmen, and no, nobody has seen the paintings. Nobody knows about them except Eli. I called him last night."

"Good," Indigo said. "This should go without saying but—"

"I know," Tess said. "I'm not about to tell anyone else about this."

"You know the wall safe in the drawing room?" Indigo said. He was referring to a rather large wall safe hidden behind a bookshelf that swung open. It was really more of a small room than a safe, built by Indigo years ago to hide valuables during the off season. Like paintings.

"Yes, I know it, but not the combination," Tess said.

"I'm going to send it to you. Put the paintings in the safe. Right now, honey. Hang up the phone and do it right now."

"But, Dad," Tess said, "I wanted to ask you about—"

"Nothing else is important at this moment, honey," Indigo said. "Get those paintings into the safe, and then call me back."

"Okay, Dad," Tess said. "I will."

But he had already hung up. A moment later, a text message from him came through. A series of numbers and symbols. The combination to the wall safe.

Tess hurried up the stairs and to the studio door. After her odd experience the previous night, she was none too excited to go back inside, but she shoved the steamer trunk out of the way, her "alarms" falling to the floor and clanging as she did so.

Everything was as it had been when she left the previous night. She held her breath and walked across the room to where she had set the paintings. They were in the same order . . . weren't they? As she viewed them, she realized they took a rather strange progression.

First the ominous image of the cliff, then the woman posing in the studio, then the woman on the street, then the series of images of looking into the windows of Wharton houses, and then the depictions of Wharton's streets at night.

It was as though the paintings were a series, telling a story. But what could it be?

Tess stared at the images for a long moment, and then she realized. She was looking at the series backward. It started on the streets and progressed, at last, to the cliff. The realization sent a cold shiver through her. What could it mean? Did it mean anything?

She shook off those wonderings and got to the business at hand. Her father had told her to take the paintings down to the wall safe, and that was what she was going to do. He was right. She needed to get them out of sight before anyone else, even Wyatt, came back. As nice as the people were that she had met in Wharton—Wyatt, Hunter, Grant, and even Jim and Jane—the prospect of $100 million might turn any of them into a thief. Or worse.

So, Tess carried the paintings down to the drawing room, making several trips, walking slowly and carefully. She pressed the combination of numbers and letters her father had sent into the keypad, and the lock clicked.

As the safe swung open, Tess saw it was empty. Her parents must've taken their important papers and anything else with them to Florida when they moved permanently, she reasoned. That was just fine with her. She slid the paintings into the safe—they all fit inside, just barely—and closed it.

Her heart was racing. She could feel eyes boring into the back of her neck, as though someone were watching.

CHAPTER FOURTEEN

Tess sank onto the sofa and dialed her father.

"Everything's in the safe?" he asked her. Not even a hello.

"Yes," Tess said. "They all fit. Closed and locked."

"Good," Indigo said. "Don't do anything with them. Just leave them in there. They sat inside Dad's studio for all of these years undisturbed. They can sit in the safe a little longer until your mother and I can make the trip back to Wharton. We can make arrangements to come just as soon as—"

Tess shook her head. "Dad, this weather has been crazy. The worst winter here in a long time. You stay put until we can make sure you're not going to get caught in another blizzard driving all the way to Wharton from the airport in Minneapolis."

Indigo sighed aloud. "You're right, of course," he said. "I was thinking—the sale of these paintings is going to substantially change the foundation. I'll meet with Eli to talk about it when we get there, but what I think we should do is bolster your and Eli's personal accounts—your mother and I don't need anything—and then figure out with Eli how best to use the rest of those funds. You should be in on those conversations, too. You get a say in how we use this money. And it goes without saying, honey, but I'm paying for all of the renovations on the house. That shouldn't come out of your pocket."

"Oh, Dad, no, I—"

"I don't want to hear another word about it, okay? You just hire whoever you need to hire to transform that studio into an owner's suite for yourself. You have my blessing to do it. It's about time."

Tess's stomach knotted at the thought of it. Yes, renovating the studio had been her plan. But after the previous night? Now she wasn't so sure. And what the foundation was going to do with the money from the sale of the paintings was the last thing on her mind.

But she said, "Thanks, Dad," anyway.

"So, what are the images in the paintings?"

Tess's stomach tightened. The words caught in her throat as she tried to get them out. "Scenes from Wharton," she said, her voice wavering just a bit. "Streetscapes at night. There's a portrait of a woman. And an image of the cliff at night. They're kind of . . ."

"Kind of what?"

"Disturbing, I guess you'd say."

"Hmm," Indigo said. "It's true Dad could get a little dark. Maybe he was exploring that side of his creativity."

"Maybe," Tess said. "And you've never seen them before? You didn't know they were in there?"

"I had no idea, honey," her father said. "If I had, they'd have been in the safe or sold long ago."

That made sense. But why would her grandmother have stashed them away? She was going to ask her father, but for some reason, she bit her tongue. Not now. When he was here, in person, and could see them for himself.

"Now," Indigo began. "You said you had something else to mention."

Tess cleared her throat. And down the rabbit hole she went. "Okay, you might think this is a strange thing to ask, but, Dad, is this house haunted?"

Her father huffed. "Haunted? No. Not that I know of. I've certainly never thought—I mean, sweetie, you know I grew up there." And then, to Tess's mother: "Tess thinks La Belle Vie is haunted." The tone of his voice was one of amusement.

"Haunted?" she heard her mother say. And then laughter.

So, that was how it was going to be, then. Tess understood the subject was closed. Her parents had a certain set way about them. Talk of hauntings, ghosts, or anything unexplainable wasn't exactly on their roster of acceptable conversation. Another reason to not mention more about her thoughts about the paintings.

So, she chatted with her parents for a bit about other things— doings in Florida, what Eli had been up to, the latest news of the world, something about a bridge tournament they were participating in—and soon they hung up.

Tess pushed herself up from the sofa and wandered over to the window. It looked cold outside. The snow had the sort of bluish hue that always seemed to reflect out on the coldest of days. Not a single car was driving down the streets that Tess could see. It was like Wharton was a ghost town.

She made her way back into the kitchen and turned on the flame under the kettle. Tea sounded like just the thing. And then what?

Tess looked around for Storm. He was usually by her side. But now he was nowhere to be seen. She carried her tea mug up the back stairs, somehow knowing where he would be. She found the dog lying in the hallway outside the still-open door to the studio. Not growling. Not threatening. Just lying there. A sentry.

She peered over his shoulder into the studio. With the paintings gone, it was just a room in disarray.

"What do you think, Storm?" she asked the dog, scratching behind his ears. "Should we clean it up?"

A moment later, she was opening the closet at the end of the hall, at the top of the back stairs. Her family always kept cleaning supplies there for the second floor so they wouldn't have to haul brooms and dust mops from the kitchen all the way up the stairs.

She grabbed a spray bottle of wood cleaner, a broom, and several bags and started back down the hall. Storm scrambled to his feet and followed her into the studio, where she set about gathering all the bottles, dried paint canisters, papers, and other debris that had been strewn around the room. She made the executive decision to throw away the glasses—many were broken anyway—instead of washing them. It felt a bit unseemly to think of using them again. They had been shut up, out of time, for decades. Who knew what might come from drinking out of them now?

Tess had always been a touch superstitious. She didn't have a firm belief in things otherworldly, but she was the kind of woman who wanted her bases covered, just in case.

She was finishing sweeping the floor when Storm rushed out of the room and down the back stairs, barking. Then she heard the rapping. Someone was at the back door.

Tess made her way down the stairs and into the kitchen and saw Wyatt's smiling face peering in through the window.

She opened the door to let him in.

"Hi!" she said. She furrowed her brow at him and cocked her head to the side. "Did we have an appointment today? Am I forgetting something?"

Wyatt smiled. "I'm afraid this is an unauthorized stop-by," he said. "Do you hate that? I was doing a little job down the block and thought I'd come by to talk about the renovations you want to do in the studio. We could talk over lunch?"

Tess didn't particularly love the idea of people stopping by unannounced, but somehow, this felt okay. More than okay. She smiled back at him.

"Lunch?" she said, glancing at the clock. It was indeed about that time. The morning had flown by. "That sounds great. I haven't been out to eat anywhere since I got here."

"The Superior Café is open," he said. "One of the few places that is open this time of year. They have great food."

He gave her an expectant grin.

"Why not?" she said. "I didn't know they were open in the winter. Sounds like fun. Just give me a minute to clean up. The coffee's hot if you want to pour yourself a cup while you wait. Make yourself at home."

Wyatt unzipped his parka and pulled off his hat and gloves. "I'll do that. Thanks!"

Tess skittered up the stairs to her room and hurried over to her closet. She didn't have time to take a shower, but she'd do what she could. She grabbed a flax-colored fisherman's-knit sweater and a light denim shirt to wear under it, and a pair of soft—clean—jeans. Wriggling out of the clothes she was wearing and into the fresh outfit took just a minute, and then she was in the bathroom in front of the mirror, chagrined to find a streak of dirt on her forehead. *Awesome.*

She washed and moisturized her face and applied a little makeup and lip color and brushed her hair. She popped in a pair of earrings and eyed her reflection. Not exactly fit for a night on the town, but an afternoon in sleepy Wharton? She was good to go.

Back in the kitchen, she saw Wyatt placing his cup in the sink. He turned to her and smiled. "You clean up pretty good," he said.

"Wait until you see me after I've actually showered," she said, pulling on her jacket and boots.

Wyatt laughed out loud.

Tess looked around for Storm, who came trotting into the kitchen. She bent down and scratched behind his ears. "You be a good boy," she said. "Guard the castle."

"Oh, he will," Wyatt said, as Tess pulled the door shut behind them. "You can bank on that."

The Superior Café sat on the corner of Main and Front Street, just a block off the lake. As they walked in, Tess saw a long bar running the full length of the paneled room, with a fireplace on one end. It reminded her of a lodge in the woods she and Matt had visited before Eli was born. A second area, through French doors, was a sort of sunroom affair, with large windows on three sides. Tess could imagine all these opened on breezy summer days, the cool lake air wafting through. But today, it was warmed by the sun shining in. On such a cold afternoon, it felt like heaven.

A handful of people were enjoying their lunches—Beth St. John from the Just Read It bookstore; the police chief, Nick Stone, and his wife, Kate, who was the cousin of Tess's friend Simon and helped him run Harrison's House. There were a few others, whom Tess didn't recognize. But Wyatt knew everyone.

"You all know Amethyst Bell?" Wyatt asked the room. "She's renovating La Belle Vie into an inn."

Hellos, waves, and greetings all around.

Kate pushed herself up from her chair and came over to Tess. "Welcome to the community," she said, taking Tess's hands. "I'm sorry I haven't been in touch before. Simon is over the moon that you're here permanently."

"I am, too," Tess said.

"How are the renovations going?" Kate asked.

Tess tried to suppress a wince as she thought about the scratching. And the paintings. "Great!" she said, with much more enthusiasm than she felt. "We're starting on an owner's suite now, and once that's done, I'll be ready to open. I'm hoping to be done with it all by summer."

"Simon hooked you up with his antiquing mafia, I'm told," Kate said, chuckling.

"He did," Tess said. "We found some gorgeous furniture and accent pieces. The main part of the house looks really good. It's this owner's suite . . ." Her words stopped in midair. The very thought of transforming her grandfather's studio into her private lair felt . . . wrong somehow. A desecration. That had been the plan all along, but now she was feeling unsure.

"You're helping her out with that, I hear?" Kate said, turning her gaze to Wyatt.

"I don't know how much help I've been, but yes," he said.

A genuine warmth swirled through the air between them.

They made promises to get together for coffee soon, as Kate went back to her table. Tess and Wyatt found a spot by one of the windows. After ordering—a turkey, bacon, and avocado sandwich for him, a bowl of squash-and-apple soup for her—they sipped on their drinks and Tess realized, as she stared across the table at this man, that she didn't know the first thing about him.

Well, she knew he had dogs. And that he was a friend of Jim's. And that he knew just about everyone in Wharton, from the reception he got when they walked into the restaurant. She knew he helped people with their various projects and problems around their homes. He called a Scottish animal wrangler a friend. But that was about it.

"What brought you to Wharton?" she asked before blowing softly on her spoon filled with steaming soup as she brought it to her mouth.

A chuckle, then, from Beth St. John, who was passing by their table on her way out. "How long have you got?" she said to Tess with a grin. She winked at Wyatt and patted Tess on the back. "It's a great story."

Tess turned to Wyatt. "Oh?" she said, raising her eyebrows.

He smiled and shrugged. "My great-great-great-grandfather was John Wharton," he said, and took a bite of his sandwich. "I guess you could say he founded the town."

Tess's spoon hung in midair on its way to her mouth. "You're kidding."

His grin grew wider. "Nope. Interested to hear about it?"

"Absolutely!"

Wyatt took a sip of his drink. And then he began to tell his tale.

CHAPTER FIFTEEN

More than two centuries ago, John Wharton was a fur trapper and trader on the land that would become the town that bore his name. Long before LuAnn's boarding house was built a hundred years ago to house them, long before there were streets and buildings and restaurants and anything else that made up the town of Wharton, John Wharton's canoe found its way to this rocky shore.

Back then, it was pristine wilderness, filled with pine trees reaching up to the sky, wide beaches where the waves crashed, and otters, beavers, and other furry mammals scurrying up and down the shoreline on the prettiest bay on this side of the lake. Moose strode elegantly through the forests; wolves stole silently behind them. Foxes played in open meadows.

That was what John Wharton found when his canoe was blown off course during a storm on the other side of the lake in Canada. It was as though the lake itself had taken John's canoe and, after a few harrowing days, set it gently on the shoreline that would become the Wharton ferry dock more than one hundred years later.

His canoe was filled with goods to trade for furs—blankets, metal tools, firearms and ammunition, even brass kettles. He also had traps of his own. The fur trade was big business around the Great Lakes during this time.

But the day that John Wharton's canoe slid onto shore, he found something astonishing, something completely unexpected.

John had been battered by rain and wind, baked by the sun. So he wasn't altogether himself when he was greeted by several men. Englishmen. Or Canadians. John wasn't sure. They roused him from the canoe bottom and helped him to their village, a neighborhood of domed structures covered with bark where their people lived. It was nestled in the forest on the hill overlooking the water, safely protected from the lake's harsh winds and crashing waves.

There, the people gave him food and drink, and after sleeping the night through, maybe longer, John awoke, refreshed, if a bit sunburned and sore.

He wasn't completely sure where he was, but after some conversation with the men of the village he understood that he had been blown all the way across Lake Superior. It didn't quite seem possible for him to have survived such a journey, but there he was, in a land he had never before seen, nor imagined.

The very woods seemed different here. It was almost as if they were enchanted, buzzing with an energy John couldn't define. The sky seemed a deeper blue, the stars closer and more brilliant. The furs more plush, as though the animals themselves were of another ilk. The people themselves were kind—almost unnaturally kind—welcoming him for as long as he wanted to stay. There were long nights by the fire trading stories and laughter instead of goods and furs. They told him of the Indigenous peoples, Ojibwe, who were expert trappers and traders and taught them how to survive in this land. He took long walks in the forest or along the shoreline, marveling at the magnificence of it all.

But the most magnificent of all was Elizabeth. One of the women from the village. With her silky, dark hair, which she wore down, unlike most of the women of the day, she was the most beautiful woman John had ever seen. But there was more than that, so much more. Her smile. Her laughter. The touch of her hand.

John saw children happily running through the village, and soon he began to imagine children of his own.

John didn't quite grasp how much time had passed. Days? Weeks? Years? It was as though he were caught out of time, somehow. But he didn't much care about that. He didn't care about getting back to his trading post. He only cared about Elizabeth and making a life for her.

And so they were married one summer evening on the shores of the lake that had brought him to them. It was the happiest John had ever been. He had a home, with a loving wife, and a loving and kind community around them. Soon, there would be children. Month after idyllic month passed.

Until that day. That horrible day.

John awoke to find himself lying on the rocky ground. Outside. He blinked and looked around, confused. Where were his cozy furs? Where was Elizabeth? He scrambled up to his feet and turned in a circle. Where was the village? Everything was gone. Every person. Every dwelling. Every tool and bucket and hide and fur.

What in the world was going on? How could this have happened? Did they all leave, every single one of them, during the night while he was sleeping? But how could that be? Did they take the houses, too?

A coldness wrapped itself around him then, as the realization of the impossible began to take hold. As he looked around, he saw that it was just the forest, undisturbed. As though the village had never been there at all.

But that could not be. John ran through the woods, calling for Elizabeth. Everyone else might have left, but she would not. His wife. His love. He ran down to the shoreline. There was nothing there, no canoes from the village. Only his own, pulled up onto shore. He hurried up to it and saw it was laden with his supplies. The very supplies he had brought with him when he washed up on shore all those months ago.

But then, he saw it. Lying on his pile of furs, as though it had been lovingly placed there. A single leaf from a maple tree. He took it as a sign. A terrible, horrific sign.

John dropped to his knees and let out a wail of anguish so fierce and so deep, all the birds and animals fell silent.

He was tempted to climb into that canoe and paddle fast and long to get far, far away. But then, as he looked around what had been the only happy home he had ever known, he knew he could not go.

"Please come back to me, Elizabeth," John said, tears streaming down his face, his words carried away on the breeze.

John used what he had learned from the people of the village to build himself a dwelling. He made a roof out of bark and hides, as he had seen the villagers do, and lined the floor with cozy furs. He built a shelf where he stored his supplies and a firepit outside where he could cook his food—just as the people of the village had done. He had all the traps and tools he needed to survive—he had come with it, and somehow it had all ended up in his canoe after everything else disappeared.

He fished and hunted and took only what he needed, using the ways of the land. He spent many of his days gathering berries and mushrooms and wild onions and cattail roots, drying them in the warm sun.

He knew the ways of the forest and the water. The people of the village had taught him well. He would stay and wait for his love to return.

Weeks later, a long canoe of voyageurs—legendary French Canadian trappers—pulled up onto John Wharton's rocky shore. They were there to trade with the Ojibwe, who lived a day's paddle away. He invited them to stay the night and share a meal.

Around the fire, John told them of his experiences, how he had been blown off course and ended up here, in a strange land. How the whole village had taken him in and enraptured him with the beauty of the woods and the water. And then, just like that, it was all gone. Disappeared one night, as though it were never there.

"*Oui,*" one of the voyageurs said, nodding solemnly. "We have heard of a strangeness in these woods. Tales of shape-shifters enchanting travelers. I have heard of it happening elsewhere, as well. Entire settlements, vanishing without a trace."

"Are you saying they were shape-shifters? Even my wife?"

"It is not for me to say. But will you stay? You are welcome to come with us. We have room for you in our longboat."

John thought of the lake and all its moods, the animals scurrying up and down the shoreline or playing in the water, the graceful moose with their enormous racks, the steely wolves. The bounty of the land. The view as the sun rose.

"I will stay," John said, gazing into the flames. "Even without my wife, my place is here."

Because the area was so rich in furs and John was such a skilled trapper, the voyageurs made plans to help transport John and his furs to a trading post, a three days' journey down this side of the shoreline. Soon, it was a thriving trade route. And since the man whom the traders were coming to see was John Wharton, the name stuck. "We're traveling to Wharton," they would say.

Then the fishermen came, when they heard tell of the bounty of these waters. More settlers arrived. Hands to repair the boats. Women to cook meals for the fishermen. A general store opened, to sell goods from the trading post. A town was growing. And John Wharton was growing older. Nearly a decade had passed since his village and his beloved Elizabeth had vanished.

One day, John rose from his cozy house to take a cup of coffee down to the lakeshore, as he did every morning. But on that morning, a young woman was standing on the shore, looking out over the water. He hadn't seen her before, but when she turned, she looked so familiar, he gasped aloud.

"Elizabeth?" he said, his voice a whisper.

She squinted at him. "No," she said. "I'm Cecelia Brown." She held out her hand. "You must be John Wharton."

✦

"And that's the tale of Wharton," Wyatt said. "And of my family."

Tess was listening with her chin in her hands.

"So, what? Did they get married? Have children?"

"That's how the story goes," Wyatt said. "They had four kids. Two girls and two boys. John lived to a ripe old age and is wholly responsible for this town being here."

"Wow," Tess mused. "How cool to know that part of your family history. What an immense connection you must feel to this place."

Wyatt took a sip of his drink. "Yes, I do. My whole family does. We've still got some furs from that time and other mementoes of his. Diaries, too. That's how we know the story. Apparently, his children were unaware of . . ." Wyatt stopped, choosing his words carefully. "Unaware of the whole village disappearing."

"That was in his diaries?"

Wyatt nodded. "Exactly. They weren't found until a generation or so later. He didn't talk about that part of his life to his family. He kept it hidden."

Tess could understand that. Every family had secrets, things they'd rather not see the light of day. Many of those secrets involved family members who had simply vanished, left for whatever reason, were never heard from again, made new lives elsewhere, with new people, rejecting what—and who—they had for the allure of something new.

She thought of her uncle Grey's sudden disappearance, decades earlier. Her dad never talked about it, never speculated where his brother might have gone, or why. It was like he was erased, not just from holidays or family gatherings, but from existence. The only picture Tess had ever seen of him wasn't a picture at all. It was the painting, *Picnic at Mermaid Cove*, that hung above the fireplace at La Belle Vie. Now that she thought about it, she wondered why her father insisted that the family hold on to it, given that he never spoke of his brother. Perhaps it reminded him of gentler times.

Tess brought her thoughts back to the moment and smiled at this man across the table. "Do you believe it? The disappearing part, I mean. One person, sure. But a whole village?"

"I don't know," Wyatt admitted. "You know how these tales tend to get taller over time. But I do know that he believed it to his dying day."

He took a sip of his drink and looked off into, perhaps, the past. "I've always been sort of torn about it. I'm a pretty practical-thinking person, so, you know . . . Shape-shifters. Enchantment. The whole thing disappearing like Brigadoon."

"That doesn't happen so often these days." Tess smiled at him.

"Not every day, no," Wyatt said. "I've speculated about it a lot over the years. I've thought that maybe Elizabeth left him—although that didn't happen back then too much, either. Or she died suddenly. That's the more likely explanation. In childbirth, perhaps. Or, I mean, this is a little darker, but maybe she was killed. Maybe he killed her. Then, when more people started coming to the area, maybe the village moved on, went deeper in the woods, to not be bothered by this new town that was springing up. He could have concocted a fantastical explanation. The bottom line is, we just don't know. It just disappeared."

"Like Brigadoon." Tess smiled. "And Wharton has been enchanting people ever since."

"True enough," Wyatt said.

"Has your family always lived here?" Tess asked him. "Or did you come back to your roots more recently?"

"We've always been here," Wyatt said. "Members of my family have lived other places, of course, but there's always somebody in Wharton. It's as though the whole place might disappear if one of us wasn't here anchoring it down."

CHAPTER SIXTEEN

Something wasn't right at La Belle Vie when Wyatt and Tess returned after their lunch. She had invited him in for a cup of tea and, immediately after walking through the door, Tess felt an itchy, hot veil of unease settle around them. It lurked in the air as they hung up their coats, prickling its way through her hair, down her neck, and into her spine. Storm was nowhere to be found. No greeting when they came inside. That alone made the hairs on Tess's neck stand up.

Wyatt looked around the kitchen. Apparently he was wondering about the dog, too, because he asked, "Where's Storm?"

And then they heard the growling. It was coming from the hallway, toward the front part of the house. Tess caught Wyatt's eye, and the two of them walked toward the low and menacing sound. They found Storm standing at the doorway to the drawing room, facing inside, teeth bared, a terrifying growl rumbling through the air. Tess's heart jumped into her throat as she hurried to the dog's side and peered into the room.

She gasped at what she saw. The wall safe was wide open, and the panel that hid it from view had been torn off and flung across the room. The paintings were laid out on the floor, side by side. As though they had been carefully placed there by a curator.

The room went ice cold. Tess could feel it penetrating her thick sweater until it reached her skin. Storm began to bark and reared up on his back legs, jumping and biting at something unseen in the air. He'd twirl around midair and jump again, barking all the while. An angry, raging-dog ballet.

She looked at Wyatt with her mouth agape.

Wyatt walked toward the dog with his arms outstretched, his palms open. "Easy, boy," he said, his voice calm and soothing. "Easy, Storm."

Storm stopped the jumping and crept to each of the paintings in turn, sniffing them all. His ears were pricked. On high alert.

Wyatt's eyes followed Storm. "What is this?" he said, his voice low, as though he didn't want whoever—or whatever—had done it to hear. "What are these?"

So much for keeping the existence of the paintings a secret, Tess thought. She stepped gingerly into the room, wincing, not quite wanting to see if the paintings themselves had been marred or defaced or destroyed in some way. She took a deep breath and looked.

The paintings were intact. She let out the breath she was holding in one great sigh. She could feel the relief radiating off her shoulders.

"Are these . . . ?" Wyatt's words evaporated as he stared at the paintings.

"I found them in the studio," she admitted. "After we opened it up. We're assuming—my parents and I—that they were painted by Sebastian Bell."

All at once, she had the feeling again of eyes boring into the back of her skull.

"Wyatt," Tess said, slowly. "These paintings were in the wall safe when we left for lunch."

They locked eyes for one long and terrible moment that seemed to last forever. The room, the paintings, even the dog's growling dimmed and faded into watercolor. Only their eyes, locked together, were crystal clear.

"Who else has the combination?" he said.

She shook her head. "Only my dad," she said, her voice wavering. "In Florida. And it's one of those Wi-Fi-enabled locks that he can change from his smartphone. So, it never remains the same for too long."

Wyatt slid his phone from his back pocket. "We should call the police. Whoever did this might still be in the house."

Tess shook her head. "No," she said, the words coming out harsher than she meant them. The intensity of it surprised her. She cleared her throat and tried again. "No, Wyatt. Let's you and I and Storm check the house to see if there has been a break-in. He'll know if someone is hiding. I don't want anyone else in here. Not even the police."

Wyatt's expression melted from concern into confusion.

"These are undiscovered works by my grandfather," Tess said. "The world doesn't know they exist. I told only my son and my parents that I found them. I got strict orders from my dad to keep all of this under wraps. Nobody else was supposed to know about them."

"Why?" Wyatt asked.

Tess stared at him, open mouthed, for a moment. "Do you have any idea what they're worth?"

Clarity on his face, then. "Of course. Millions. Now I get it."

"When I told my dad about finding the paintings, he instructed me to put them in the safe right away. He absolutely does not want any hint of this to get out. It could be—"

"Dangerous," Wyatt continued her thought, nodding. "For you. I absolutely agree. Nobody can know about these until you—well, I don't know what one does at a time like this. Get them into the right hands, I suppose. But, Tess . . ." he continued, staring at the paintings, "something doesn't make sense, here."

Nothing much had made sense since they had opened the studio, she thought.

"What?"

"If somebody broke in and ripped open this wall safe to get at the paintings . . ."

All at once, she realized. "Why didn't they take them?"

"Exactly." He thought a moment before he went on. "The only people here yesterday were Grant and Hunter. I would bet my life neither of them would do anything like this. They've been inside every house in Wharton, and let me tell you, some very wealthy people call this town home for the summer or year round. Grant and Hunter are as trustworthy as they come."

That might be true, Tess thought. But not being tempted to steal some family heirloom candlesticks or expensive jewelry was one thing. An undiscovered Sebastian Bell was something else entirely. The heady thought of what it would fetch at auction was enough to turn anyone's head. People had killed for much less.

She took one step toward the row of paintings, Storm watching her every move. As she looked closer, she saw they were in the same terrible order they had been in the studio when she found them.

First, the images of Wharton's streets at night, then the ones that were views into the windows of homes, then the woman on the street, then the same woman posing in the studio with the angry red streak on the wall behind her, and finally that ominous, haunting image of the cliff. A darkness, an anger running through all of them.

"My God," Wyatt whispered, taking a step closer, too, seemingly lost in the world the paintings depicted. "They're so . . ."

"Disturbing?" Tess finished his thought. "I know. Sebastian's work always had sort of ominous undertones, but deliciously so. These . . ."

"These are something else," Wyatt said. "I see exactly what you mean."

Storm moved in front of Tess, positioning himself between her and the paintings.

"The way they're laid out like that," Wyatt said. "It looks like a storyboard. You know, like they use in advertising or even in movies to lay out how the scenes are supposed to go."

The idea caught in Tess's throat. That was exactly what it looked like. But a storyboard of what?

They stepped closer and took it all in. Wharton's streets on lonely, rainy nights, fog rising in the air. Views inside houses where families were going about their lives, some happily, some decidedly not. Whatever the scene, these were not an inside snapshot of family life. They were a voyeuristic intrusion. And then, a woman, on the streets alone, viewed from behind. Followed. Stalked. The same woman in the very studio where Tess had discovered the paintings. And then the cliff, deep and dark and dripping with evil.

All at once, the realization hit Tess like a freight train. She didn't want to believe it. And more than that, she wanted very much for Wyatt to be gone. He had to leave before he realized it, too.

But she turned to him and saw it was too late.

"Are these telling the story of . . ." He caught her eye, but somehow he couldn't say the words aloud.

"A predator," she whispered.

CHAPTER SEVENTEEN

Tess's body was vibrating with dread. Now that she had seen it, she couldn't unsee it. These paintings, her grandfather's paintings, were telling the story of a predator who stalked the streets of Wharton, looking into windows, following women down lonely streets. Convincing one of those women to pose in his studio.

And then what? What did that red gash behind her on the wall mean? The paintings were obviously a series that told a story. But was it fiction? Or fact?

Who was the predator?

Was it Sebastian Bell?

No, no, dear God, no, Tess thought. A gnarling took hold in the pit of her stomach. He wasn't just her grandfather. The thought of him potentially being a stalker, or worse, would be bad enough. But Sebastian Bell was a favorite son of Wharton. Beloved locally, respected and admired worldwide. What would her father say if he knew?

As she stood there in abject horror, Wyatt moved closer to the paintings. He slipped a pair of glasses out of his pocket to get a better look.

After a long, horrible moment, he turned to Tess. "Am I crazy? Come closer, and look at this." He pointed to the painting of the woman on the street, then to the one in the studio.

"They're obviously the same woman, right?" he asked. "At least it appears they are. But are we sure?"

Tess looked more carefully. The image of the woman on the street was painted from behind. She had the same hair as the woman in the studio. It certainly looked like they were the same person. Didn't it?

Then, Wyatt pointed to the other paintings, the ones depicting scenes of families, as if seen from outside, through their windows.

"All of these feature women," he said, his voice low.

"They all look sort of similar, don't they?" Tess said, realizing it for the first time.

She focused on one of the family-life scenes. The woman crying at the stove as she made dinner while her angry husband sat with a drink in the living room, staring off with a stony expression on his face.

Something about that painting made her skin crawl. It seemed to be the moment before an argument, even a violent one. She could almost feel the tension in the air in that house, the moment before it all ignited. Was this the calm before a woman was beaten by her husband? Was that what the painter was trying to depict?

Why in the world would her grandfather have devoted so much time to painting such ghastly scenes? It was as though all of them had a common theme running through them.

Impending doom.

"These are really disturbing," Tess said, finally. She shook her head. "I have no idea why he would've painted these subjects."

The two of them just stood there for a moment, staring at the dark and disturbing images.

"Will you help me get them back into the safe?" Tess said.

Together, they gathered up the canvases and placed them into the enormous wall safe one by one. Tess closed the door and heard it click shut. She tried the combination her dad had given her earlier in the day, plugging the numbers in to the keypad. The handle didn't budge. Her father had already changed the combination, as she thought he might.

Safe and sound. For the moment.

"I really think we should call Nick Stone," Wyatt tried again.

But Tess shook her head. Even though the paintings were back in the safe, something in her gut told her to keep quiet about them.

"Only if we find evidence of a break-in," she said. "If the front door was forcibly opened, or if any windows are broken. That kind of thing."

"Okay," Wyatt said, but Tess could tell he wasn't happy about it. "Let's go check the house."

He agreed to split up, but only if Tess would take Storm with her. She'd check the main floor of the house while he went upstairs to the bedrooms.

"Open closets, look under stuff," he said. "And especially down here, look for any sort of evidence of a break-in."

"Got it," Tess said, and she made her way, Storm at her heels, to the front of the house, walking from room to room, noticing if any windows were opened or broken—although she'd have felt the cold air if they had been—opening closets, glancing under furniture, looking for anything amiss.

In the dining room, she saw all her grandparents' china still stacked neatly in the ancient hutch. The crystal chandelier hung silently, undisturbed. Her study was just as she had left it, not a book out of place.

She stepped into the living room and heard the soft hiss of the radiator and saw the lights of the street streaming in through the windows.

She glanced at the bay window with its curved seat at the front of the house, looking out onto the street below. Nothing out of the ordinary there. Finally, she ended up at the old, heavy wooden front door, which had always reminded her of something out of Middle Earth. It stood fast and strong, the windows beside it intact.

All was peaceful and quiet. The house was tight as a drum. Not one thing was out of place, apart from the scene in the drawing room.

Tess opened the front door and peered outside onto the snowy porch. No footprints there. She decided to check for prints around the outside of the house—*good luck covering your tracks if you're trying to break into a house in Wharton during the winter*, she said to herself. She opened the closet door and pulled out her boots and, forgoing a jacket, stepped out into the cool air.

Storm romped through the snowbanks and into the yard, jumping like a deer. His joy brought a smile to Tess's face. After all that growling, he was clearly happy to get outside.

It wasn't yet four o'clock, but the sky was already slipping into twilight. Tess noticed the snow had taken on the bluish hue she loved at this time of day. She trudged through the snow, looking for tracks, trying to discern if anyone had been peering through the windows of La Belle Vie. Nothing. Not a snowflake out of place. She saw only the tiny tracks of animals that flitted here and there, but no human footprints. She was stomping the snow off her boots on the porch when she heard Wyatt calling her name.

"Tess!" he called out again. "You had better get up here."

Her stomach dropped. What had he found?

She called for Storm as she hurried inside the house. After shutting the door behind them—and locking it—she kicked off her boots and rushed up the stairs. She found Wyatt in the studio.

He was pointing at the wall.

She turned to look in the direction he was pointing and gasped aloud. A long red brushstroke. A slash. Just like the one in the painting.

"That wasn't there before," she said, walking up to it to touch it. She had expected it to be fresh and wet, but it wasn't. The streak was dry as a bone.

She turned to Wyatt and shook her head. "I don't understand this," she said. "Shouldn't it be wet?"

She looked around. The twilight was shining in through the wall of windows, its pinky-purply glow casting an almost magical aura on the room. Dust floated in the air. Everything was as she had left it earlier when Wyatt had interrupted her cleaning. The broom stood leaning against one wall, its dustpan sitting neatly beside it. The brown bag of recycling—bottles and glasses—sat on the table next to her dust rags.

A feeling of utter serenity came over Tess then, draped around her like a hug. Her heart swelled as she gazed at the long table where the paints had been. She imagined dabbing the brushes into the paints and caressing the canvas with brushstrokes. This was where it all happened, the genius, the artistry, the—

"Tess!"

She jolted awake and blinked her eyes. Wyatt was holding her by the arms.

"Where were you just then?" Wyatt asked, a mask of concern on his face. "You were completely zoned out."

"I . . ." Tess looked around. "I don't know. That was weird. I don't know what it was. I just started feeling so happy to be in this room."

Wyatt was silent for a moment. "Let's go downstairs," he said, finally. He led Tess out of the studio and pulled the door shut behind them.

"Help me push this trunk back into position," he said. They arranged their makeshift alarm system on top of it.

They made their way down the back stairs to the kitchen, where Tess sank into one of the armchairs by the fire. She let out a great sigh.

"How about a glass of wine?" Wyatt asked her.

"Perfect," she said, snuggling a little deeper into the chair and putting her feet on the small ottoman.

Wyatt retrieved two glasses from the cabinet. Then he opened the fridge and pulled out the wine and a bottle of beer. He filled both of their glasses, handed one to Tess, and settled into the armchair on the other side of the fireplace.

"I hope that wasn't too forward, but you did say earlier to make myself at home, so . . ." He grinned.

"No, that was great," Tess said. "Thank you." Suddenly she felt bone tired. But she managed a toast after raising her glass. "Here's to ancient vanishing villages and reappearing ghoulish paintings."

Wyatt gave a small smile. "Just another day in Wharton."

They sat in silence for a moment, sipping on their drinks, Storm curled up at their feet. Then Wyatt turned and leaned forward, his elbows on his knees.

"I'm not crazy about everything that happened here today," he said, narrowing his eyes.

"Yeah," she said. "It was really bizarre. I mean, there I was at lunch questioning your story about John Wharton and whether or not that village really vanished, and we get back here to find . . . whatever this was."

"Did you notice any evidence of a break-in?" Wyatt asked. "I'm assuming you didn't, or you'd have said something before now."

Tess shook her head. "Nope. I even looked outside for tracks in the snow."

"Nobody hiding in the closets upstairs, either."

Tess sighed. "I guess we might as well admit that this is . . . weird. I asked my dad this morning if this house was haunted. He laughed. I chuckled along with him. But now I'm not so sure it's funny."

"I also didn't love the way you zoned out in the studio," he said. "Do you remember that? I said your name a couple of times, but it was like you didn't even hear me until I took hold of your arms."

The thought of it was rather hazy, as if it had happened in a dream. Tess shook her head. "Not really," she said. "I can't explain it. I just sort of . . ." She sighed. "I don't know. I felt happy."

Wyatt furrowed his brow. "Happy?"

"I know," Tess said. "A completely out-of-place feeling. Considering the circumstances."

"There might be a very plausible, real-world explanation for it all, but whether it was a ghost or a person, there's one thing for sure," Wyatt said.

"What's that?"

"They wanted you to notice the story told by that series of paintings."

Tess nodded. He was exactly right. It was the only thing that made sense out of all this.

But who? And why?

Wyatt took another sip of his beer. "Do you feel safe staying here by yourself?" he asked.

Tess didn't quite know how to answer that. If she was honest with herself, and with Wyatt, that answer would be no. But what was the alternative?

"I don't know," she finally said. "I guess if I had to put it into words, I'd be more afraid of a real-life threat than a ghostly one. And I just don't think there's any sort of real-life threat here."

Wyatt nodded. He was eyeing her as though sizing her up, judging the truth of her statement. "I'd have to agree with you," he said. "Give me a ghost over a live person any day."

As Tess sipped on her wine, she thought about that. "How about neither?" she said, grinning at him. "Neither would be good."

"Listen, I should be getting home to feed the dogs," Wyatt said. His witching hour, Tess was noticing. "But I just want to make sure one more time. I'm not crazy about leaving you here by yourself, but I don't quite know how to convey that. I'd ask if I could stay, but you'd think I was terribly forward, and plus we don't really know each other very well. You could be just as nervous having me in a room down the hall as having a ghost in the studio."

Tess chuckled. But he was right. She really wouldn't feel comfortable being alone with Wyatt all night under her roof. Yes, she was going to be an innkeeper, so strangers would be sleeping under this roof regularly. That was the point. But it was also the point of making the owner's suite.

"And I'd ask you to come back to my house, but you'd think that was even creepier," Wyatt went on.

"I'll be okay," she said, his concern warming her from the inside out. "I have my bodyguard, remember?"

She reached down and gave Storm's head a pat.

Wyatt pushed himself out of his chair and set his beer glass in the sink. As he was pulling on his coat, he turned to her. "Thanks for coming out to lunch today. I hope I didn't yammer on too long about my family."

"Not a bit." Tess smiled. "I hung on every word."

He pulled her into a hug, his arms around her waist. As she slipped hers around his shoulders, their cheeks touched. A sizzle of electricity shot through Tess, and she closed her eyes for a moment, remembering what it was like to feel that way. It had been such a long time. Opening her eyes, she pulled back slightly and put a hand on his cheek. And then she raised up onto her toes and put her lips on his, pulling him into a kiss that was, at first, hesitant, and then deepened into something real and tangible and important. Tess felt as though she should remember this kiss. It was a beginning.

"Tess," Wyatt said, his voice rough and low.

They stood there for a moment, their faces close together, gazing into each other's eyes. It was as though they were both recognizing and marking the same moment in time.

Wyatt cleared his throat. "Why do I have my coat on again?"

Tess smiled. "You were leaving. Something about the dogs and food."

"That's right," Wyatt said. "I'm going to call you later. You have been warned."

"First the unauthorized stop-by and now this," she said.

After she closed the door behind him, she turned to Storm. He was standing by his food dish. A not-so-subtle hint. She scooped some food into it, poured herself a second glass of wine, and settled back down into the armchair by the fire.

Just another day in Wharton, indeed.

CHAPTER EIGHTEEN

Later that night, after she had lit a fire in her bedroom fireplace and switched off the light, Storm curled up at the foot of her bed, and Tess lay back thinking about the events of the day.

Her familiar routine with Eli, their "so what?" exercise, ran through her mind. The wisdom gleaned from simply asking "so what?" had guided her through many hard times in her life, opened up ideas, and showed her the way when she thought she was at a dead end. She'd lean on it now to unsnarl the thoughts that were knotting up in her head.

She had found a treasure trove of unknown paintings by one of the world's most celebrated modern artists. So what?

The art world would be overwhelmed with delight. So what?

The paintings would sell at auction. Her family would come into multiple millions of dollars from the sale. So what?

So what, indeed. They already had everything they needed. Her father and Eli were running a foundation with the bulk of Sebastian Bell's estate. More money could be funneled into that, Tess supposed. They could pay for arts education for children who couldn't afford it. More scholarships. They could even build an artists' retreat in Wharton. Or endow a magnet school dedicated to the arts. The sale of those paintings would be a good thing. A wonderful thing. A positive thing.

But then, Tess's thoughts went down a different path. The paintings were disturbing. Would people think they were somehow a reflection on her grandfather? These paintings depicted someone—in all likelihood, her grandfather—stalking the streets of Wharton. She let that thought percolate for a moment. So what if it showed that? What would happen when the world realized it? When her family realized it?

His reputation, and that of the family, might be tarnished. Would certainly be tarnished. Sebastian Bell was a beloved Wharton son. The paintings might shatter his gilded image. At the very least, it would raise uncomfortable questions.

So what? What would happen then?

The family would have to deal with the aftermath.

Tess adjusted her pillows and snuggled deeper into her soft bed. There was a fine line between genius and madness. Great artists had long histories of mental illness, bad or even criminal behavior, and all manner of flaws. Genius does not preclude one from misdeeds, nor does it protect one from their consequences. Van Gogh was troubled. Picasso had his moments. Hemingway was a notorious misogynist with mental-health issues. Fitzgerald was an alcoholic. When these paintings came to light, when the world saw what Tess had seen, would Sebastian Bell be judged harshly in the face of all who had come before him? Didn't he deserve to be if he'd been stalking some woman?

And, Tess reasoned, the paintings might not show that at all. They might simply be products of her grandfather's imagination. Nothing more.

Tess's eyes fluttered closed as she made peace with it. She'd call her father and Eli tomorrow, explain her thoughts, and as a family they'd move forward together. She didn't have to bear it all on her own.

Her eyes didn't stay closed for long.

For all her "so what-ing," she couldn't get one thought out of her head.

The red streak on the wall. The portrait of a woman who, if Tess was honest with herself about her impressions of the painting, didn't seem like she wanted to be posing at all.

And then, there was the last painting, the one of the cliff. The cries of anguished souls the image seemed to evoke.

Tess realized there was another thought on her mind. One that she had been trying to tamp down. Or keep away. Or banish. But as she lay in her bed, with the shadows of the firelight dancing on her walls, she let it come.

Maybe Sebastian Bell wasn't just a voyeur or a stalker. Maybe he was a murderer. The paintings didn't show anything of the kind, not exactly. But the feeling that Tess got when she looked at them . . .

Her familiar "so what" exercise wasn't going to reason that away.

Tess sat up with a start and reached for her phone. Wyatt answered on the first ring.

"Tess," he said, his voice heavy with sleep. "Are you okay?"

"Sorry to call so late," she said, taking a big breath in. "I think you might be right."

"As much as I love to hear that any time, from anyone, I am getting a rather bad feeling about this," Wyatt said. "Right about what?"

"I think maybe we should call the police," Tess said. "Not right now. This is not an emergency. But I couldn't get the portrait of the woman in the studio out of my mind. The red gash. And the last painting of the cliff. Wyatt, could we be looking at a confession?"

Wyatt cleared his throat. "What do you mean, a confession?"

"The paintings, the storyboard, as you aptly called it, tell a story," Tess said. "What if that story is of a murder? What if those paintings are my grandfather's confession?"

Tess heard Wyatt gasp. "It makes a terrifying kind of sense," he said. "I mean, just looking at the paintings in order. Right?"

"Exactly," Tess said.

"Do you know when your grandmother closed off the studio?" Wyatt asked.

Tess tried to think back. The truth was, she didn't know. It had been shuttered her whole life.

"When did Sebastian Bell die?" Wyatt pressed on. "And how did he die?"

"I'm not sure the exact date, but I'm sure it's on the foundation's website, or any number of websites about him. He died when my dad was a young man. Away at college, if I'm remembering it correctly. It was a heart attack, that much I know, but nothing more. My dad rarely talked about it, and my grandma never talked about it. That was one subject I knew never to bring up with her. That's odd, isn't it?"

"Not really," Wyatt said. "It was common back in the day, especially if something scandalous happened. Or if someone had cancer. Or even had an accident that would sort of bring shame to the family. I know of a guy who had always heard that his grandfather died in the Cliffside tuberculosis sanatorium that used to be just outside of Wharton. Truth was, the grandfather was coming home from a tavern in the winter after having one too many, or several too many, and he froze to death in the snow. Back in the day, people covered up things like that. Spoke about it in whispered tones. As though if you spoke of death, it would hear. And come for you."

It made a strange kind of sense to Tess. She thought of a friend from college whose grandmother had cancer, but the friend didn't even know what type. In some families, that just wasn't spoken of. Something like this? It certainly would have been covered up.

"And about your grandmother closing off the studio," Wyatt went on. "You don't know when she did it. And you don't really know why, right?"

"Exactly right," Tess said. "She always had these flimsy excuses about it being too expensive to heat. When I was a kid, I never thought twice about it. But now? That's just ridiculous."

"I think so, too," Wyatt said. "I mean, it could be nothing more than grief. Her beloved husband had died, and she wanted to close that room off, just as he left it, as a sort of—I don't know—shrine that would live out of time. Or something. I know that sounds dramatic. But what if that's not the reason. What if—"

Tess could almost see his thought coalesce into a tangible play in front of her eyes. "What if," she said, "my grandmother found those paintings and shut up the room to keep them from the world? That would certainly explain the studio's state of disarray. She did it in a hurry and didn't even take the time to clean up."

"That sounds right to me," Wyatt said. "Not that I know anything. But as someone just hearing it for the first time, it sounds sensible. She found the paintings, realized what they were—a confession—and locked everything up tight to make sure that confession never saw the light of day."

"She couldn't have the world knowing her husband, the great Sebastian Bell, was a stalker. Or worse."

Wyatt sighed. "If all of that is true, you have a decision to make."

Tess's stomach knotted up. "What do you mean, exactly?"

"Given that your grandmother went to all of that trouble to make sure the world didn't ever see these paintings—she didn't destroy them, she couldn't bear to, it seems to me—but she made sure they stayed hidden."

"Yes, she did," Tess said, her mind flying in many directions at once.

"Are you going to show them to the world in defiance of those wishes?"

Those words wrapped around Tess and constricted. She hadn't considered that. "You've already seen them," Tess said, weakly.

"I'm not exactly the town gossip," Wyatt said. "If you decide you want to permanently shut that door again with the paintings inside, I won't say anything to anyone. It's not my place. This is your family's decision."

Tess thought about this. Somehow, she believed Wyatt. He was a good man. A man of his word, it seemed to her. If he said he was going to keep quiet about something, she trusted him to keep quiet. It made her wonder what other types of secrets, whose secrets, he might be keeping, but she was sure she'd never know.

Tess's train of thought seemed to have hit a snag. If she wasn't prepared to share all this with the world, should she call the police about a possible murder, even if that murder had taken place decades earlier?

But then, she thought back to her conversation with Wyatt at lunch. And just like that, the light bulb went on above her head.

His family had been in Wharton since before there was a town. They would know about a decades-old murder, if indeed there had been one.

"Wyatt," she began. "It seems to me your family knows Wharton's history better than most people."

"I'd say that's true," Wyatt said. "My parents and grandparents for sure."

"I'm sorry if this sounds indelicate, which it will for sure, but . . . are they still alive?"

"And kicking," he said. "My parents go to Arizona every winter for a few months. My grandma passed about a decade ago, but my grandpa is still with us. He's in the assisted-living complex in Salmon Bay."

Tess's thought caught in her throat. "Can we go see him?" she asked. "Tomorrow?"

⊱⋆⊰

Tess didn't get much sleep that night. She tossed and turned, and when she did nod off, her dreams were wild and unhinged and violent. And she heard the scratching, but when morning finally came, she wondered if she had dreamed it.

She wasn't quite sure what she wanted to ask Wyatt's grandfather when they met. But one thing was for certain, the man would know Wharton's history. He had lived at the time of Sebastian Bell's heyday. They probably knew each other. And if there had been any disappearances or murders or scandals back then, he would know about them. Getting him to talk about it would be the difficult part.

The clock said it was six thirty-five. After trying in vain to will herself back to sleep, Tess gave up the effort. She pulled on jeans and a sweater, and bundling up in her down coat and mukluks, she snapped on Storm's leash. Together they set out into the predawn darkness.

Jim and Jane's lights were on. Tess figured Jim was up early to open the store. But most other houses in the neighborhood were dark. Sensible people, sleeping until the sun touched the sky. As she walked through Wharton's dark, deserted streets, she couldn't help conjuring up the images in those paintings. Her grandfather, or someone, had walked these same streets. They had left La Belle Vie just as she had, closed the door behind them just as she had, and had set off into the darkness.

What compelled you? What were you looking for? What made you long to observe people without them knowing it?

As an artist, her grandfather had painted moments in time. Captured those moments on canvas, interpreted through his eyes. He needed to be a keen observer, whether it was taking in an idyllic scene of his own family at the lakeshore having a picnic, or the second before tension erupted into violence in a house occupied by his neighbors.

Tess knew her mind was going in all kinds of hypothetical directions at once, but she wondered—if domestic violence had occurred, had Sebastian watched it? Had he seen what was happening in the household? Did he feed off it? Or was he repelled by it? Did he help the woman? Whether or not he felt it was for art, Tess couldn't shake how wrong it was, watching from the shadows.

Tess sat on a bench by the lakeshore, watching the frozen lake, imagining the deep, dark water below. She was so entranced by it that she didn't hear Jim come up behind her.

"Hey, neighbor," he chirped. "You're up early." He reached down and patted Storm's head.

Tess managed a smile. "No rest for the wicked," she said.

Jim chuckled. "That's what they say. Need anything? I'm just about to open the store."

Tess pushed herself up from the bench with a groan.

"Actually, yes," she said, perking up a bit. "I could use some coffee beans. And I don't suppose you've got any fresh croissants?"

Jim smiled, pointing to a delivery truck that was pulling into the alley behind the store. "Rene is right on time," he said. "They might even still be warm."

That was all Tess needed to hear. They walked to the store together, Storm at their heels, and she waited as Jim opened the front door and disabled the alarm. Jim met his baker, Rene, at the back door, flipping on the lights as he went. He emerged from the back room carrying a big box—croissants, muffins, and bagels—that he always offered fresh, every day from the French Canadian–run bakery that was down the shoreline a few miles.

"One plain, one almond, please," Tess said with a grin. "Can you put it on my tab? And not tell anyone I'm going to eat two of these?"

"You got it," Jim said, double bagging the pastries. "Your secret is safe with me. Hurry home before they get cold."

❧

After a hot shower, Tess settled into her warm kitchen with a cup of freshly brewed coffee and the plain croissant, which she buttered decadently. One bite sent her into culinary nirvana. That alone was a reason to wake up early in Wharton. She wondered if she should start making croissants, but then thought better of it. She couldn't compete with this baker. She'd just buy them from him, when the time came.

She turned on the morning shows, waiting for a decent time of day to call Wyatt. After the news, a cooking segment (she made a note to try an interesting rub for steaks), and a celebrity promoting a new movie Tess had no desire to see, she figured he would be awake.

"Hey," she said.

"Good morning," Wyatt said. "How was your night?"

"Long," Tess said. "I didn't sleep much. I took Storm for a walk early this morning, and as a bonus, I ran into Jim just as his baker was arriving with the croissants."

"Rene makes the best this side of Quebec," Wyatt said.

"I can neither confirm nor deny that I have eaten two this morning."

"Now you're just bragging."

Tess chuckled. This man was easy to talk to. "Are you still up for a visit with your grandpa today?"

"Absolutely," Wyatt said. "But I just want you to go in knowing that . . . well, he has some memory issues. Not Alzheimer's, exactly, but he's got some mild dementia for sure."

"That's okay," Tess said. "I'm not expecting much. But he was living in Wharton at the time Sebastian was here. They were contemporaries and certainly knew each other in such a small town. He might have a perspective, a view of that time that my dad doesn't."

"I know you're wondering about the woman, too. The one in the portrait."

The words caught in Tess's throat, not wanting to be said aloud. But she forced it. "Your grandfather would know if anyone went missing or died in Wharton back then. Any woman. I mean, I could research this online, but without having a specific year or name or . . ."

"I get it," Wyatt said. "A firsthand memory would be the place to start."

That's right, Tess thought. But why was her stomach in knots? Why didn't she want to know what Wyatt's grandfather might tell her?

CHAPTER NINETEEN

The ride to Salmon Bay was uneventful compared to Tess's last drive on that road. Plows had cleared the snow, and the salt they sprayed to melt the ice had done its job. The car was rolling on dry pavement.

The Salmon Bayview complex was adjacent to the hospital and included apartments for active seniors who needed no help, those who needed some help throughout the day with things like medicines and bathing, and those who needed more help than that, including round-the-clock care. The idea was to allow seniors to stay in their apartments for the duration and let the care come to them as they needed it. A great concept, Tess thought, wondering if her own parents would benefit from such a setup someday soon.

It was just before eleven thirty when Wyatt pulled his truck into the parking lot. They thought taking his grandfather to lunch in one of the three restaurants in the complex would be a relaxed setting for their conversation.

Before they got out of the car, Wyatt turned to Tess. "I just want to make sure you're not expecting too much," he said. "I told you he has dementia. It's really not too bad yet. But sometimes, he gets mixed up about things."

"I understand that," she said, reaching over and taking Wyatt's hand. "I'm just grateful you were willing to do this. If he doesn't have any insights or information for us, that's okay. We'll have had a nice lunch together."

Wyatt eyed her. "It depends on your definition of *nice*. Be warned that you're not going to get the best lunch you have ever had. Do not, I repeat, *do not* get the tuna sandwich. I'm not sure if there's any actual tuna in it, or if it's just tuna-flavored mayo on bread."

Tess chuckled. "These sorts of places aren't known for their culinary prowess," she said. "But why? These folks should be getting the best food, if you ask me."

"You know," Wyatt said, "we could bust him out of here for lunch and take him to the brewpub on the main street. He'd love that."

"I would, too."

They walked through the doors, and Wyatt led her through the hallways to his grandfather's room. When a quick knock didn't get any answer, he tried the knob. It was unlocked. He pushed open the door, and they found his grandfather sitting on the couch, dressed in a crisp striped shirt that was buttoned up to the neck, a maroon cardigan, and tan slacks. His sparse hair was neatly combed, and his face was bright and alert.

"Wyatt, my boy!" he said, pushing himself up from the couch. A walker was nearby, but he didn't use it. "Hello! Come in, come in! Who is this enchanting girl you've brought to my door?"

He shuffled his way toward Tess and reached out for her hand. She gave it to him, and he brought it to his lips.

"Welcome, dear lady," he said, his eyes shining. Tess actually blushed. *What a flirt.*

"Pop, this is Amethyst Bell," Wyatt said. "She goes by Tess. And Tess, this is my grandfather, Joseph Wharton."

"I go by Joe," he said to Tess. "My friends call me Joe."

"Joe it is," Tess said.

"How about getting some lunch at the brewpub downtown?" Wyatt asked. "We'll bust you out of this joint for the afternoon."

Joe's face lit up. "Wonderful!"

Wyatt found his grandfather's coat and boots and helped bundle him up as though he were a little boy. As Tess took in the sight, she found there was indeed a childlike innocence on the old man's face. An almost vulnerable look of excitement and joy in his eyes. It made her own sting with tears. She turned and quickly brushed them away.

"Where's my hat?" Joe asked.

Wyatt reached into the closet and found a wool herringbone cap that reminded Tess of something you might have seen on a Scottish golf course a century ago.

Joe popped it on his head and grinned. "All set!" he said. "Let's go!"

"Do you want your walker, Pop?" Wyatt asked.

Joe waved his hand. "I've got you next to me. Don't need that old thing." He turned to Tess and said in a stage whisper, "The ladies will think I'm old if I use a walker."

Tess chuckled.

Wyatt locked the door behind them, and Joe took his arm. The hallway was long, but the old man's pace was surprisingly swift for someone in his nineties. When they got to the front desk, he smiled brightly at the woman sitting behind it.

"There she is!" he said to her.

"Where are you off to, Joe?" she said with a big smile on her face. Tess got the feeling that was how most people reacted to Wyatt's grandfather. His positive energy was infectious.

"These two kids are taking me to lunch," Joe said. The pride in his voice tugged at Tess's heartstrings. "At the brewpub downtown!"

"I love that place," the woman said. "They have great burgers."

"I'll sign him out, Connie," Wyatt said.

She nodded, sliding a clipboard toward him. "And in, when you get back," she said. "You know the drill by now, but every now and then people forget to sign in, and the staff has to go looking for a resident."

"You don't want anybody MIA," Wyatt said, raising his eyebrows.

"No, indeed," Connie said. "Have a nice lunch, Joe!"

Joe waved at Connie as Wyatt trotted off to the parking lot. Tess waited with Joe inside the vestibule. He watched intently as Wyatt made his way to the car.

"Here he comes," Joe said. "He's coming right now."

"He sure is," Tess said, patting Joe's arm.

After Wyatt pulled up to the door, Tess helped Joe into the front seat and hopped into the back. The same arrangement happened in reverse when they reached the restaurant, just a couple of blocks away. Tess helped Joe out of the car and then stayed with him while Wyatt parked the car. *It takes a village,* she thought.

Inside, Tess saw that the pub looked like it might have been transported from old-world England. A huge wooden bar dominated the room with an intricately carved bar back, bottles gleaming on shelves above it. Booths with black-leather seats lined the walls, and heavy wooden tables and chairs with the same black leather sat in the center of the room.

Tess couldn't remember ever having been there—with so many great restaurants in Wharton, she had never made the trip. She settled Joe at one of the tables, easier to get into and out of a chair rather than a booth, and hung up his coat, along with her own, on the close-by hook on the wall.

When Wyatt joined them, Joe asked, "Can I have a beer?"

"Hell yes, you can have a beer, Pop." Wyatt grinned at him. "Two, if you want."

Their server appeared and they ordered their lunches—split-pea soup for Joe, a burger for Wyatt, a French dip for Tess. When their drinks arrived, Joe held his aloft.

"Happy days," he said.

"Happy days," Wyatt said, clinking glasses with his grandfather and Tess.

What a beautiful toast, Tess thought. It said it all, everything important, in two little words.

Joe turned to Tess. "Speaking of beer, did I ever tell you about the time I broke my leg and wound up in the hospital here in Salmon Bay and my best friend smuggled some beer into my room?"

"No!" Tess said. She leaned forward and put her elbow on the table, resting her chin on one palm. "What happened?"

Joe went on to relate how he had been playing high school football back in the 1940s and broke his leg after getting tackled on the field. He was taken to the hospital just down the street from where they now sat, which was run by nuns at that time. He remembered everything—how his best friend came to the hospital with a six-pack, and how one of the nuns discovered it.

"The nun took the six-pack and said, 'Now, Joe, you know you can't keep this in your room,' and I thought that was it, I was caught red handed, and she was confiscating it," he said with a twinkle in his eye. "But then she winked at me and said, 'I'll keep it in the refrigerator in our break room for you. You just tell me when you want one.'"

He let out a great laugh, and Tess did, too. She glanced at Wyatt, who she was sure had heard this story a thousand times. But he was smiling at his grandfather with tears in his eyes.

"Was that your friend George, Pop?" Wyatt prompted, clearly knowing the answer.

Joe nodded. "That was George. Best guy I ever knew."

Tess wondered if this George was still alive. But given Joe's age—midnineties, she guessed—she thought she probably knew the answer to that. As she gazed at this dear man, she wondered what it would be like to outlive most of the people who grew up with you, shared your most pivotal experiences, loved you throughout your life. She imagined a kind of stark loneliness without your contemporaries, even if you were blessed with children and grandchildren. All the people who not just shared but participated in your memories were gone.

She wondered, too, if that was what dementia was all about.

Nobody was alive to remember your important moments, your pivotal experiences, the people who you lived with and loved or even peripherally knew. Nobody else alive remembered what Joe's childhood was like. Or what it was like to go to high school in Wharton in 1942. Or grow up there during the Great Depression.

Only Joe remembered asking his wife to marry him—the only other person there had gone long ago. Only Joe remembered their honeymoon. Or buying their first house. Or the happy news of a baby on the way.

Joe alone was the keeper of those memories, and so many more like them, Tess thought. It was a great responsibility, holding all that history inside one's head. An important vigil. Maybe that was why newer experiences faded as one neared the end of a long life. The brain simply couldn't hold the lifetime of memories it had stored, and the most precious took precedence over those that came after. Who cared what he had for lunch the day before? His mind was otherwise occupied.

The server brought their lunch, and the three of them dug in.

Joe took a spoonful of soup and smiled. "This is the best pea soup I've ever had," he said. "Really good! And this beer is wonderful!" He raised his glass.

His positive energy warmed Tess from the inside out.

"Pop," Wyatt began, eyeing Tess across the table. "Speaking of the old days in Wharton, do you remember Sebastian Bell?"

Joe's spoon stopped in midair. "Sebastian Bell," he said. "You bet I do. He was a few years older than me in school, but a good fella."

"Tess is his granddaughter," Wyatt said.

Joe's eyes grew wide, and he grinned. "Is that so? Great!" He squinted at her. "You're Indigo's girl?"

Tess smiled. "That's right. Indigo is my dad. He and my mom are down in Florida."

"Tess is renovating their house into a bed-and-breakfast," Wyatt said.

"Wonderful," Joe said. He gazed off into the past as he sipped his beer. "Sebastian Bell. Haven't thought about him in years. He was a quiet sort. I imagine all artists are, to a certain extent."

"He passed away before I was born, so I never knew him," Tess said. "It's fun to hear from people who did."

"Oh, yes," Joe said, dipping a piece of French bread into his soup. "Bastian was quite the ladies' man, too, before he met Serena. Did you know that?"

"No!" Tess said, chuckling at Joe's mischievous expression. "Was he really?"

"Oh my, yes," Joe said, nodding. "The strong, silent type. All the girls were wild about him. But when he met Serena, that was that. All the fellas had eyes for her, but she only saw him."

Tess's heart swelled. "Is that so?"

"Oh, yes, indeed," Joe said. "She was one of the prettiest girls in school. Not as pretty as my Sophie, mind you. But Serena turned all the heads, that's for sure."

Tess noticed Wyatt taking a deep breath. "Pop, Tess and I are trying to get some information about a mystery we've uncovered."

"Oh?"

"We thought maybe you could help with that."

Joe took a sip of his beer. "I don't know how much help I can be, but I'll try."

Wyatt smiled at the old man. "Do you remember anything about a murder that might have happened back in those days? A woman."

Joe stared at his grandson for a long moment. "A murder? In Wharton? I don't think there's ever been a murder in Wharton."

But Tess knew that wasn't true. A few years earlier, the truth had come to light about the murder of Wharton resident Addie Stewart, which had happened a century ago. Joe would certainly know about that. Wouldn't he?

As Joe was enjoying his soup, Tess noticed Wyatt slip his phone from his jacket pocket. He eyed her. A moment later, she heard her own phone beep. She fished it out of her purse and saw a message from him.

Should we take him to see the paintings? He might be able to identify the woman.

Tess caught Wyatt's eye and nodded.

If Joe knew anything about any possible murders in Wharton, maybe his memory needed a kick start. Seeing the woman in the paintings might be just the thing.

CHAPTER TWENTY

After finishing their meals and bundling up, Tess helped Joe into the car. He dozed during the drive back to Wharton—Tess supposed that was common at his age.

As they drove, Tess remembered her father had changed the combination to the wall safe. She'd need that if Joe was going to get a look at the paintings. She grabbed her phone and texted her dad, not wanting to wake up Joe.

Dad, I need the combination to the wall safe.

Why?

I want to take a quick look at a couple of them. I'll put them right back and text you when I've done it.

She didn't tell him about showing the paintings to Joe. Her father had been so adamant about nobody else seeing them, that bit of information caught in her throat.

He didn't text back right away. Tess sat there staring at her screen. She should've thought of this before they headed out of Salmon Bay. They might be making the drive for nothing.

She looked at Wyatt. "I need the combination to the safe," she said, her voice low. "Otherwise . . ."

Wyatt nodded, understanding. He pulled the car onto a side road, and they waited for a moment. And then, it came. A complicated series of numbers, letters, and symbols, along with a message.

Honey, while you have them out, will you take photos of each one and send them to me? Front and back, please. Dying to see what they look like.

Sure, Dad.

She should have done that immediately, she thought.

Also, I contacted Bill Parsons and adjusted the home insurance to account for the paintings being there.

Insurance! She hadn't even thought of it.

Tess responded, "Got it," to Wyatt before he pulled back onto the road. But that exchange with her father rattled around in Tess's head for the rest of the drive. Something was off, but she couldn't put her finger on quite what.

Joe stirred when they pulled into the driveway. He looked out of the window and smiled. "The old town looks the same," he sang. Tess knew it was a line to an old song she had heard her dad sing from time to time.

She and Wyatt helped the old man into the house, then shook the cold off their coats and hung them up in the entryway.

"Look at this good boy," Joe said, scratching Storm behind his ears. The dog happily curled around him.

"Pop is great with animals," Wyatt said.

"This is one good dog right here," Joe said. "He reminds me of a dog Sebastian had, back in the old days."

"Is that so?" Tess asked.

"A white dog. Just like this one. He used to walk the dog all around town. At all hours."

A tingle snaked its way down Tess's spine. So that was how he got a look in people's windows.

"Can I offer you gentlemen anything? Tea? Coffee?" she asked.

Joe's eyes twinkled. "I don't suppose you've got a beer?"

Tess glanced at Wyatt. The old man had had one at the restaurant. Should he have another?

"Why not?" Wyatt said. "I'll have one, too."

He helped his grandfather get settled in the armchair by the fireplace and took a moment to stoke the fire as Tess poured their drinks.

"I've got something I'd like to show you, Joe," Tess said. "It's a painting of my grandfather's. Wyatt and I came upon it during renovations."

"I'd love to see it," Joe said.

"I'll go get it," Tess said, locking eyes with Wyatt, who nodded back at her. "Two, actually."

Tess hurried into the drawing room and opened the wall safe. The paintings were stacked inside, just as she had left them. At the utterly normal sight, she let out a breath she hadn't realized she'd been holding. No mysterious arrangements of the paintings today. She pulled out the portrait of the woman and the one depicting a view through her window on the rainy night. *Okay,* she thought. *This is it.*

If Joe had any information about this woman, who she was, or what—if anything—had happened to her, the mystery might be solved. As easy as that. As she carried the paintings from the drawing room to the kitchen, Tess hoped that Joe would recognize her and say she had lived a good, long life. But somehow, she knew that simply wouldn't be the case.

Back in the kitchen, Tess set the paintings against the wall, facing out.

"Pop," Wyatt said. "We're wondering if you know who this gal is. The woman in the portrait."

Joe squinted at the image for a moment that seemed to drag on forever. It was as though the house itself were holding its breath, listening.

"Why, yes," he said, finally, nodding. "I believe I do know her. That's Daisy. Daisy Erickson."

CHAPTER TWENTY-ONE

Wyatt and Tess locked eyes. Neither of them spoke for a moment. Then Wyatt said, "Do you remember anything about her?"

"You bet I remember," Joe said, looking closer at the painting. "She was a schoolteacher. And a friend of your mother's."

Wyatt's mouth dropped open. "Mom knows the woman in this portrait?"

Joe nodded. "They were great friends. All throughout school."

Tess squinted at the painting to get a better look. She had assumed the woman was a contemporary of her grandfather's. From his era. Joe's era. But Joe was telling them this woman, Daisy, was much younger. Her parents' age.

That shone a whole new light on things.

"Is she still here in Wharton?" Tess asked, raising her eyebrows. "She might like to see this painting by the great master." Maybe this whole mystery would evaporate into thin air, just like that.

But Joe shook his head. "No, Daisy has been gone from here for a long time. Decades, I think. Kathy was upset when she left."

"Oh," Tess said, drawing out the word. "Do you know where she went? The Twin Cities, maybe?"

Joe looked off into the past. He shook his head. "That, I couldn't tell you," he said.

"What about this one?" Tess said, pointing to the second painting. "Is that her, too? Daisy? And her husband?"

Joe looked closely at the second painting. "You know, I think it is. That looks like old Frank right there." He pointed to the dour, angry figure depicted in the living room.

The old man turned to Tess and Wyatt then, a look of confusion on his face. "What a funny thing for Sebastian to paint. It's not a very happy scene, is it?"

No indeed, thought Tess.

Joe sighed and leaned back in his chair. He looked from Wyatt to Tess. "It's been a nice day, kids."

Wyatt glanced at the clock on the wall. Nearly two thirty. "We should get you home, Pop," he said, pushing himself to his feet. "I'll bet you're getting tired out."

"That's probably a good idea," Joe said, looking at his watch. "Sophie will want me home for dinner. You're both welcome to have a meal with us, of course. You know how she loves company."

His sweet face tugged at Tess's heartstrings. She knew from Wyatt that Joe's wife had been gone for many years. But who could say she wasn't still with him? Watching over her vulnerable, kind husband as his mind slowly faded. Tess brushed away a tear.

Wyatt turned to her as he helped Joe into his coat. "Why don't you ride along?" he said, raising his eyebrows. "We can call my mom on the way back. Maybe she can shed some light on the situation. She might still be in touch with Daisy, for all we know."

That was a good idea, Tess thought, but she had something to do first.

"You warm up the car and get Joe buckled in," Tess said. "My dad wants me to take some photos of the paintings. I'll go do that now and get them back into the safe. Then I can join you."

With that, she carried the two paintings back into the drawing room, pulled the others out of the safe, and propped them up against the wall, side by side. In order. If she was going to send these photos to her dad, she wanted him to get the full impression of the "storyboard."

❧

During the drive, the three of them chatted about the weather, how odd it was to have so much snow in Wharton.

"Back in my day, we used to shovel a path on the ice all the way to the island," Joe said. "We used to skate back and forth. Drove our mothers crazy. The ice was never safe, you see. But we were rascals." He gazed out the window with a slight smile on his face, remembering. "Where are we going?" he said, finally.

"We're going back to your apartment at Bayview," Wyatt said, his voice tender. "We had a nice lunch, took a drive to Wharton, and now we're headed back to Salmon Bay."

"Salmon Bay?" Joe asked. "But . . . why are we going there? We've always lived in Wharton. On Front Street. Sophie is waiting for me."

"No, Pop," Wyatt said. "You live in a nice place in Salmon Bay now. It's real swanky. You'll see when we get there."

Confusion washed over the old man's face. All at once, he wasn't the impish flirt he had been all day. Tess's heart broke a little bit to see it. Wyatt had warned her about the dementia. She hadn't seen too much of it during their lunch. But now she knew what he had meant.

"Don't worry, Pop," Wyatt said. "We'll get you home just fine."

"Okay, son," Joe said, turning his trusting eyes to Wyatt. Tess could see he was still confused, but, almost like a child, he trusted his grandson to get him home. Wherever that home might be.

When the conversation lulled, Joe nodded off.

Tess remembered how Eli used to do that, as an infant. He'd be gurgling and smiling one minute, drifting off to sleep the next. It wasn't so different with elderly folks. It was almost as if, the nearer people are to the other side, whether they've just come into the world or are close to leaving it, the more sleep they need. And she wondered, too, if it was really sleep at all. If it wasn't simply their way of touching what was behind the veil. Infants reaching back to where they had been. Seniors reaching forward to where they were soon going.

As she watched Joe, his head back, his mouth slightly open, a faint snore wafting through the car, Tess wondered what his spirit was doing. If he was talking with Sophie about dinner that night; if she was giving him a glimpse of where he might go, soon enough.

Back at the senior complex, Joe perked up. "Brrr!" he said as they walked into the building, a big smile on his face. Connie still sat at the front desk. "There she is!" Joe chirped. Tess was learning this was a favorite greeting. Maybe his way of compensating for not remembering their names.

"Welcome home, Mr. Wharton," Connie said as Wyatt signed him in.

"Thank you!" he said. "I go by Joe. All of my friends call me Joe."

She nodded. *She's heard that before,* Tess thought.

They walked down the hallway, and Joe stopped at his door. So, he did remember. Wyatt fished the keys out of his pocket and unlocked it, ushering the old man inside.

Joe shrugged off his coat and hung it up neatly, placing his hat on the shelf above it.

"Pop, it's been a good day," Wyatt said, enveloping him in a hug and patting him on the back in the way men did.

"Yes," Joe said. "Yes, it has."

"Thank you for including me," Tess said, hugging him. She hoped it would be the first of many visits with the old man.

With Joe settled in his armchair in front of the television, they said their goodbyes. As Tess looked back at him from the doorway, she saw his expression droop. He seemed impossibly tired, as though he felt every one of his ninety-plus years.

Walking down the hallway with Wyatt, she threaded her arm through his.

"What a wonderful man," she said, her voice cracking. Tears were stinging at the backs of her eyes, and she didn't fully understand why. "Thank you for today. It was a real treat."

"No, thank *you*. Pop had a great time."

"So did I," Tess said.

"He was the mayor of Wharton for many years," Wyatt said. "You probably didn't know that. He was involved with city government all of his life. He was one of the first people to push for the zoning ordinances that keep Wharton the way it is now—no tall buildings, no chain stores or restaurants. Developers tried to come in many times, and he blocked them. Sometimes singlehandedly. So we're the sleepy little tourist town with all of the charm. That's because of him."

Tess smiled. "Not only did his family found the town, he preserved it," she said. "He had a lot of foresight."

"He always has," Wyatt said. "I've learned so much from him. Not just about the ways of the world, preserving our history, keeping this town's magic alive, but he taught me how to not just live, but to live well."

Wyatt's eyes were welling up with tears. Tess could almost see the love he had for the old man, as if it were a tangible thing, floating in the air around them.

"As you probably noticed, he is the very definition of living in the moment," Wyatt continued. "Every dinner is the best he's ever had. Every beer or glass of wine is more delicious than the last. Every day is a cause for celebration, whether it's a holiday or any random Tuesday. I don't know anyone who enjoys life more than he does."

"It sort of makes you realize that the little things—a glass of wine, a great meal, the company of friends—are actually the big things," Tess said.

"They're everything," Wyatt said. "I learned that from him. His perfect day would be sitting on the deck at the house in Wharton, looking out over the lake, steaks on the grill, with family and friends gathered around the table. Laughter, good food, storytelling. Nothing better than that, for him."

"Or for anyone. What was your grandma like?"

"Wickedly funny and highly intelligent. I've never met anyone as smart as she was, and she never went beyond high school. And, wow, their marriage."

"Good?"

"The best. Don't get me wrong, my parents have a good marriage. But Pop and my grandma—that was a love story for the ages. He worshipped her. And she loved him right back."

"He must miss her so much," Tess said. "You too."

"It'll be ten years this spring," he said. "It's still hard to believe she's gone." But then he shook his head. "It's such a cliché. Everyone says that. But it's true. I can't believe he survived one day without her. They were soulmates. Yet another cliché." He chuckled. "But they were. I don't know how else to describe it. It was like they were two halves of a whole. You couldn't imagine one without the other."

Tess looked into Wyatt's eyes. "I've never had that," she said. "I thought I had a good marriage to Eli's dad. He thought otherwise."

"I'm divorced, too," Wyatt said, shaking his head. "We haven't had this conversation. It's weird, isn't it? It seems like we should know all about each other already."

It did seem like that to Tess, oddly enough. It was as though they had skipped the getting-to-know-you stage and gone right to just being together. And they had only known each other a couple of days.

"We've been sort of busy with other things, I guess," Tess said. "We really should have those conversations sometime soon."

"We'll do that," Wyatt said. "When we're not trying to solve a mystery."

They climbed into the car, and as Wyatt started it up, he turned to Tess. "So, should we call my mom?"

CHAPTER TWENTY-TWO

The call came through the car's speakers.

"Honey!" Wyatt's mother said, laughter in her voice. "You called your mother! What a good boy. How's tricks?"

Wyatt chuckled. "Tricks are good, Mom. I took Pop to lunch today."

"Oh, bless you," she said. "I'll bet he loved that."

"We went to the brewpub near the hospital," Wyatt said. "He had a beer!"

"Now I know he loved that."

"It was fun. How's Dad?"

"Keeping himself out of trouble," she said. "He's out playing golf with some of the guys. He'll be sad he missed your call."

"Tell him to give me a buzz later when he gets home if he wants to chat," Wyatt said. "And how are you, Mom? Everything good?"

"I'm great! Can't complain. So, what's up, honey? I know you're not calling to inquire about our health. I just talked to you last week."

Wyatt caught eyes with Tess. "Mom, I have someone in the car with me, and the call is on speaker."

"Okay, I won't swear, then, or blurt out my Social Security number," she said.

"A good policy all the time," Wyatt said, smiling broadly and shaking his head. Obviously, this man loved his mother. "Mom, this is Amethyst Bell. Tess, meet my mother, Kathy."

"Hi!" Tess said.

Kathy was silent for a moment. "Tess! I haven't seen you in ages."

Tess and Wyatt exchanged a curious glance.

"You've met Tess before?" Wyatt asked his mother.

"Of course, honey," Kathy said. "I knew Indy and Jill back in the day. We went to school together and sort of lost touch after they moved down to the Twin Cities. But we've gotten together on and off when they've been in Wharton over the years."

It made sense, Tess thought. Wharton was a small town. Of course, people of around the same age would know each other. She had only vacationed in Wharton but wondered if she and Wyatt had crossed paths in the past. That would certainly explain the instantly familiar feeling between them.

"I'm doing some work for Tess at her house," Wyatt went on. "La Belle Vie. She's turning it into a bed-and-breakfast."

"Oh!" Kathy said. "How nice. Giving the old place new life. I love it. So, you'll be in Wharton permanently?"

"That's the plan," Tess said.

"Wonderful," Kathy said. "I'll stop by when we get back in the spring."

"Please do," Tess said. "My parents will be coming to Wharton around that time, too." She stopped short of telling her why.

"Great!" Kathy said. "It will be great to catch up with them."

"Mom," Wyatt said, his words coming out slowly. "While we were doing some renovations, we came upon something that has created a sort of mystery. I think you might be able to shed some light on it."

"Well, that sounds intriguing. What is it?"

"Do you know someone named Daisy Erickson?"

Silence, then.

"Mom?"

"I'm here," she said. "That just took me off guard. I haven't thought about Daisy in years. What about her? Why would you bring her up?"

Tess winced. She and Wyatt hadn't talked about what, if anything, they were going to tell his mother about the paintings. Her father had given her strict orders to keep their existence under wraps until he could make the trip to Wharton in the spring. It was sketchy enough showing the paintings to Joe, but really, who was he going to tell about them? Wyatt's mother was another matter.

They exchanged a quick glance, and somehow Tess knew Wyatt was on the same page.

"Daisy came up in relation to something going on at La Belle Vie right now," Wyatt said. "Pop said you and she were friends, and she left Wharton many years ago."

Kathy was silent for a moment. "Okay, so you're not going to tell me exactly what it is, right?"

Wyatt smiled and shot Tess a look. "Well. Right. Not at the moment. It's sort of a mystery we're trying to solve. Very hush-hush."

"Okay, Hercule Poirot," Kathy teased. "What do you want to know?"

"Pop said she left town," Wyatt said. "Do you have any idea how to contact her?"

Kathy was silent for a moment. "I haven't thought about this in a long time," she began. "But no. I don't know how to contact her. I haven't heard from Daisy since the last time I saw her in Wharton."

Tess's heart sank. So, they were no closer to solving this mystery after all.

"And you don't know where the family moved?" Wyatt asked.

"The family?" Kathy asked. "Oh, honey, she didn't leave with her family. She left them. Ran off, people said. What a terrible term. But that's what people called it. The talk was pretty ugly, I can tell you that."

"She ran off," Wyatt said, elongating the word. More of a statement than a question. "Do you know why?"

Kathy sighed. "This is ancient history," she said. "But I really don't feel good about airing my friend's dirty laundry, even after all of these years."

Tess and Wyatt exchanged a glance.

"It could be important," Wyatt said. "It might even help us find her, or at least find out what happened to her."

"I don't know how," Kathy said. "Listen, honey, I have to run—"

"No, Mom," Wyatt said. He caught Tess's eye, and she nodded. What's one more person knowing, she thought. The word was getting out fast. "You don't understand. Tess found a couple of portraits of Daisy at La Belle Vie during the renovation."

"What?" Kathy said, her voice a harsh whisper. "Paintings of Daisy?"

"Yeah," Wyatt said. "They seemed rather . . . disturbing."

Kathy was silent for a moment. "How so?"

"One is from the point of view of someone standing on the street, looking into the windows of her house. It's really disturbing, Mom, as though her husband was going to erupt at any minute. Is that accurate, do you know? Was Daisy's husband that kind of man?"

More silence from Wyatt's mother, as though she were turning the thoughts over in her mind.

"Okay, kids," she said. "I haven't said this out loud for a few decades, but yes. Yes, he was. Daisy's husband, Frank—that bastard—was not a good man. He was abusive. To her and the kids. We didn't use that term back then. But that's what it was. She confided in me . . ." Kathy's words trailed off. "But I think it's okay now, after all of this time, for me to tell you."

Tess's stomach knotted. The vision of the painting, the view inside Daisy's house with the husband glowering in the living room and her crying by the stove, screamed in her head.

"Can you shed any light on what was going on during that time? When she was married to this Frank and had young children?"

"She was talking about leaving Frank, but I thought it was just her venting to a friend, you know?" Kathy went on. "Back then, women just sort of stuck it out. That's the way it was. But she did go."

"She never contacted you afterward?"

"No," Kathy said. "It really hurt for a while, if you want to know the truth. We were good friends. I thought she'd come to me. Or let me know where she was. That she was safe. But she just vanished one night, and I never heard from her again. Like she was in witness protection or something."

"Was she?" Wyatt said. "Do you think she was in witness protection?"

"Oh, goodness no," Kathy said. "We had no idea about anything like that back then."

"So, then what?" Wyatt asked. "She went missing. Did her husband—Frank—ever file a police report?"

"He did," Kathy said. "All of us were questioned. He was investigated by the police. At least that was the rumor around town."

Kathy was quiet for another moment, as though deciding whether to voice her next thought. Both Wyatt and Tess stayed quiet, too, allowing her the space to make that decision.

"I've always suspected he killed her, to tell you the honest truth," she said, finally. "I hate to say it out loud, but that's what I've thought, in the back of my mind, over the years. I really didn't believe Daisy would leave her children. No matter how bad it got with Frank. The police sort of thought that, too."

"So, they knew he was abusive?"

"Honey, this is a small town. Everyone knew everything. And yes, we all—including the police—knew Frank was a wife beater. Again, another horrible term. This story seems to be full of them. But that's what abusers were called at the time. And I told the police that, too. I didn't sit silently by. You should know that. They investigated but didn't find anything."

"What happened to him?" Tess wanted to know.

"Frank? Nothing. He took the kids and left Wharton a year or so later, and nobody has heard from him since, that I know of. Good riddance to him. But not the kids. I would've loved to have seen Daisy's boys grow up. I've worried about them over the years, living with that monster without Daisy there to get in between them."

Wyatt winced at Tess before posing his next question. "Mom, this may sound like an off-the-wall question, but do you know if Daisy ever had a relationship with Sebastian Bell?"

Kathy was silent for a moment. "A relationship? What do you mean?"

"Well, you know. A *relationship*."

"Daisy knew him. We all did. Everyone in town did. The world knew *of* him. He was already famous during those days. They had just opened the art gallery, if I'm remembering correctly. But a relationship? You're talking a romantic one?"

"Yeah. That's what I was asking."

"No," Kathy said. "Kids, I don't know if I should be saying this, but after all this time . . ." She sighed. "Sebastian wasn't the Bell Daisy was involved with." Kathy paused for a beat. "It was his son."

Tess took a quick breath in. "My dad?" she squeaked out.

"No," Kathy said. "Not your dad. His brother. Grey."

"What?" Tess said, looking at Wyatt and shaking her head. "I had no idea."

"There's no way you could have known," Kathy said. "This is ancient history. Way, way before your time. Daisy and Grey were high school sweethearts. She wound up marrying Frank—a huge mistake—and broke Grey's heart. But I know for certain they never stopped loving each other. I was right there. I was her best friend."

Tess's thoughts were racing. "But, if she loved Grey, why did she marry Frank?"

Another sigh from Kathy. "You might know," she said. "It feels like I'm opening the barn door and letting all of the horses out, but . . . this was a long time ago."

"Pregnancy?" Tess asked, wincing.

"Yep," Kathy said. "You got it. She and Grey had broken up, and Frank swooped in. Nobody could understand it. I couldn't understand it. He was a high school jock. Football star. Popular and handsome, but we all knew he was an egomaniac and sort of a jerk. As it turns out, worse than that. I think Daisy was just going with him to make Grey jealous. But by the time Daisy realized what a bastard Frank really was, and how much she still loved Grey, she was trapped."

Something was scratching at the back of Tess's mind. "Grey went missing, too," Tess said, drawing out the words, reaching to try to remember the circumstances. "I think it happened around—"

"The Fourth of July," Kathy finished the sentence. "They disappeared at the same time. I hope I'm not talking out of school, here."

"Mom, do you think they went away together?" Wyatt jumped in.

"I really don't know, honey," she said. "This is terrible to say, but I've had two thoughts about it all of these years. Like I said before, part of me thinks Frank killed her and Grey left town out of grief. But part of me has held on to the hope that maybe they left together. Maybe they've been living happily ever after somewhere, in some little town halfway across the country. Or halfway across the world."

Tess and Wyatt held each other's eyes for a moment. "Mom, thanks for all of the info," Wyatt said. "You've been really helpful."

"Okay," Kathy said. "I should go and start dinner for your father. And by *start dinner*, of course I mean *make reservations*."

Wyatt chuckled. "Love you."

"Love you, too."

Wyatt clicked off his phone. And that was that.

The knot in Tess's stomach told her that Daisy and Grey did not have the kind of happy ending Wyatt's mother hoped they did.

Her mind was racing, and everything—all the weirdness of the past few days—was coalescing into a dark miasma of ugliness.

Her grandmother Serena shutting up the studio abruptly, never really explaining why. The strange paintings that seemed to Tess to be a sort of unhinged confession. Of stalking. Of looking in people's windows. Daisy's windows. Daisy and Grey disappearing at the same time.

What did it mean? Why had Sebastian painted that sad portrait of his son's love?

Tess thought about her disturbing dreams. The scratching, only at night. The red slash across the wall in the studio that hadn't been there before.

It seemed to point to only one thing. La Belle Vie was haunted by the ghosts of the past. And Tess had the sinking feeling she was starting to discover just who those ghosts were.

CHAPTER TWENTY-THREE

They drove in silence for a bit. Tess noticed the sky melting into the purple and pink hues of Wharton's spectacular twilight. The lake shimmered in the distance as the sun itself seemed to soften.

As magical as it was outside, Tess knew it would be but a fleeting moment until darkness fell. And she was growing more and more anxious at the thought of the strange happenings inside her own house.

As Wyatt rounded the corner into Wharton, she turned to him.

"I suppose you have to get back to the dogs . . . ?" she said, a hopeful lilt in her voice.

"It's getting to be about that time, isn't it?" Wyatt said. "I'm sure they're circling their dishes wondering where I am."

Tess managed a smile. Wyatt narrowed his eyes at her and smiled.

"Why don't you come with me? They can enjoy their supper while you and I enjoy a drink, and then I can walk you home with them. I live just a few blocks from you—you probably didn't know that."

"Oh, what a relief," Tess said, exhaling. "Not about you living close by, though that's nice, too. I really wasn't excited about facing the house alone right now. Not after what we learned today."

"I figured as much," Wyatt said, pulling into his driveway. "I don't blame you."

As Tess got out of the car, she saw that Wyatt's house was typical of the grand homes in Wharton: a Queen Anne Victorian with a curved turret, dramatically angled rooflines, and a wraparound porch. The exterior was painted a smoky green, accented with a red-tiled roof and multicolored stained-glass windows. She knew this home well.

"I've always loved this house!" Tess said, smiling up at it. "My dad calls it the mayor's house. That's because it literally was, right? Joe lived here?"

"That's right," Wyatt said as they walked up the porch stairs. "Come on in and meet the girls."

Wyatt opened the door, and they were greeted by two enormous malamutes, one black and white, one red and white. They had great smiles on their faces, and their tails were wagging furiously as they curled around their man.

"Luna is the black one, Maya is the redhead," Wyatt said.

"They're beautiful," Tess said, marveling at Luna's bright-yellow eyes. "And big."

But not much bigger than Storm, Tess thought. They would make quite the trio. She wondered if they'd get along.

Tess looked around. The living room, just off the front door, was elegant but lived in. Wyatt definitely used those "front rooms," as they were called back in the day. Many people didn't. They had been saved for company. But Tess saw a book here, a coffee cup there, a sweatshirt thrown over a traditional wingback chair, slippers by the couch. Dog toys all but destroyed on the floor. This man lived in this elegant house. He didn't tiptoe through it.

"Come on, girls," Wyatt said. "Let's get you out."

Tess followed them through the house to the back door, just off the kitchen. Not unlike hers. She noticed the houses were very similar in layout and design—probably built during the same era, if not by the same builder, she thought.

Wyatt opened the back door, and the dogs scrambled outside. He filled their bowls from a big plastic bin in the corner of the room and topped off their water dishes. By that time, the girls were ready to come in for their supper.

All that handled, he turned to her.

"Glass of wine?"

"Sure," she said. "Why not?"

He reached into the fridge for a bottle and poured a glass for her and a beer for him.

"Let's go into the den," he said, leading her out of the kitchen through another door and down a back hallway. They emerged into an enormous room lined with floor-to-ceiling bookshelves. A heavy wooden desk sat at one end of the room, a black-leather sectional couch at the other, in front of a huge flat-screen television that hung above the fireplace. Two dog beds sat on either side. Tess noticed a couple of afghans strewn across a black-leather ottoman, along with a couple of books. A coffee cup sat on one of the end tables.

"I spend most of my time in here," Wyatt said, sinking onto the couch.

Tess joined him. "I can see why. It's really comfortable. The whole house is, Wyatt. It suits you perfectly."

"Thanks," he said, smiling. "It's home. I moved back in here about five years ago or so. Maybe a bit longer than that. I was just coming out of a divorce, and Pop needed a watchful eye on him."

Tess settled back into the couch and took a sip of wine. "What kind of fool woman would let you go?" she asked, smiling at him. "You seem like a pretty great guy to me."

Wyatt smiled, and Tess thought she caught a glimpse of a blush. "One who didn't really like Wharton."

Tess leaned forward and put her elbows on her knees. "You're kidding."

"No," Wyatt said, shaking his head. "I needed to come back here for Pop, but I always knew I'd end up living here again. Wharton is in my blood, quite literally. I could have compromised by getting a vacation home up here and, I don't know, spending the summers. But she didn't even want to do that."

"I'm astonished," Tess said.

"I was, too," Wyatt said. "And so let down. Yeah, there were other things wrong but . . . that was the nail in the coffin, so to speak."

"Wow, unreal," Tess said.

"She was more of a city person," Wyatt said, sipping his beer. "I knew it from the start, too, if I'm being honest with myself. You can't change people, no matter how much you try."

"So, did you—" Tess stopped her thought in midair. She didn't want to ask too much. It seemed intrusive.

"Yeah, I think I know what you're getting at. We lived in the Cities and came here for vacations, which was fine to begin with," Wyatt said. "But when my grandma died and Pop started going downhill, I knew I had to be here more."

"And she wasn't okay with that?"

He shook his head. "She never came with me. And as Pop needed me more and more, my visits got longer and longer. She stayed at work."

"Could she have worked remotely?"

Wyatt raised his glass. "Yes, she could have. She just didn't want to."

"With your family history . . ." Tess said, afraid to finish the sentence.

"It was sort of crazy, wasn't it?" Wyatt finished that thought. "I see that now. It made me realize we just couldn't have worked, in the end. Family, roots . . ."

"It's so important," Tess said. "Eli's dad didn't really get it up here, either. He liked visiting, but I don't think there was any way he would have agreed to live here full time."

"When did you guys split up?"

"It's been going on a decade now," Tess said.

"Your son was how old?"

"Twelve."

Wyatt winced. "That's hard."

"It was," Tess said. "For both Eli and me. But we got through it. And Matt was great when Eli was hospitalized."

Wyatt's eyes grew wide. "Oh no."

"Yeah," Tess said. "Car accident. Actually, his dad, Matt, came in from Las Vegas, where he lives now with his new wife, and spent several weeks with us as Eli got back on his feet."

"It sounds like your relationship is okay now, then," Wyatt said.

"Oh yeah," Tess said. "It has been for a long time. We needed to be good coparents for Eli. And we were. It's sort of wonderful now because so much time has passed, we can just appreciate what we genuinely liked about each other and don't have to deal with what we didn't."

"Not all divorced couples are so civil," Wyatt said. "I haven't so much as talked to my ex since we split."

"I get that," Tess said. "You didn't have any kids to tie you together."

The conversation turned to other things, then. Where they went to college, significant experiences. Funny tales from childhood. Painful ones, too. "The great telling," Tess's grandmother used to say. The time in a relationship where you reveal who you are through the important stories that shaped who you were. Tess thought of Joe then, and realized these were the stories she'd remember if she were lucky enough to reach his age. She had a feeling that this night, with the way Wyatt was looking at her, and the way she was looking back, could become one of those stories.

She had a vision just then, a picture of the two of them snuggling together on this black sofa, a bowl of popcorn on Wyatt's lap, and the three dogs curled up by the fire.

Was this a flash of their future? As she sat listening to this man talk about a crazy trip he had taken with some high school friends, the world seemed to melt away. All Tess could see was his chiseled face, his green eyes, and his infectious grin. And for the first time in a very long time, she had hope.

CHAPTER TWENTY-FOUR

The walk back to La Belle Vie was chilly. Tess could see her breath. She took Wyatt's arm and snuggled close to him as they walked.

She noticed his dogs pulled their leashes taut, straight out in front of Wyatt, as though they were pulling a sled side by side.

"They love this weather, don't they?" Tess asked, warmed by what seemed like smiles on the dogs' faces.

"They are in their glory in the winter," Wyatt said. "If it's not below zero, I'll let them stay out in the backyard for hours. This year, there's so much snow, both of them dug snow dens."

"Just like wolves," Tess said. "Or sled dogs on the trail."

"Exactly like that," Wyatt said.

Snow began to fall then, a light, dusty snow that clung to the branches of the majestic pines lining the streets and settled on Tess's hat and eyebrows. She put her head back and stuck out her tongue to catch a few flakes. Wyatt did the same.

"December snow," he said, grinning. "Nothing better."

The two of them stopped for a moment, there on the sidewalk, and took in the scene around them. Snow frosting the pines and the malamutes' fur. Lights burning in the windows of the grand and not-so-grand homes in the neighborhood, evoking thoughts of happy families enjoying meals around the table together. Utter silence—not a car or a pedestrian or even another dog traveling on the streets of town—as the snow fell lightly around them. It was like Tess and Wyatt were in their own magical, snowy world, inside a snow globe depicting the perfect winter night.

"This is so beautiful," Tess murmured in a whisper.

"Yes, you are," Wyatt said. He pulled her into a kiss, their mittened hands curling around each other as the snow fell. A surety descended upon her then, a certainty about what was electrifying the air between them. *This is the man I'm going to grow old with.* It was early in their relationship, and despite Tess thinking it was foolish to rush in so quickly, she simply knew he was the one for her, as surely as she knew Eli and her parents would love him. His humor. His steadfastness. His love of and loyalty to family. How easy he was to talk to. How she wanted to hear his voice first thing in the morning and last thing at night. And the intangibles, too, like the way he made her feel, deep inside.

As they walked, then, arm in arm, toward La Belle Vie, Tess silently decided she would ask Wyatt to stay. It had been a long time since she had slept next to a man, let alone done anything else, and a sizzle of nervousness flashed up her spine. She hoped her bathroom was clean and that her bedroom wasn't strewn with yesterday's clothes and underwear. But even if her bedroom was a mess, she knew she didn't want this day, and evening, to end.

Tess realized it was time to get on with it, already. She had left the false hopes of reconciling with Matt well behind her. Now it was time to admit there was more to her life than being a single mom to a now-adult son, and begin to live again with, perhaps, this incredible man who was right in front of her. As the snow fell around them, it seemed like a blessing of that realization, an impossibly romantic blessing.

She and Wyatt shared a smile, and she wondered if he was thinking the same thing.

Two blocks away, they rounded the corner to Tess's house, and the magic that had been swirling in the air between them took a dark turn, as magic often can. Whatever enchantment had been floating around them vanished. The snow globe fell onto the sidewalk with a thud and cracked.

All the lights in La Belle Vie were off, except one. The studio. The light was blazing there, and it shone through the whole wall of windows. It stopped Tess and Wyatt in their tracks. Even the dogs stood still.

"Wyatt," Tess said. "I don't remember leaving the light—"

Just then, Tess's phone rang. She grabbed it out of her purse and slid her hand out of her mitten to answer it.

"Hi, Tess, it's Jim," he said. "This may be an odd question, and I hate to seem like the nosy neighbor, but are you in the house? I thought you were out today."

Tess locked eyes with Wyatt. "Yes—I mean no," she said. "Yes, I was out today, and no, I'm not in the house. In fact, if you look out your side window, you'll see Wyatt and me with his dogs."

A moment's pause, then. "Okay, yes, there you are," Jim said. Tess spotted him in his window, waving. She waved back. "Again, an odd question, but do you have any houseguests?"

Tess locked eyes with Wyatt. "No. Why do you ask?"

Jim took an audible breath in. "Tess, I don't want to alarm you, but there is someone inside your house."

His words were calm. Measured. Careful. So as not to cause panic. "In the back room. I can see him—or her—clear as day. A dark figure, silhouetted. I knew you had gone out earlier and wanted to check with you before calling the police, just in case you had a houseguest."

Tess looked up at the studio, and there it was. She saw what Jim was seeing. A person, a figure, standing in one of the windows.

She pointed to the window. "Do you see what I see?" Tess whispered to Wyatt.

Wyatt nodded, slowly and deliberately. "We're calling Nick." He slid his phone out of his jacket pocket to contact the town's chief of police.

"We see them," Tess said to Jim. "I'm going to call Nick Stone right now. Stay tuned. And please keep watching."

Tess rang off and was ready to make that call when she noticed Wyatt's phone was already at his ear. "Hey, Nick. Wyatt Templeton. We need a squad at La Belle Vie. Tess and I are outside walking my dogs and we can see somebody walking around on the second floor of the house." Wyatt put the call on speaker so Tess could hear the chief's response.

"La Belle Vie," Nick repeated. "I'll be there in a minute. And I'll call for backup on the way. You two stay outside until I get there."

As they both watched the figure moving around near the second-floor windows, Tess tucked her mittened hand into Wyatt's. They stepped closer to the house, until they were standing on the sidewalk just past the driveway.

A moment later, Nick Stone pulled up.

As he jumped out of the car, Tess pointed to the windows. "Look," she said. The figure was moving back and forth along the wall of windows, as if pacing.

A loud, long scream pierced the night air.

"What the hell . . ." Nick growled, his eyes trained on the window. "What in God's name is that?"

The three of them hurried toward the kitchen door as Tess fumbled with her keys. The scream continued, a screech of the damned. Tess's shaking hands dropped the keys in the snow. Wyatt scooped them up and unlocked the door.

"You two stay out here," Nick said, drawing his gun.

But the dogs had other plans. They followed Nick inside the house, pulling Wyatt as they went. He tried to hold them back, but they broke free from his grasp on their leashes and bounded into the house. Tess watched as they raced around Nick to the back stairs as though they knew the layout already, and pounded up the stairs. Nick followed closely behind.

Tess looked around wildly for Storm. He was nowhere to be seen. The screaming that came from upstairs rang in her ears, as though someone were being mauled alive. Or burned.

A cacophony of barking and snarling and rage then. Tess and Wyatt locked eyes, and despite what Nick had said, they ran up the stairs and down the hallway toward the studio.

The noise was unbearable.

They burst into the room to see Nick standing there, gun in hand, but his arm hung limply by his side. His mouth was agape, and he was shaking his head.

All three of the dogs seemed to have an invisible enemy cornered on the back wall. Storm, Maya, and Luna were standing in a row, snarling and barking, biting the air, shaking their heads back and forth like they had caught something in their jaws. The screams rang out, like the wail of a demon on a dark night.

And then it was done. Silence fell across the room, an eerie, empty silence. The three dogs sniffed the air. Storm patrolled the perimeter of the room, sniffing and emitting a low growl. Maya and Luna gazed around, their ears up.

Tess's heart was pounding in her throat.

Nick shook his head. "I know some pretty odd things tend to happen here in Wharton," he said. "But I've never experienced anything like that." He turned to Tess and Wyatt. "Nobody was here."

"We all saw—" Tess began.

Nick cut off her words with a raised hand. "I know. I saw a person at the window, too. Plain as day."

"What was making that god-awful noise?" Tess squeaked out, her voice wavering. Tears were welling up in her eyes. Wyatt wrapped an arm around her and pulled her close.

Nick ran a hand over his closely cropped black hair and sighed. "It's the damnedest thing I've ever heard. Like someone was being tortured."

"Or attacked," Wyatt said, raising his eyebrows. "By a pack of dogs."

The three of them stood silently for a moment, looking from one to the other. Tess was shaking. She felt cold on the inside.

Just then, a police car pulled into the driveway—Nick's backup squad. He slipped his gun back into its holster. The simple reality of it, a car pulling into the driveway, broke the otherworldly spell that had descended around them.

"So, let's go down this path," Nick said, clearing his throat. "We all saw a person in the window. But nobody was here by the time I entered the room just a moment later."

"Right," Wyatt said.

"Okay," Nick said. "How could that possibly be? The dogs got up here before I did—this white dude was already in the room, I'm thinking." He nodded his head toward Storm. "In theory, someone could have run out of here and down the hallway toward the front stairs as I was running up the back stairs. But, if that happened, how did they get past the dogs?"

Wyatt shook his head. "They couldn't. There is no possible way an intruder got past a German shepherd guarding his home. And if, in the highly unlikely event that he did, the dogs would have chased him, not stayed in the room barking at nothing."

Nick nodded, considering this. "Absolutely right." He squinted his eyes and walked to one of the walls, running his hand along it.

"Many of these grand old Wharton homes have things like secret passageways and false wall panels. Does yours?" he asked.

Tess shook her head. "No," she said.

"You're sure?"

"I'm sure," she said. "I remember my dad telling the story about how, when he and his brother were little, they wished there were secret passageways. But there weren't. So instead, they used to climb into armoires, pretending they were the gateways to Narnia. They drove my grandma crazy with it all. Every time she'd open an armoire to get a sweater or something, she'd find my dad and his brother huddled in the back of it. Nearly scared her to death."

"Okay then," Nick said, with a slight smile. "I don't see how someone could've gotten out of this room without me seeing them or the dogs chasing them. But I'm going to have my officers search the house anyway."

"Great," Tess said. "Thank you, Nick."

"I'll go fill them in," he said over his shoulder on his way out of the studio. "And then, let's meet downstairs to talk a little bit more."

With Nick occupied, Wyatt enveloped Tess in a hug. She rested her head on his shoulder. "You're shaking," he said, his voice low in her ear.

"What just happened, Wyatt?" Tess whispered.

He shook his head. "I have no idea," he said. "But I do know one thing. There is not a chance in hell a person could've gotten out of here past the dogs."

CHAPTER TWENTY-FIVE

Downstairs in the kitchen, Tess put on the tea kettle with shaking hands. Her heart was still racing. Wyatt had snapped off his dogs' leashes, and the three of them—Maya, Luna, and Storm—were curled up by the fire. So different from the snarling three-headed Cerberus they had been moments before.

"I guess we shouldn't have wondered if these three would get along," Wyatt said. "It's like they're family already."

Tess managed a smile. "Comrades in arms."

Wyatt raised his eyebrows. "That's right. They were battling something. The question is, What?"

Nick came through the kitchen door to join them.

"Okay," the chief said, pulling out a chair and sinking into it. "My guys are looking around the place. I don't think any of us has any idea what was making that noise."

Tess shook her head, looking from Nick to Wyatt and back again. "What do you think it was?"

Neither man spoke. Nobody knew quite what to say.

"How about we start at the beginning?" Nick said, finally. "When did you leave the house today?"

Tess winced. "That's not really the beginning," she said.

Nick raised his eyebrows. "Oh?"

All at once, Tess wasn't sure how much to tell the chief of police. Should she mention the paintings? It seemed to her that something wholly otherworldly was happening, but . . . what if it wasn't? What if a real person was creeping around inside the studio? There could be only one reason. The paintings. And there were only two people in Wharton, other than Wyatt, who could potentially know about them. Hunter and Grant.

Should she say all that? Should she cast those doubts on these men who were, in all likelihood, guilty of nothing but helping her with some demolition?

She looked at Wyatt, trying to somehow project her thoughts into his.

He nodded, as if reading them. "It started a couple of days ago when Tess asked me to help open up the back room of the house, which we now know is the studio, which we were just in."

"Open it up?" Nick asked. "Why? It was locked, and no key?"

Tess shook her head. "Not exactly. It was locked, yes, but my grandmother had shut off that part of the house a long time ago. There wasn't even a knob on the door. So, it had to be opened by force, so to speak."

Nick looked at her and then cast his eyes up, as if remembering the room. "Why did she shut it off?"

"That's unclear," Tess said. "She always said it was because the whole house was too expensive to heat, but that never really made a lot of sense to me."

"Okay," he said. "And you wanted it open now because . . . ?"

"Because I'm renovating the house into a bed-and-breakfast," she said. "And I thought of turning that area into an owner's suite. A sort of living room–bedroom–bathroom arrangement, even eventually putting in back stairs going outside, so I could stay out of the guests' way."

Nick nodded. "Got it. Then what?"

Wyatt picked up the ball from there. "I had two of my buddies, Grant and Hunter, help me open up the door."

Nick nodded. "I know those two clowns," he said, grinning. "They're good folk. Help a lot of people here in town."

"Hunter was included, actually, because Tess had heard some . . ." Wyatt's words evaporated.

"Some what?"

Tess picked up where he left off. "I had been hearing noises coming from that room," she said. "Loud scratching. At night. I thought an animal had somehow gotten in there."

"What kind of scratching?" Nick asked.

Tess shrugged. "I don't know. But it was really loud. As though something was trying to claw its way out. So that's why Wyatt called Hunter. He specializes in getting animals out of houses, I guess."

"Did he find one?"

"No," Tess said. "There was no animal. And no place for it to have gotten in or out."

"So, what was causing the scratching?" Nick asked.

"We don't know," Tess said. "We haven't been able to figure that out. But according to Hunter, it wasn't an animal."

"Okay, this just keeps getting weirder," Nick said. "Not that I haven't done 'Wharton weird' before. Trust me. I have."

Tess raised her eyebrows. With all these old houses and the town's long history, she didn't doubt it.

"But let's get back to some more real-world stuff," he continued. "Let's talk about today. When did you leave the house?"

"About eleven," Tess said. "We went to Salmon Bay, had lunch with Wyatt's grandfather, brought him back here for a bit, and then took him home. We were walking back to the house with Wyatt's dogs when we saw the person in the window."

"Okay, so from about eleven to what time were you out of the house?"

"From eleven until about two," Tess said, trying to remember exactly. "Then from about three until now."

Nick turned to Wyatt. "And you were with her the whole time?"

"Yes," he said.

Nick took a deep breath. "Did Grant or Hunter have any reason to want to get back into the house? Did they leave any tools or . . . anything?"

"If they had left any tools—which they didn't—they'd have called me or Tess," Wyatt said. "Neither of them has keys to the house. I know people sometimes give them to workmen, but not this time."

"So, to your knowledge, there was no reason for either of them to come back to the house."

Tess caught Wyatt's eye. Neither knew quite what to say, but they both knew what the other was thinking. Tess's father had made it abundantly clear to her that she was to keep quiet about the paintings. But now things had changed. In a frightening way. First the paintings being arranged like a storyboard the day before, and now this.

It might be best to let the police in on it.

"Okay," Nick said, "you know that when people are looking at each other with guilty, secretive glances, the police know something is up, right? I mean, come on, guys. What's going on?"

Tess managed a weak smile and took a deep breath. "I'm not sure," she said, finally. "But we discovered something when they opened up that room."

Nick leaned forward. "What was that?"

"Paintings by my grandfather. Previously unknown paintings."

Nick's mouth dropped open. "Wow, I really lost my poker face on that one," he said, giving a small smile. "Why don't you tell me a little more about that?"

"I'm under strict orders from my dad to keep this quiet," Tess said. "It can't be getting out all over town that I've got some undiscovered Sebastian Bell paintings here."

"Understood," Nick said. "It could be dangerous for you. And, if those two clowns know about the existence of the paintings—"

Tess held up her hand. "I don't think they do," she said. "I found them after they were done getting the door open. The paintings were in the small bathroom in the studio. To my knowledge, Hunter and Grant hadn't been in there."

"But you said Hunter was checking around for animals," Nick said. "Why wouldn't he have looked in there?"

Now it was Tess's turn to gape. She went cold, as though she were outside in the snow. Of course he would have.

But Wyatt shook his head. "There's no way either of them would have done anything like that. I've known them for decades."

Tess didn't want to suspect Grant or Hunter, but it very well could be they had seen the paintings and had something to do with it all. You can know someone for decades, but when millions of dollars are at stake, people can surprise you.

"Where are they now?" Nick asked. "The paintings."

"In our wall safe," Tess said.

"Show me," Nick said, pushing his chair back from the table.

Together, they walked down the hallway to the drawing room. Tess flipped on the light—nothing was amiss. All was as she had left it hours earlier. Just to make sure, she keyed in the code to the safe, opened the door, and saw the paintings safely inside. She closed the safe door quickly.

"They're in there," she said.

"Does anyone else have the code to the safe?" Nick asked. "Anyone who could've seen you open it?"

"Other than Wyatt, no," she said. "And my dad can change the code remotely—actually, I'm surprised he hasn't done that already. So even I won't be able to open it."

"Chief?" a voice came from down the hallway. "Nick?"

"In here," Nick said, poking his head out of the doorway. Two of his officers came into the room.

"I take it you didn't find anyone," Nick said. "Nothing suspicious?"

One of the officers shook his head. "No," he said. "Nobody broke in, as far as we could tell. And obviously we didn't find anyone, or any evidence they had been here and left. No footprints in the snow, that kind of thing. But . . . can we have a word?"

Nick held a hand up to Tess and Wyatt, as if to say *stay*. Then he joined his officers in the hallway.

A moment later, he reentered the room.

"Tess, do you have someplace else to stay tonight?" Nick asked.

She and Wyatt exchanged a glance. Before she could say anything, he said, "Yes. She can stay with me."

"The dog, too?" Nick asked.

"Of course."

"What is this all about, Nick?" Tess said. "Why do I need to leave my own house?"

Nick crossed his arms and leaned against the doorframe. "Tess, the studio is a crime scene."

CHAPTER TWENTY-SIX

Tess just looked at him, her mouth agape. "What?" she said, finding her voice. It sounded thin and far away. "What are you talking about?"

"Tess, the bathroom up there is covered in blood," Nick said. "Dried blood. We need to get a forensics crew over here and analyze—"

"Blood? That has to be a mistake. Are you sure?" She looked at Wyatt, who seemed equally as stunned.

"Pretty sure," Nick said. "You had to have noticed it when you were in there. The stains on the walls and the rags and, well, everywhere."

Tess shook her head. "It was a painter's studio," she said, drawing her words out slowly. "My grandfather's studio. Yes, we saw the stains. But we assumed it was paint."

Nick raised his eyebrows. "A reasonable assumption. But until forensics does its work, we're not going to know for sure. We've already made the call to the cop shop in Duluth, and a team will be here within a couple of hours. They're on their way."

He continued to talk, and Tess continued to answer—

"And I can't be home while they work?"

"No," Nick said. "I'm sorry, but you know the drill."

—but her mind was someplace else.

Blood. The word rang in Tess's ears and then engulfed her, the realization wrapping around her like a shroud. It wasn't paint on the rags and the walls as she thought it was. It was blood.

What had happened in that room? Was that the real reason her grandmother had closed it off? Did she know? Her sweet, funny, wickedly intelligent grandmother. What had Serena known? What had she experienced? Had she come upon a murder?

And what was the scratching? The screaming? What were the dogs barking at? A shadow of what had happened in that room? Were they trying to protect a ghost? Prevent a murder? Had opening that room unleashed the pain of what happened there long ago?

"It's okay, Tess, you can come and stay with me," Wyatt said, pulling Tess back into the moment. "Storm, too. Not a problem at all."

Tess looked from Wyatt to Nick and back again. She sighed. Whatever had happened in that room, it was in the hands of the police now. The veil was lifted. There was no hiding it anymore. If her grandmother had shut that room up to bury a secret, it was going to see the light of day whether anybody liked it or not.

"Okay," she said. "I'll just go and pack a bag. How long am I going to have to be out of here?"

Nick shrugged. "It shouldn't take more than a day."

Tess was headed up the back stairs when Nick stopped her. "How long did you say that room was closed off?"

She put her hand on the doorframe. "I don't really know. I think since before I was born. I don't ever remember it being open."

"Okay, then," Nick said. "We're dealing with a decades-old crime. If indeed it was a crime. You go on and grab a few things. My officers are still up there."

Back in her room, Tess wasn't sure what all to take. Pajamas, for sure. Slippers. A change of clothes. She grabbed some makeup—minimal—and her hairbrush. Was that all? Oh! A toothbrush, too. Nick said it would only be a day.

She made her way back down to the kitchen, where Wyatt was scooping some of Storm's food into a plastic container.

After Tess grabbed Storm's harness and leash, she and Wyatt bundled up in their coats, hats, and boots. As they were ready to make their way out of the side door, Tess handed Nick her spare house key.

"One of my grandfather's paintings is hanging above the fireplace in the living room," she said. "It is protected by a very sensitive alarm system. Sneeze loud enough in that room, and it will go off."

Nick nodded. "Okay," he said.

"Listen, you might as well know that I'm not comfortable opening this house up to strangers without me being here," Tess said. "I understand you and your people have a job to do. And I don't want to sound like a jerk. But I just want to make perfectly clear that I am holding you personally responsible for protecting my things. My family heirlooms. And especially that painting."

Nick put a hand on Tess's shoulder. "Don't worry," he said. "I get it. I will not leave here until the forensics team is done with its work. If it takes all night, so be it. Kate won't be happy, but this is what she signed on for."

Tess smiled at the mention of the chief's wife. "Tell her I'm sorry," she said, squeezing his arm. "And thank you."

"Nick, we'll be at my house if you need either of us for anything," Wyatt said. "Call us tonight if need be, but if not, we'll give you a call first thing in the morning to see what's what."

With that, Tess and Wyatt wrangled the dogs and made their way out of the door, a whoosh of cold air nipping at their faces.

Jim and Jane were standing at their open door, looking out.

"Everything okay over there?" he asked. "We saw the squad cars and heard the commotion. Did they get the guy?"

Wyatt took Storm's leash as Tess crossed the driveway to talk to her neighbors. Wharton was a small town. Many people had probably noticed the squads at La Belle Vie. Best to discuss it all openly. Or, at least some of it. Secrets had a way of festering in a town like this. Maybe that was the problem. Maybe that was why Tess found herself in this situation in the first place.

Still. She didn't want word to get out . . . did she? She would have to think fast.

"No," she said. "They didn't find anyone, nor did they find any evidence someone had broken in."

"But we saw—"

"I know," Tess said. "So did we. That's one of the reasons I'm leaving the house tonight."

Jim nodded and put an arm around his wife's shoulder. "That's sensible, Tess," he said. "Good for you. Anything we can do?"

"Thanks, but the police are investigating," she said. "We may have found evidence of an age-old crime after opening up the back room."

Jim raised his eyebrows. "Oh?"

"It's nothing urgent, nothing dangerous, but something we found in the room may indicate . . . well, it's a mystery right now, I guess you'd say." Tess stumbled over her words. "That room has been boarded up for decades, and I just wanted to make sure, to get the police's opinion, before going ahead with the renovation."

"And they didn't find evidence of a person being in the house?" Jim pressed. "We all saw it."

Tess shook her head. She could feel herself shaking inside. "This may sound crazy, but no," she said. "There was nobody. The police checked the whole house. We don't know what it was that we saw in the window. And we don't know what was making that awful noise."

Jane reached out and put a hand on Tess's arm. "You probably do," she said. "I had a feeling you weren't going to find a person had broken in. These old Wharton houses are filled with spirits. You start doing renovations, and it can disturb them."

Tess just stared at her. Someone had said it out loud. Finally. Should she acknowledge it? Admit it? Give it a voice? All this time, she had been trying to explain it away, brush it off, or otherwise not think about it. But here was Jane, standing clear eyed in front of her, putting the possibility out there. It floated in the chilly air between them. As much as Tess wanted to deny it, she couldn't help saying the truth. Her truth.

"What do I do about it, Jane?" she asked, her eyes pleading for help. "I don't know if it's a . . . a spirit, as you say. But I do know this is my house. I can't have all of this happening with guests when and if the place is ever ready for them to come."

Jane tapped her arm. "I see you're headed out right now while the police do their work," she said, her voice calming and smooth. "Let's talk tomorrow. I can help."

Tess nodded. "This isn't the first thing that has happened." After all this time trying to hold it in, now she longed to let it all out.

"I'm sure it's not," Jane said, with a small smile. A knowing glance. "We can deal with this, Tess. Wharton is famous for haunted houses. We're also famous for getting the ghosts out, if that's what we want."

"Okay," Tess said. "I'll give you a call or stop by tomorrow, and we can talk about it."

With that, she, Wyatt, and the dogs set off. They walked in silence for a while.

"Police discovering a crime scene, and a ghostbuster offering her services," Wyatt said, taking Tess's arm in his. "That's some kind of day."

"Not to mention finding out my uncle and the woman in the painting were lovers. Don't forget that."

Wyatt pulled her close. "It's a lot. You must be exhausted."

Tess leaned her head onto his arm as they walked. He was right. She was exhausted. Bone tired. Yet her mind wouldn't shut off. "Did you have any idea it was blood?" she asked, finally.

"No," Wyatt said. "We both thought it was paint. That's totally reasonable. But what I'm wondering is . . ."

"Whose blood?" Tess said.

"Exactly." Wyatt took a deep breath and let it out, the steam visible in the chilly air. "I mean, this seems like delicate territory that we've stumbled into. Your grandmother shut up that room. Now, knowing what we know, it seems obvious that this is the reason. Blood was shed there. She found it."

"Agreed," Tess said. "We can't ask her why."

They crunched along on the snow, the dogs straining at their leashes, until they reached Wyatt's door.

Before he unlocked it, he turned to Tess, a grin on his face. "This isn't exactly the way I imagined asking you to spend the night with me."

She couldn't help but smile. "So, you didn't think a disembodied scream piercing the night air and the police finding a crime scene in my house would be romantic? Weird."

Wyatt unlocked the door, and the dogs ran inside in a flurry, with Wyatt turning on lights as he went.

They stood in the entryway for a moment, just looking at each other. "What now?" Tess said.

Wyatt shrugged. "Pizza and a movie? The Superior Café delivers."

Tess exhaled a long breath. "That sounds absolutely perfect," she said. "Do you mind if I put my things away and change into my sweats first?"

"No! That's great!" Wyatt said, a little too loudly. "Uh—the guest room is the second door on the right upstairs. While you're doing that, I'll get the pizza ordered."

Tess smiled at him, rather weakly, over her shoulder as she climbed the wide oak stairs. She ran her hand along the ornately carved banister as she went. The hallway was long, like hers, a deep-red Oriental runner spanning the entire length of it. She counted six doors. Squelching the desire to peek into every one, she opened the door to the guest room Wyatt had specified and found it to be just as she imagined it would be—a bed with a grand headboard and footboard, and what looked to be a hand-carved dresser with an enormous cloudy mirror on top. She wondered how old it was.

It seemed fitting the family of the town's founder should live in one of Wharton's most beautiful homes. What would John Wharton think of it? What would Elizabeth think of the town that had sprung up where her village had been, and mysteriously disappeared? If it had ever been there at all.

She set her bag on an old, threadbare, shabby-chic wingback chair in the corner of the room and drew out the leggings, soft sweatshirt, and slippers she had packed, laying them on the bed. She noticed the en suite bathroom door was ajar. She flipped on the light to find a claw-foot tub, fluffy towels, and an old-fashioned pedestal sink with hot and cold faucets. Next to it was a glassed-in shower, with fixtures that looked equally as old. She wondered if it was original. But could that be? Did they put showers in houses back when this was built?

Tess set her travel kit on the side of the sink and opened it up, staring into it for a moment. She had intended to do a quick touch-up—splash some water on her face, brush her teeth and hair, apply some moisturizer—but instead, on impulse, she pulled her hair back in a ponytail, peeled off her clothes, and turned on the shower.

She stood under the warm water and drank in the steam, breathing in and out, allowing the day's stress to wash off her and into the drain. Tears came then, as they often did. Tears of stress and frustration, of fear at the unholy scene they had just witnessed, and even of anger at the knowledge that there was *something* in her house, something she would have to deal with. On top of everything else. Part of her wished she had never opened that door. But then again, the scratching had started before the door was opened and the room disturbed. It was almost as though her *intention* to open it had brought the studio's old trauma—whatever it had been—to life.

Smelling fresh from the body wash, she toweled off and slipped into her comfy things. She ran a brush through her hair and applied moisturizer to her face. And then she walked out of the door and into the hallway, turning back to flip off the bedroom light. Then she thought better of it and left it on.

CHAPTER TWENTY-SEVEN

Back downstairs, Tess found Wyatt at his kitchen table, the dogs nowhere in sight. She noticed the oven was on, and the intoxicating smell of pizza filled the room.

"That delivery was quick," she said.

"It doesn't take them long. I kept it warm in the oven." Wyatt pushed himself up from his chair and crossed the room to the cabinets, where he grabbed two plates. He held them out to Tess, along with a roll of paper towels. "You take these. I'll take the pizza. Into the den we go. I suspect that's where the dogs are."

Tess followed Wyatt down the hallway to his cozy den and saw that the fire was already blazing. And sure enough, there were the three dogs, curled up together like a pack of wolves in the snow. What an impressive sight they were, tails curled around their noses. All three pricked up their ears when Tess and Wyatt walked into the room, but none stirred. Even Storm was as content as Tess had ever seen him.

"I guess all of that barking tired them out," Tess said, reaching down and giving Storm a little scratch behind the ears.

"It's not every day they get to do battle with the unseen," Wyatt said. A big tray with a tiled top emblazoned with a drawing of a chef was positioned on the sectional, and he set the pizza box on it. Then, he poured glasses of wine from a bottle chilling in an ice bucket on the side table.

The pizza, the wine on ice, the fire—he had done all this while Tess was in the shower?

"I'm sorry I took so long up there," she said, wincing a little. "I couldn't resist washing some of the day away."

"Think nothing of it," he said. "I'm glad you made yourself comfortable."

Wyatt sank onto the sofa and motioned for her to do the same. And with the pizza and wine on the tray between them, their first evening together at Wyatt's house began. Somewhere in her heart, Tess knew it wouldn't be their last.

She took a bite of her first slice and closed her eyes in food rapture. "This is delicious," she murmured. "Small-town pizza. There is nothing better."

"The best," Wyatt said.

Tess took a sip of her wine. "I really should call my dad to tell him about what the police found," she said, wrinkling her nose and resting her back against the sofa's soft cushions.

"And yet, she makes no attempt to pick up the phone." Wyatt raised his eyebrows.

"Is that bad?" Tess said, with a sigh. "After all that's happened today, I just feel like . . ." She didn't finish her thought. She didn't quite know what she felt like.

Wyatt took another slice of pizza. "You don't have to call him tonight if you don't want to," he said. "I get it. It's a lot. You should take a little time to process it before you bring it up to him anyway. I'm thinking you don't know quite what to say. I know I wouldn't. And plus, it's an hour later there right now."

Tess thought about this for a moment. Wyatt was right. She didn't know what exactly she'd say to her parents. A lot of information had been thrown at her that day, from Joe and his stories about Daisy, to

Kathy and her stories about Grey and Frank, to the police and their revelation that the studio bathroom had been covered in blood. And not to mention the figure in the window and the unholy screaming. She wanted it all to stop, even for just a few hours.

"I'll call him in the morning," she said. "It would be ideal if I could wait to see if the police could identify the DNA. But can they even do that after so many years? Does it degrade or anything like that?"

"I'm no expert in police procedure, but I have watched every episode of *Law & Order*," he said with a grin. "Seriously, though, I think they can extract that information after many years, yes. I mean, we hear all the time about the police opening cold cases after decades and solving them using DNA evidence, right? They've even exhumed bodies to do DNA matches."

He was right, Tess thought. The police would surely run DNA tests on the blood at the crime scene. She wondered how long it would take. Weeks, maybe?

She grabbed another slice and noticed her hands were still shaking. So, the shower hadn't washed the day away, after all.

While Tess and Wyatt were chatting about real-world matters like blood samples and DNA, what they weren't talking about hung in the air around them, just as a ghost would, filling up the room with unseen dread.

Tess held Wyatt's gaze for a long time. "What was that, in the studio, Wyatt?" she said, her voice not much louder than a whisper. Tears were pricking at her eyes.

He leaned back into the sofa cushions and took a deep breath, considering his answer. "I can't tell you what it was," he said, finally. "But I can tell you what it wasn't. It wasn't a person. It wasn't an animal. It wasn't any type of sound that could be made by water running through pipes or old houses creaking or anything like ancient wood splintering from the cold. Nothing like that."

"It was not of this world, is what you're saying," Tess said.

"Yeah, like Jane said before," Wyatt said. "It's a pretty safe bet your house is haunted."

"But I've been coming here my whole life," Tess protested. "I've never seen or heard anything like this at La Belle Vie."

Wyatt nodded. "I know," he said. "But what Jane said is really true. Renovations sometimes disturb things."

Tess took a deep breath and scratched her head. "You're talking like you believe all of this stuff—ghosts, spirits. Do you?"

"I guess I do," he said, propping his feet up onto the chaise. "It's not something I go around spouting off about, but—"

"Has anything like this happened to you before?"

"I've seen some things," he said. "Experienced some things I can't quite explain. Jane's right about the fact that this whole town seems to be haunted. Or enchanted. Or something. It's like the veil that everyone talks about, the separation between this world and the next, seems very thin here. Like a person could pass right through without even knowing it."

This sent a chill up Tess's spine. She had always felt Wharton was a magical place. Not a malevolent one. "Why is that?"

Wyatt took a sip of his wine. "It's hard to coalesce it into one reasonable explanation, but look at the strange things that have happened here. You know that, a few years ago, the Cliffside Manor, a Retreat for Artists and Writers, burned down, just outside of town."

"I had heard about that," Tess said. "It was on that stretch of road . . ."

"Yeah," Wyatt said. "*That* stretch of road where so many people have gone off the cliff. Rumors have been circulating for years about the strange circumstances around that place burning down. People say it was haunted. And not by your dearly departed aunt, so to speak. Something more sinister than that. It doesn't surprise me, what with the building starting its life as a tuberculosis sanatorium. All of those people dying there . . ."

Tess shivered. She had indeed heard the rumors.

"And then there's the story of my family and the origins of this town," Wyatt went on. "A whole village disappearing, John Wharton awakening as though he was in some sort of old Irish folktale and finding all of the people he had been living with, and loving, maybe weren't people at all. Maybe he had somehow inadvertently stepped through that thin veil into—I don't know—another time. An ancient time. And somehow, during the night, he crossed back over into his own."

"Do you think that's what happened?"

"I don't know," Wyatt said. "Like I said before, it might just be an old tale. But what if it wasn't? What does it say about this place?"

Tess let that sink in. What, indeed?

"And then," he said, leaning forward, his eyes widening, "there are stories from almost every old place in town about resident ghosts, strange happenings. Harrison's House—I'm surprised Simon hasn't told you about it—and LuAnn's boarding house top the list. Her cook—and husband—Gary, calls the ghosts in their place 'passers-through.'"

"Passers-through?"

"Yeah, like they're traveling, on their way to somewhere else," Wyatt said. "And to get there, they pass through LuAnn's."

"That's crazy," Tess said. "Maybe not so crazy in Wharton. My family has gone to LuAnn's for the fish boil on Friday nights in the summer. I've been there a few times, actually. It's quite the production."

Wyatt smiled. "You know, maybe that's where I've noticed you before. You looked familiar when I met you, and I'll bet that's why."

Tess remembered how crowded those fish boils got, with people in the restaurant and spilling out into the backyard and even the parking lot. Being at the same crowded event with Wyatt at some time during her past, not knowing she was across the room from the man who would become her . . . her *what*, exactly? She didn't want to get ahead of herself, but she couldn't shake the feeling that this might well be something important.

It all rang true to Tess, the magical, strange, and otherworldliness about Wharton. She had never quite thought about it before, but that could be why the town was so special. So apart. Growing up visiting Wharton, she hadn't been aware of all the strangeness that swirled in the air here. Maybe now she was a part of that swirl. She was slipping into the enchantment.

CHAPTER TWENTY-EIGHT

After cleaning up the dinner things, Wyatt turned on a movie, and the two of them settled in in front of the fire. Tess made it through a grand total of about fifteen minutes before falling asleep. She woke up snuggled next to Wyatt, his arm around her shoulders. The television was off, and he had a book in his lap.

She lifted her head and sighed. She noticed the fire was just a small flame on a bed of embers. "How long was I asleep?" she asked, blinking the sleep out of her eyes.

He smiled at her. "Long enough for the movie to be over, and for me to take the dogs out," he said. "I was going to roust you in a bit to move you upstairs. I figured you didn't want to sleep the night down here."

"I'm sorry I passed out like that," she said, running a hand through her hair.

He pushed himself up from the couch and held out his hand to Tess. She took it, and he helped pull her up. "I sort of liked you curling up with me," he said. "It felt good. And you were exhausted. I was glad you could drift off. I wasn't surprised at all."

He led her down the hallway, turning out lights as they went. Storm appeared from another room and followed them up the stairs.

"Your guardian is following you to bed," Wyatt said.

Tess smiled. "He always does."

At the door to the guest room, Wyatt hesitated. "Tess, I . . ." His words stumbled over each other. "I guess I should leave you here. Right?"

He was adorably nervous, Tess thought.

"I wouldn't mind it if you tucked me in," she said, leaning against him.

"Give me a second," he said, and stepped down the hall to what Tess presumed was his bedroom. She took that time to brush her teeth and slide under the covers, her stomach knotting up. Was this going to happen? Did she want it to happen? She hadn't so much as slept in the same bed with a man other than her ex-husband for a long time.

Wyatt returned in a soft T-shirt and plaid flannel pajama pants. He slipped under the covers and leaned on his side facing her.

"You're sleeping over at my house," he said, his voice soft.

"I know," she said, turning to him.

"It's nice to have you here," he said.

"It's nice to be here," she whispered.

He stroked her hair. "I have to tell you, Tess, that from the first moment I saw you . . ." His words drifted off into the air, replaced by a look of love and vulnerability on his face as he gazed down into her eyes.

"I know," she said. "From the first moment I saw you, too."

He kissed her, then, and she wrapped her arms around him. She didn't care about any paintings or mysteries or ghosts in her house, or anything else. She was here, now. And it was the most important thing in the world.

※

The next morning, Tess awoke to sun streaming in through the blinds on the windows. Wyatt was sound asleep beside her. She snuggled back down and closed her eyes, not wanting to leave their warm bed, but despite trying for a while, sleep would not return.

She looked at Wyatt's handsome face and noticed his profile. A perfect nose. Strong jaw. He really was quite beautiful, she thought.

Tess slid out of bed, careful not to wake him, and put on her slippers. Storm was nowhere to be found. Downstairs with the girls, she guessed. She brushed her teeth and hair, splashed some water on her face, and with Wyatt still snoring softly, she retrieved her phone from her purse and padded out of the room and down the hall toward the stairs.

On her way past his bedroom, she saw his door was open, so she peeked inside. Another wooden head- and footboard and massive dresser from the same era as the one in "her" room.

The walls were lined with lovely fading, old-fashioned patterned wallpaper in deep reds and creams. The nightstand held a stained-glass lamp and several books. She could make out a couple of thrillers, a popular title about race relations, and a political insider's tell-all about life in the White House. She smiled at his reading choices.

Wyatt's clothes from the day before were strewn on the bed, which was not made, and a round Oriental rug sat on the floor between the bed and the fireplace. An afghan, which looked hand crocheted, was slung across an overstuffed armchair in the corner by one of the windows; a book lay open on its ottoman.

Comfortable, Tess thought. Everything about this man felt comfortable to her. She inexplicably felt at home with him, and had since the first day they met. Was this what love was? She mulled it over in her mind as she padded down the stairs and headed for the kitchen.

She eyed her phone—it still had a charge, thank goodness—and dialed her parents. Best to get this conversation over with early, she thought. The phone rang five times.

"You've reached us. Sorry we're not here to take your call. Please leave a message."

Tess glanced at the clock. They were probably on the golf course by now, she thought. She'd call them a bit later.

The dogs materialized from wherever they had been curled up and headed for the kitchen door. Time to go out, she realized. Wyatt's backyard was fenced in, so she opened the door and was greeted by a whoosh of chilly air as the three of them scrambled around her. She watched as they romped in the snow, Storm joining in with the girls like they were old friends. *We're all comfortable here,* Tess thought.

She looked around for the dogs' food, filled their bowls, and then set about making breakfast for Wyatt. In the fridge, she found eggs, swiss and goat cheeses, sweet red and yellow peppers, and fresh spinach. She spied tomatoes and a Vidalia onion on the counter. Perfect for an omelet. In the fridge, breakfast sausage. She piled all of it onto the counter and hunted around for coffee. Before she set about slicing and dicing and whisking, she let the dogs in. They headed for their dishes, and she got to work.

First, she put the breakfast sausage into a small frying pan with a little water, covered it, and turned on the burner so the sausage would start steaming. Then, she sliced the peppers and onions very thin. While they were sautéing in another bigger pan, she sliced the tomatoes and whisked six eggs, beating them for at least two minutes. That was the trick to fluffy, silky eggs she had learned from her favorite Julia Child cookbook. With the peppers and onions softening, she added the tomatoes and spinach, sautéed for a minute or two, and then added the eggs.

At the very end, she folded the mixture over the goat and swiss cheeses to create the perfect cheesy omelet and sprinkled some of the cheese on top, just in time for Wyatt to walk into the room.

"What's all this?" he said, a huge grin on his face.

She poured a cup of coffee and handed it to him. "Breakfast," she said, kissing him on the cheek. He set the mug down on the table and drew her to him. She draped her arms around his shoulders and kissed his lips, loving the feeling of being held by this strong man.

"I could get used to this," he said. "I can't tell you the last time someone made breakfast for me. I really can't remember."

Tess smiled at him and turned back to the stove. "I love doing it," she said.

He came up behind her, wrapped his arms around her waist, and rested his head on her shoulder. "So, what have we got here?"

Tess lifted the lid off the sauté pan, and steam arose, along with a savory aroma. "Omelet with sweet peppers, onions, goat and swiss cheeses, spinach, and tomato," she said.

"It looks great," Wyatt said. "Where's yours?"

She chuckled and took the lid off the fry pan where she had been browning the sausage after the water had evaporated. "Sausage, too."

"I had all of this stuff on hand, just waiting to be made into a gourmet breakfast?"

"You just needed someone to throw it together."

"That was my ulterior motive all along," he said.

He opened the cabinet, slid two plates out of it, and grabbed silverware, setting it all on the table. Then he looked around. "The dogs are suspiciously absent," he said.

"They've been out and fed, and trotted off to points unknown in the house," she said. "I'm guessing the den."

Wyatt refilled his coffee mug and topped hers off, too. "You can come over anytime," he said.

She bent down and kissed him on the cheek. "Oh, I intend to," she said.

Tess cut the omelet in half in the pan and served it up on their plates, along with the breakfast sausage, and then sank into the chair next to Wyatt.

"Will you make this omelet for me every day?" Wyatt said after taking a bite. "Good Lord, this is delicious."

Tess smiled. This was homey, she thought. Having breakfast with someone you were falling for. It had been so long, she had forgotten what this feeling was like. Even though so many other things were tapping at the corners of her mind—the house, the studio, the paintings, Daisy and Grey, the blood—she took a lesson from Joe and concentrated on the moment. This moment. Sitting next to a man she was peacefully, contentedly excited about letting into her life, eating a delicious meal, drinking a rich cup of coffee. It was everything.

They ate in silence for a moment, but something else about Joe was nagging at her. Something she'd been wondering about since the day before. She wasn't sure she should bring it up, but in the end, she did.

"Can I ask you a question that's highly inappropriate and really none of my business?" Tess asked.

Wyatt raised his eyebrows. "Those are the best kind. Fire away."

"How did you decide it was time to move Joe into senior living? I don't want to sound, I don't know, insensitive or even accusatory, but I'm just sort of wondering how that process happens," she said. "You came back here to help care for him, and he seems pretty capable still, so I'm wondering if something happened or . . ."

The look on Wyatt's face—guilt, mixed with sadness—made Tess wish she hadn't asked. Maybe it was too personal. She didn't want to seem like she was judging Wyatt or making some sort of comment about his ability to care for a grandfather he obviously adored.

"He is pretty capable of taking care of himself during the day, you're right," Wyatt said, taking another sip of coffee. "At night, it's another story. He'd regularly wake up and go wandering around the house, thinking it was daytime, even though it was the middle of the night and pitch dark outside."

"Oh no," Tess said. Thinking about dear Joe, such a great man, being so confused, tore at her heart.

Wyatt nodded. "Yeah. He'd wake up and think it was morning, get dressed and ready for work, and head out of the house to his old office, the mayor's office. In the middle of the night."

She leaned over and put a hand on Wyatt's thigh. "I'm so sorry. And sorry I brought it up."

"Not at all," Wyatt said. "My parents were doing the heavy lifting with him for a couple of years on their own, but they're getting up there in years, too. It was really hard on them, especially my mom, watching the father she looked up to all of her life fade, bit by bit. That's why I came back full time. They needed help helping him. So I came to give them a break, to let them be off the clock for a while. Back then, they'd go to Arizona for a couple of weeks to a month in the winter. I'd be caring for Pop by myself, and that's when things started to get tougher."

"How so?"

"Sometimes, I'd wake up when he got up in the middle of the night. Sometimes, I wouldn't. And he'd be outside on the dark streets, lost. It got so I barely slept at all. I tried everything. I'd stay up until well after midnight, just so I'd be up when he got up. I put a digital clock in his bedroom with huge numbers on it, and a sign next to it. 'Check the time. It is night, not day. Not time for work until morning.' I put different locks on the doors, thinking that might confuse him. It didn't do any good. I even hung a bell on his bedroom door, as if Pop were a damn cat or something. I didn't know what else to do. I was terrified."

"Oh my God," Tess said.

"There were times when I'd be watching *The Late Show*, and he'd come downstairs all ready for the day. He'd say, 'Good morning!' with a big smile on his face, happy as a clam. I had long since stopped trying to convince him it was nighttime. So, I'd say good morning, ask if he wanted a glass of wine, which he always did, and we'd sit and watch *The Late Show* together. After about ten minutes, he'd announce it was time for bed, and he'd go back upstairs. Those times were kind of sweet, you know? He was just so damn happy."

"Oh, Wyatt." It became clear to Tess that Wyatt wanted, and needed, to talk about this. Maybe he hadn't felt comfortable enough with anyone else to let it out.

"Nick and his officers knew about it," Wyatt went on. "They started to ride around on patrol at night, just to look for him. Especially when they knew my parents were out of town. It was getting to be a huge burden on them, but nobody ever said that."

"It's what people do in small towns," Tess said. "Take care of their own."

"Yes, we do. But I knew it was just a matter of time. I couldn't let it go on for much longer. It was a hard decision, getting him into that facility. But in the end, Pop made the decision for himself. It was after the fall."

"He fell?" Tess's heart sank at the thought of it.

"Yeah," Wyatt said. "More than once. But the last straw was when he left 'for work' well after midnight, last winter. About a year ago now. One of Nick's officers found Pop flat on his back on the sidewalk. He could have frozen to death out there while I was sleeping."

"Oh no," Tess said, tears welling up in her eyes. Wyatt was tearing up, too.

"He was in the hospital for several days, almost a week. He had broken ribs and a broken shoulder. And some mild frostbite. When he was nearly ready to come home, he told me he wanted his home to be in the senior facility next to the hospital. He didn't want to burden me anymore. To tell you the truth, I was relieved. But I also felt like a failure, you know? My parents were upset about it, too, but we all knew it was the best thing."

"You couldn't care for him at home anymore," Tess said. "As much as it hurts to say that. It was time. Joe knew it."

Wyatt wiped away a tear. "Sometimes, he forgets he lives there," he said. "Like yesterday. He gets mixed up. But he's always happy when he gets back. And the most important thing—he's safe there. The staff is on duty twenty-four seven, and the doors are locked. Nobody gets in or out after five o'clock without a staff member opening the doors."

Tess squeezed Wyatt's hand. "You are a good grandson," she said, her voice shredded by her own tears. "You did right by him, the best you could. He's very lucky to have you."

Wyatt smiled. "Oh, I don't know about that. I'd say I'm the lucky one."

Tess knew how he felt. Such a caring man, devoted to his family. She felt that same kind of luck sitting across the breakfast table from him.

They were finishing their breakfast when the dogs came rushing into the kitchen barking, just before a knock at the back door. Tess saw him through the window. It was Nick.

And just like that, their idyllic night and morning, away from the mystery and horror surrounding La Belle Vie, was over.

CHAPTER TWENTY-NINE

Wyatt poured a cup of coffee for Nick as Tess cleared the dishes off the table. They all took seats around it.

"Sorry to have to displace you last night, Tess," Nick said. "You're free to go back anytime you like."

"Okay," Tess said. "It was no trouble. So, what did you find? Do you know anything yet?"

"Only that it's blood," Nick said. "Old blood."

"Are you going to do a DNA test on it?" Wyatt wanted to know.

"Yeah," Nick said, and sipped his coffee. "It may take a week or so to get the results from the lab in the Twin Cities, but it's on its way there now."

"Anything else you can tell us?" Tess asked. "I mean, are you doing an investigation . . . or what?"

"Well," Nick said, scratching his head. "That's a yes *and* no answer. There were fingerprints all over the place, and we're going to run those, but I really don't think those are going to reveal much. We know for sure it's not a *recent* crime scene. But, for that matter, we don't know if it even *is* a crime scene. We don't know how that blood got there. For all we know, your grandfather or somebody else could have cut themselves somehow, had some sort of bad accident, and bled all over the place, sopping it up with the rags."

While that made perfect sense to Tess, the tightness in her stomach and the darkness that was closing in around her told her it simply wasn't the case. It was no accident.

Nick went on, "Whatever happened, it is likely the reason your grandmother sealed off the studio. But again, without her around to tell us anything, we'll probably never really know. We can talk to your dad to see if he can shed any light on it, but that's about as far as the trail will go."

Tess and Wyatt exchanged a glance. He nodded. So he had been thinking the same thing.

"There might be another way," Tess said.

Nick looked from Tess to Wyatt and back again. "What way?"

Tess took a deep breath. "The paintings we found," she said. "They seem to tell a story. And not a very pretty one." She caught Wyatt's eye. "I—we—think it might be related."

"Okay," Nick said, elongating the last syllable. "Why don't you tell me about it?"

"It would be better to show you," Tess said. "But only you. No other officers. I'm not supposed to show them to anyone." Although, to be fair, so many people knew about them now, they were hardly a secret. She thought for a moment before continuing. "I have some pictures on my phone, but they don't really do the paintings justice. Better you see them in person."

"Got it," Nick said. "I need to take care of some things right now, but I can be to your place in about an hour, if that's convenient."

"Sure," Tess said. She turned to Wyatt. "Will you come, too?"

"Of course," he said.

And with that, Nick pushed his chair back from the table, stood, and zipped up the jacket he hadn't even bothered to take off. He had known he wouldn't be there long.

"Okay," he said, his hand on the doorknob. "I'll see you at La Belle Vie in an hour or so."

When the door had closed behind him, Tess looked at Wyatt. "Do you think this is a good idea? Showing him the paintings, I mean? I just blurted it out, but I'm not sure I should have."

"It's out there now," Wyatt said. "And, I think you were right to do it. Those paintings do seem to tell a strange and ugly story. A story of obsession, if you want to know my opinion. And obsessions never end well."

❧

After getting changed and leashing up Storm, they hopped into Wyatt's car for the short ride to La Belle Vie. Once there, Tess unlocked the side door, and the three of them, Tess, Wyatt, and Storm, stepped over the threshold into the kitchen. Nobody moved.

Silence hung in the air around them. It was a different kind of silence than Tess had ever felt at La Belle Vie before. Something electric seemed to be behind it. An inaudible sizzle. It was similar to the kind of tangible, yet invisible heaviness you could feel hanging in the air after two lovers had been fighting in a room. But not the same. This felt alive.

Something had been awakened here.

Storm let out a low growl.

"I'm going to put the tea kettle on," Tess said, breaking the silence, her words stumbling out of her mouth too quickly. "Do you want some tea?"

"Tea sounds good," Wyatt said, shrugging off his coat and hanging it on one of the hooks by the door. "Yeah. Tea." His eyes were darting back and forth.is His

"Do you feel it, too?" Tess asked, doing the same with her coat.

Wyatt nodded, looking around the room. "The remnants of yesterday are still in the air."

That sent a shiver through Tess.

"Nick will be here soon," she said, taking the tea kettle off the still-warm AGA stove and topping it off with water. In just a moment, the water was boiling (the beauty of the AGA). She popped teabags into two stoneware mugs and poured.

"We'll wait here," she said, handing Wyatt a mug and settling into one of the armchairs by the fireplace. He sank into the other.

"Sounds good to me."

The spicy cinnamon tea infused calm with every sip. Maybe it was just the strange events of the previous day that had her feeling so uneasy in a home she had grown up visiting countless times and, now, owned. It was her home now, after all. Her place in the world. She sat up a little straighter and cleared her throat. Her home. Her place. She wouldn't be scared out of it.

"When Nick leaves, depending on what happens with him, I think I should ask Jane to come over," Tess said. "We can't deny what we both saw and heard here yesterday, and no matter who or what was causing all of that commotion, no matter who the figure in the window was, I want them gone. I know everything in Wharton is haunted, or people say it is, but not like this. And it doesn't mean we have to live with it."

"Agreed," Wyatt said. "I know Jane is part of a . . . well, sort of a ghost-hunter's club. I think it's kind of hokey myself, but they go into people's houses and buildings and other places with their electrical equipment and recording devices to find evidence of hauntings. She started a Wharton Ghost Tour business, too, a few summers back. Not sure if you knew about that or not."

Tess smiled. "I must've missed that. I haven't been here too often in the past few years. I was in the catering business—"

Wyatt raised his eyebrows. "Oh? I didn't know you did that. How did I not know what you did for a living? That's crazy. Were you a chef?"

That's right. It was crazy.

"Yep," she said. "I decided to pivot and do something else. I just figured there was more to life than cooking for corporate events and fundraisers. Not that there's anything wrong with that, but I, personally, wanted something on my own."

"If you're making the breakfasts for this bed-and-breakfast inn, your guests will be in for a treat," Wyatt said, taking a sip of his tea. "I can attest to that."

Tess leaned forward. "I thought I might play that up a bit, the fact I was—am—a chef. I could have cooking-themed weekends where I teach classes on how to make the perfect . . . whatever it is."

"That's a great idea," Wyatt said. "Have you ever thought of opening a restaurant?"

"I have, actually. That's the beauty of starting over, isn't it? It seems like the world is filled with possibilities."

"I've seen more than one person's dream come true in Wharton," Wyatt said.

Tess's phone buzzed. Nick.

"Hey," she said.

"Hey. I'm on my way over," he said. "I'll be there in about ten minutes."

"Sounds good," Tess said. And there it was. Pulled back into reality once again by the chief of police. Tess was realizing he had a way of doing that.

CHAPTER THIRTY

In the drawing room, Tess had set up the paintings, in order, for Nick to see. When the chief arrived, Wyatt ushered him into the room, Storm at their heels. The two men had been chattering in the hallway, but once they stepped into the room, the conversation stopped. Nick's eyes grew wide, and his mouth hung open slightly.

"Wow," he said, stepping closer to the paintings to get a better look. "I'll be damned."

"I know," Tess said. "That's just how I felt when I saw them."

"Getting a look at these before the whole world does is, well, really a privilege," Nick said. "But why show them to me?"

"See?" Tess said, pointing from one to the other. "They're sort of like a storyboard, in a way."

Nick stepped closer still, looking at each one in turn. First the paintings of Wharton's darkened streets. Then the scene of the woman Tess now knew was Daisy, and her monstrous husband, Frank. Next, the scene following Daisy down a rainy street. The portrait, which came next, now looked ghastly to Tess. And finally, the macabre scene on the cliff.

After studying the paintings for a while, Nick looked up at Tess and Wyatt. "I'm not sure what you're wanting me to see here," he said, his words coming out slowly. "I mean, I get that these are rather . . .

disturbing paintings of Wharton. Not exactly typical of Sebastian Bell, but not that different, either. But beyond that . . ."

Tess and Wyatt exchanged a glance. Wyatt took a deep breath. "We had Pop here yesterday," he said.

Nick smiled. "Oh? How's he doing?"

Wyatt returned that smile. "Great. We took him for lunch and then back here for a bit. Tess and I were curious about the woman in the portrait. And in the rather voyeuristic paintings from the vantage point of looking into a house from a darkened street."

Nick turned his gaze back to the paintings. "Oh, yes. I see now. They do all seem to be the same woman. Family scenes." He wrinkled his nose. "Not very happy ones."

"Exactly," Wyatt said. "Tess and I were really curious, especially because of the . . . well, the strange things going on here. The scratching, for one. What we all experienced yesterday, for another. We were both just sort of compelled to find out who this woman was."

Nick nodded. "Yeah, I can see that. How does Joe fit in?"

"We thought, since Sebastian Bell was a contemporary of Pop's, this woman would be from that same era. Wharton's a small town, and we thought he might know who she was."

"Aren't you two the amateur sleuths?" Nick said, his eyes twinkling with amusement. "And?"

"And, he did know her. The woman's name is Daisy Erickson. That's her husband, Frank." He pointed to the angry man. "Those are her kids."

"Okay, it's Daisy Erickson. I still don't see . . ."

"Daisy Erickson and my uncle Grey were high school sweethearts," Tess piped up. "She ended up marrying this Frank—it's a long story— but apparently she was desperately unhappy."

Nick furrowed his brow. "Joe told you all of this?"

Wyatt shook his head. "No," he said. "He identified her, and also said she was a good friend of my mother's. So, after we dropped him off back at his place, we called her. And she told us the rest of the story."

Nick crossed his arms. "And what is the rest of the story?"

"Frank was abusive," Wyatt said. "That's what my mom said, but she also said everyone in town knew it."

Nick nodded. "Sounds like Wharton. I'm sure the cops knew it, too."

"My mom said as much," Wyatt said. "Anyway, Daisy disappeared."

Now Nick's eyes grew wide. "Okay. Now we're talking. Tell me more about that."

"My mom, who was her closest friend, believes Frank killed her," Wyatt said. "Either that, or she left town with Grey."

"Grey?"

"He disappeared around the same time," Tess said.

Nick took this in. She could almost see the wheels turning.

"But this woman, Daisy, had children, according to the paintings, right?" he said. "Would she have left them with an abusive man?"

"That's the wild card," Wyatt said. "My mother doesn't think she would have done anything of the kind. If she was going to leave her husband, she said, she would've taken her kids with her."

Nick sank down onto the sofa. "Maybe Frank killed them both."

"That's what the police thought, well, about Daisy, anyway," Tess said, joining him on the couch. "They investigated, but didn't find anything."

"And where is this Frank now?"

Wyatt shrugged. "Nobody knows. He took the kids and left town shortly after she disappeared."

Nick took his phone out of his pocket. "Frank Erickson," he said. "I can make some inquiries. We have ways of finding people now." He grinned. "Do we know any more about him? Like what he did for a living here in Wharton? That might point us in a direction."

"My mom would probably know," Wyatt said.

Nick pushed himself off the sofa and seemed ready to go. But then he turned back to Tess and Wyatt.

"Wait a minute," he said. "You found the paintings in the studio, which was covered in blood and sealed off years ago. The paintings are of a woman who went missing. Your uncle went missing. Prime suspect, Frank. Are you thinking that the blood in the studio is Daisy's? Or Grey's? Or both?"

Tess let out a heavy sigh. "I don't know. We don't know. There are so many moving parts, it's hard to keep track of it all. But we do know a couple of things. Daisy is the woman in the paintings. She went missing. And now, thanks to you, we know there's blood all over the studio."

Nick nodded. "Go on."

"We also know that my grandfather may have been standing outside Daisy's window—lurking—and painted a couple of scenes as though he had been . . . watching her and her family. He may have followed her down the street. That's what the paintings show, anyway. He might have imagined it. But we know for sure that he painted her portrait in the studio that was then shut up with no good explanation as to why."

"And we know there was some unholy terror going on in there last night," Wyatt said. "Let's not forget that."

"But what we don't know is, how are they connected?"

"I hate to even say this out loud," Tess said. "But why would my grandfather have been stalking Daisy? Why would he have painted those paintings unless . . ."

Nick nodded his head. "I see where you're going with this. Unless he was, for some reason, obsessed with her."

Tess's eyes filled with tears. "That's a difficult thought, but . . ." Her voice was faltering.

Nick shook his head and sighed. "Oh, the tangled webs Wharton weaves," he said.

Later, after Nick had gone, Wyatt and Tess were back in their kitchen armchairs. They had started a fire, and both had their stockinged feet up on an ottoman between them. It was nearing noon.

"I sort of wish we hadn't gotten Nick involved in this," Tess said.

Wyatt leaned forward and squeezed her foot. "You can't second-guess that. We both saw, plain as day, the figure in the studio. We had to call the police. It would have been foolish not to. You said it yourself—those paintings are worth millions. It very well could have been somebody there to take them. And hurt you in the process. Maybe worse."

Wyatt was right, of course, Tess thought. But why did she feel like she was betraying her family? Airing long-buried secrets? Her grandmother had gone so far as to seal off that room to make sure they didn't see the light of day. And now Tess had blundered into doing exactly what her grandmother had gone to extremes to prevent.

"They found the blood, which turned the studio into a crime scene," Tess said. "We couldn't stop them then, even if we had tried. 'Oh, no, no, no, officer! I know it's blood, but it's really a family matter. You can go now.'"

"They try that on *Law & Order* all the time," Wyatt said. "Never works. So now this mystery of ours has grown wings. But was it really ours to keep?"

"What do you mean?"

"If Daisy was murdered, doesn't that deserve to be known? Her kids are still out there somewhere, presumably. Wouldn't they like to know their mother didn't abandon them? This is bigger than just your family now."

"But it *is* also my family we're talking about. My grandfather's legacy. I have no idea why or how he would've gotten into the middle of a triangle between Daisy, Frank, and Grey, but the fact is, he painted those paintings in a studio that was splattered with blood. He very well could've killed them. If that comes out, what will it do to my family?"

"Which is probably the real reason your grandmother sealed off the studio," Wyatt said. "I hate to say it, but it makes a horrible kind of sense."

Tess laid her head on the back of the chair, closed her eyes, and sighed. But she opened them again when a thought ran through her mind. "We didn't tell him everything," she said.

Wyatt furrowed his brow. "What did we leave out?"

"We left out the story about the paintings somehow getting out of the safe, remember? We thought somebody had broken in and searched the house."

"That's right. Does he need to know it, do you think?"

Tess shrugged. "And there's something else. When I first got here, I was having these weird dreams that I was the one walking around Wharton at night. And then finding the paintings . . ."

She hadn't intended to bring that up, but it just came out before she could stop it.

Wyatt thought about this for a moment, looking into Tess's eyes. "You know what it seems like to me? It seems like someone has gone through a whole lot of trouble to make sure this *does* see the light of day."

"What do you mean?"

"You're being haunted."

"The question is, By whom? Who is haunting La Belle Vie?"

"Aren't you supposed to call Jane today?" Wyatt asked, his eyebrows raised. "Maybe she and her ghost-hunting buddies can tell us that."

Tess smiled. In all the commotion, she had forgotten. She pushed herself out of her chair with a groan.

"I'll just pop across the driveway and go talk to her. Will you wait for me?"

"I'm not going anywhere."

CHAPTER THIRTY-ONE

Tess pulled on her jacket but didn't bother to zip it, nor did she put on boots. She just scuffed across the driveway in her slippers and knocked on her neighbor's side door.

Jane opened it with a smile. "Hi, girlfriend," she said, ushering Tess inside. "I was just brewing a pot of tea. Like some?"

"That would be lovely," Tess said. "But I can't stay long. I came to follow up on what you said last night."

"Great!" Jane held out her hands. "Here, let me take your coat."

Tess shrugged it off and handed it to Jane, who opened a closet door and hung it up. Tess looked around. She had never been inside Jim and Jane's house. It was built around the same time as La Belle Vie, Tess guessed, and outwardly, shared similar features. Same Queen Anne design. Same turrets and angled roofs. But there, it seemed, the similarities ended.

Jim and Jane's kitchen was painted a bright, cheery yellow. Whereas Tess's was a nod to the past, with the great AGA stove as its centerpiece, this kitchen was thoroughly modern—stainless-steel appliances, sleek cabinets with glass doors, artsy pulls on the drawers. A painting of a whimsical otter playing in the snow hung on one wall, a nightscape filled with stars on the other. Plants sat on windowsills. A hutch was filled with what seemed to be handmade stoneware mugs.

Jane grabbed two of them and poured their tea, handing a mug to Tess. "Come on," she said, picking up the pot. "Let's go sit in the sunroom and talk."

Tess followed Jane through the formal dining room with its table for ten and deep-purple upholstered high-back chairs, and down a hallway decorated with the same sort of original, whimsical artwork as the kitchen. They walked past the living room—walls a deep red, black-and-white photos adorning them—to the back of the house, where they had a gorgeous sunroom. Tess had seen it from the outside and always admired it. The perfect way to bring a bit of light and warmth into a Wharton winter.

The room was filled with plants. A tall, mosaic-tiled table for two was positioned in the corner by the windows. Tess imagined Jim and Jane enjoying their coffee there, taking in the morning light. A comfy white couch strewn with brightly colored throw pillows sat in the middle of the room across from two overstuffed armchairs; a huge, square ottoman covered by a long tray was set between them.

Jane motioned to one of the armchairs, and Tess nestled into it while Jane settled into the other. Tess took a sip of tea.

"Your house is great," she said.

"Thank you," Jane said. "We love it."

Jane was wearing a navy-blue cotton sweater with several long silver chains around her neck and gray pants, with multicolored slippers on her feet. Her dangly silver earrings and bright-red-framed glasses completed the artsy look. Tess could never pull it off, she thought, but she admired it all the same.

"So," Jane said, crossing her legs. "You're here to talk about a haunting. Why don't you start at the beginning and tell me what happened."

Tess took a sip of her tea—she tasted turmeric and ginger and lemon in the savory, deeply satisfying brew—and couldn't help but smile at how similar Jane's question was to Nick's. Only he was trying to get to the bottom of a real-world mystery, while Jane wanted to dive into the otherworldly part of it all. Yin and yang.

So, there in the sunroom as the two women sipped their tea, Tess told Jane everything. She didn't know how to tell the whole story without bringing the paintings into it—her father's warnings be damned. She knew he meant well, but this was her life.

So, she started with the scratching that kept her up at night, the strange way Storm reacted to things, her dreams, what happened when they opened up the studio, the paintings, the fact that they were somehow out of the safe and displayed the next day. She told her about the blood they found in the studio, Daisy, Grey, Frank, all of it.

Jane listened intently without interrupting, nodding, shaking her head at times. A look of anger flashed across her face at the mention of Frank and his purported abuse.

"And that's about it," Tess said, with a slight smile. "I know. It's a lot."

Jane reached for the teapot and topped off both of their mugs. She didn't say anything for a moment, seeming to be digesting everything Tess had told her. "So, the first thing is," she began. "You've definitely got a haunting. There's no question about that, right? You're not still wondering about it, are you?"

Tess sighed. "I guess not," she said. "I tried to shrug it off and explain it away, but what other explanation could there be?"

"None," Jane said. "Definitely some spirit action happening over there. The next question is, What do you want?"

This question surprised Tess. She thought about it for a moment. "I want it to stop," Tess said.

"You want the ghosts out of there," Jane said. "I get that. But is that all you want?"

Tess squinted at her. "I'm not sure what you mean."

"I mean, it seems like what you really want, in addition to some peace in your house, is to find out the 'why' in this whole situation. Why this is happening. This isn't just about a random ghost haunting your house. This is about your family. Your past. You. I think you want some answers, not just a ghost-free house."

Tess let this sink in. Jane was right, of course. She wanted whatever was disturbing the peace at La Belle Vie out of there. Certainly. But she also longed to know why it was happening in the first place.

"It seems like that's the whole point," Tess said. "The 'why.'"

"Agreed," Jane said. "I think the spirit wants you to know. That's what it's all about. And all the smudge sticks and ceremonies in the world won't get that restless spirit out of there until you do."

Tess nodded, her stomach tightening into a knot. "Now what?"

Jane leaned back in her chair. "I'll rally my ghost-hunting crew, and we'll try to contact it."

Taking another sip of tea, Tess had a thought. "Wyatt says you do ghost tours of Wharton in the summer."

"I do," she said. "It's a hoot, and tourists love it. But everything I tell them is true, from the haunting at Harrison's House to the passers-through at LuAnn's. Then there's the library and the high school and . . . well, most of the old buildings in this town have a story. Certainly, all of the inns do."

"I'd rather La Belle Vie not end up on your tour," Tess said, wincing. "Depending on what we might find out. This might look very bad for my family, and my grandma specifically tried to hide it away. I feel like I'm going against her wishes already. I couldn't bear to betray her any more, just to entertain tourists."

"Understood," Jane said. "And I agree. We need to honor your grandmother in all of this."

Tess pushed herself out of the armchair. "I should get back," she said. "Wyatt is waiting at my house for me."

Jane raised her eyebrows and grinned. "So? Do tell? What's going on with the handsome Mr. Wyatt?"

Tess could feel the heat rising to her face. She put a hand to her cheek but couldn't suppress a grin.

"That good?" Jane said, gathering up the teapot and leading Tess out of the room.

"It's something, but I'm not sure what yet," Tess said. "It's been a lifetime since I was in the first stages of a relationship."

Jane gave her a mock scowl. "Oh, you're sure. I can see that as plain as day. But is he? That's the question."

"I think he is," Tess said. "Put it this way, I'd be really surprised if he wasn't."

Walking together down the hallway toward the kitchen, Jane squeezed Tess's arm. "Me too. You two seem like an old married couple already. You're so comfortable with each other. It was obvious to me yesterday."

"Really?"

"Oh, definitely," she said, setting the teapot and mugs onto the kitchen counter. "Jim noticed it, too."

Tess smiled as she pulled on her coat.

"I'm happy for you," Jane said. "You deserve someone who loves you as much as you love everyone else."

This stopped Tess short. Tears stung her eyes. "What a lovely thing to say."

"It's true," Jane said, pushing her white, angled bob behind an ear. "You are a very kind, loving person. That'll come back to you. It always does."

Tess grinned. "It's taken its sweet time."

"Or maybe just waited for the right time," Jane said, enveloping Tess in a hug. "Now, go on and enjoy the day with your man. I'll call my ghost crew and set up a time. Is tonight too soon?"

CHAPTER THIRTY-TWO

Back home, Tess filled Wyatt in on the latest with Jane, omitting the parts about him.

"They might be able to come tonight," Tess said. "Tomorrow at the latest, she said."

Wyatt took a deep breath. "There it is, then," he said. "We're climbing onto the roller coaster and getting belted in."

"I think we've been on it since we opened that door," Tess said with a grin. "I know I have. But now we're at the top, waiting for the drop."

"You know something?" Wyatt said. "I hate roller coasters."

Tess laughed at this. "I do, too. I hate all rides, actually."

"Me too," Wyatt said. "All I ever think about when I get on a ride is somehow flying off and dying, and what a terrible way that would be to go. 'Flew off Space Mountain,' the obit would read."

They stood there, smiling at each other for a moment, when Wyatt said, "Do you have outdoor gear?"

What an odd question, Tess thought. "Gear?" she asked. "Of course I have gear. Well. Wait. What do you mean by *gear* exactly?"

Wyatt chuckled. "Like, pants that aren't jeans that you can wear in the snow. Long underwear. Preferably wicking. In other words, stuff that will keep you warm and dry if we go out and play in the snow."

Tess grinned at him. "What do you have in mind?"

Half an hour later, with Tess and Wyatt suitably geared up and the dogs on leashes, they were making their way down to the frozen lake, Wyatt carrying two sets of snowshoes.

The entire big lake rarely froze over, but the channel between Wharton and Ile de Colette froze solid most years. Islanders would plow an ice road so cars and trucks with supplies could go back and forth—a lifeline for year-round residents of the island.

Every day, several times a day, people from a family who had been maintaining the ice road for generations would check the thickness of the ice before opening the road to cars. The lake was too temperamental, too unpredictable and would make that road dangerous, thin, and tenuous on a whim. That was what longtime residents thought, anyway.

The road was lined with pine trees and solar lights, so drivers wouldn't lose their way in the darkness, finding themselves snow blind and off course in the middle of the big lake, where the ice was thin. Many souls perished that way.

But on this day, the sky was clear, and the sun was bright. On their way down to the lake, Wyatt and Tess stopped at Jim's store for sandwiches—ham, brie, and arugula on French bread from the same baker who made Jim's croissants—and water for the two of them and the dogs. Jim stuffed it into Wyatt's backpack.

"A winter picnic!" Jim said. "I love it! That's the way to do Wharton winter right. Have fun, kids."

Down at the lake, Wyatt helped Tess into her snowshoes and then put on his own, and together they trudged onto the lake itself.

Tess saw that, in addition to the ice road, someone had plowed paths for snowshoers, and trails for cross-country skiers. A dozen or so folks were skiing on the trails near the shore, and she saw several more people between Wharton and Colette on snowshoes. A colorful sail whizzed by—an ice windsurfer. And dogs were running along with their people.

Tess turned to Wyatt. "This is amazing," she said. "It's as busy out here now as it is in the summer. I had no idea!"

"Winter is Wharton's best-kept secret," he said. "The channel usually freezes over, but not all the time. And when it does, people come out to take advantage of it."

They headed off, down the snowshoe path along the shoreline.

"I know of a great place about a half mile from here," Wyatt said. "Do you think you can make it that far?"

Tess grinned at him. "A half mile? I think I can manage that."

"Just you wait," he said, wagging a gloved finger at her. "Snowshoeing looks easy, but it's kind of tiring. A good workout for sure."

He wasn't kidding. This wasn't like walking. But Tess loved it, the feel of exertion in the cold, the chilly air filling her lungs, the snow on the lake glittering like it was covered in tiny diamonds. Even her newfound vantage point, standing out on the frozen lake looking back toward the shore, was a revelation. She could see the main street, Wyatt's house, the turret at La Belle Vie, and the magnificent Harrison's House on the hill, with its enormous wraparound porch, watching down over them all.

They rounded a corner along the shoreline, and Tess saw the "great place" Wyatt had been talking about. Several firepits, fires blazing in each one, were dotted along the shoreline. Hay bales covered by fleecy throw blankets were positioned around them. Tess saw a family roasting marshmallows around one firepit, and a few couples, beers in hand, around another.

On the lake, just far enough away from the firepits to avoid the heat, stood a three-sided building made entirely out of blocks of ice that had been colored in a hazy blue. Tess could see a long bar inside the building, also made of ice. A bartender wearing a heavy moose-hide jacket with a fur-lined hood was pouring drinks. Candles in ice luminaries twinkled.

Her mouth dropped open. "This is amazing," she said. "Oh, Wyatt, I can't believe this."

"I thought you might enjoy it," Wyatt said, grinning. "Come on! Let's snag one of those firepits for our picnic and then grab a drink."

They trudged their way to one of the firepits and laid claim to a hay bale with Wyatt's backpack and then headed over to the ice bar. Wyatt snapped the dogs off their leashes, and they ran together, jumping and playing in the snow, nearly unable to contain their joy. The feeling washed over Tess and worked its way inside of her, straight to her heart.

As they got closer to the ice bar, Tess saw that the bundled-up bartender was Grant.

"Hey, man," Wyatt said to him, bumping mittened fists together.

"Hey, you two," Grant said. "Tess, is this your first time out here?"

"Yes, and wow. This is so amazing," she said.

"Grant is one of the organizers of this winter park on the lake," Wyatt said. "Wharton Wonderland, they call it."

"Gotta take advantage of the season," Grant said. "We're going to be lighting the tree this weekend. Santa's coming for the kids. Fun and games for them. The whole town comes out."

He pulled off his mitten to reveal a slim glove and reached under the bar for two shot glasses, both made of ice, and a bottle of schnapps.

"Here's some fun and games for adults," he said, grinning. "In honor of your first time in our Wharton Wonderland, this one's on me." He poured the schnapps into the glasses. "In fact," he said, producing a glass for himself, "I'll join you."

They held their glasses aloft. Tess caught Wyatt's eye and said, "Happy days."

Wyatt cleared his throat, his eyes glistening. "Happy days."

The three of them clinked glasses and downed the schnapps. Not Tess's usual drink of choice, but somehow, out here in the cold, it seemed like just the right thing. It slid down her throat and warmed her from the inside out.

"Some wine with our lunch?" Wyatt asked.

Tess grinned. "You may have to carry me out of here, but sure."

"Oh, the dogs will pull you," he said. "No problem."

Grant chuckled as he poured wine into two plastic cups and popped lids on them. "Hey, I hear we may be doing some ghost hunting at your place later," he said to her.

"Oh?" Tess said. "You're part of Jane's crew?"

"I am," Grant said. "I do a little bit of everything around here. Jane does the woo-woo spirit stuff. I get the recordings on video."

Tess smiled at him. *What an interesting, quirky fellow,* she thought. She and Wyatt made their way back to their hay bales and settled down onto them, the dogs curling up at their sides.

Tess felt the warmth of the fire on her face, not too hot, but enough to take the edge off sitting in the cold. Or maybe it was the schnapps, she wasn't sure. She snuggled the heavy, fleecy wool blanket around her—it looked as though a sheep had just been sheared and she was surrounded by its wool.

Wyatt unzipped his backpack, produced their baguette sandwiches, and handed one to Tess.

As she unwrapped her baguette, she thought about the fact she had never been on a winter picnic. How could that be?

She had lived in the Twin Cities all her life—a place famous for its long, cold winters. Getting through those below-zero temperatures in style was a source of pride for Minnesotans. Every year, the capitol city of Saint Paul held its Winter Carnival in the middle of downtown, which featured concerts, activities, and an ice-sculpting contest. Its twin city, Minneapolis, just across the river, held its Holidazzle Parade, featuring lighted floats that made their way down Nicollet Mall, made famous by the intro to *The Mary Tyler Moore Show*.

In Duluth, just down the lake's shoreline from Wharton, there was Bentleyville, which had grown out of one man's light display in his own yard into a twinkling wonderland that people walked through in the city's Bayfront Park.

People bundled up and enjoyed winter in this part of the world. And yet Tess had never done much of it herself.

"Wyatt, this is perfect," she said, taking a bite of her sandwich. "What a wonderful day. So much fun."

"I thought you might like it," he said, his face softening. "I hoped you would."

"We have to come back for the tree lighting this weekend."

We. She hoped she hadn't coupled them too soon.

"Oh, for sure," Wyatt said. "It really is a lot of fun. Like Grant said, most everyone who is still in town comes out for it."

The weekend seemed a world away to Tess. There was a lot to get through between now and then.

"Do you think all of this will be over then?" she asked, wincing.

"This business at your house, you mean?"

Tess took a sip of her wine. "Yeah. I just want things to be back to normal. I'm hoping that by the weekend . . ."

"You can count on it," Wyatt said.

Tess wasn't sure where he got his confidence, but she made the choice to go with it, at least for the moment. And this moment was perfect. She wasn't about to let worry about what may or may not happen in the future—even just hours in the future—mar the beauty of this bright, sunny day, as she sat with the man she was rapidly falling for, watching the dogs run and play like puppies, and feeling the cool sting of winter on her cheeks.

Finished with their sandwiches and wine, it was time to go. Tess hated to leave their hay bale and the crackling fire, but La Belle Vie awaited them. She took a deep breath and got to her feet, ready to face whatever they might find.

CHAPTER THIRTY-THREE

They stopped at Wyatt's to drop off the snowshoes, and once inside, he turned to her.

"I thought I might come with you," Wyatt said, peeling off his jacket. "If that's okay. If you're not sick of me yet."

"I was hoping you would," she said. "I guess I was assuming you would, actually. I really don't want to face whatever Jane and her crew have up their sleeves alone."

"In that case, I have another idea," he said. "We should leave the dogs here. I don't think we want them at the house with the ghost-busters. In fact, I'm all but sure Jane would rather they weren't there."

Tess thought back to the barking in the studio the night before, how they attacked an unseen enemy. "You're probably right," she said.

"I'm going to dash upstairs and take a quick shower and put on some dry clothes," he said. "I won't be long. Make yourself at home."

Tess smiled at him. "I'll feed the dogs," she said.

"Perfect," he said over his shoulder as he scurried out of the room.

He was back in the kitchen in record time, and soon they were walking back to La Belle Vie.

"Let's hope we don't see a figure in the studio window like we did last night," Tess said with a grin, threading her arm through his.

"If we do, that's okay," Wyatt said. "That guy's time haunting your house is running out."

Back in her own kitchen, Tess heated the tea kettle and poured them both steaming cups. The house held a certain emptiness, a quietness, Tess noticed.

"It's odd to be here without Storm," she said, looking down at his dishes.

"I get that," Wyatt said. "They're a lot of company, dogs. Aren't they?"

"The best," she said.

Now it was her turn to dash upstairs to the shower, though she wished she could take a long bath. Headed up the back stairs, an uneasiness fell around her. She glanced down the hall toward the studio and could feel a sort of radiating energy pulsing from it. Or could she? Was that just a product of her overactive imagination? She wasn't sure. But she got the feeling the house, or whatever otherworldly spirits were haunting it, could sense what was coming. Maybe they were preparing.

As she stepped into the shower stream, she hoped not.

≈≈≈

Twilight had fallen over Wharton, turning the sky into its familiar pinks and purples. The snow glistened in the soft light. Tess had brewed a pot of tea and was just pouring cups for herself and Wyatt when her house phone rang.

She crossed the room to answer it and put the handset to her ear. She heard a crackling sound, like what you'd hear on a recording of a radio broadcast from long ago. In the distance, Tess could hear talking, a frantic, intense conversation between a man and a woman. But she couldn't quite make out what they were saying. Just snippets, words here and there.

Stop. It's the right thing. And shriller: *What are you doing? Who are you?*

"Hello?" she said. "Who is this?"

More muffled conversation, more frantic-sounding voices. Sirens, then. *Clear, clear, clear.* And then, one booming male voice filled Tess's ear, and her mind.

Let it go, Amethyst, the voice said. She recognized that voice. Or thought she did.

"Dad?" Tess asked, her own voice sounding very small. She and Wyatt shared a worried glance. "Dad? Where are you?"

Amethyst, you need to promise me you're going to let it go. He sounded like he was talking from inside a tin can. Or a tunnel, as his voice reverberated and bounced off the sides.

"Dad, what's going on?"

The line went dead.

Tess replaced the handset, the action feeling as though it occurred in slow motion. Or she was moving through water.

"What was that all about?" Wyatt said. "Was it your dad?"

Tess didn't bother to answer. She turned back to the phone and dialed her parents. It rang once, twice, three times. Four.

"You've reached us. Sorry we're not here to take your call. Please leave a message."

"Mom, Dad, you need to call me right away," she said, her voice wavering. "It's not an emergency. I'm fine and Eli's fine, the paintings are fine, but I need to hear from you just as soon as possible. It's important." She was about to hang up when she said, "I love you guys."

Wyatt had gotten up from the table and was at Tess's side. "What just happened?"

She turned to him and let him take her in his arms. She leaned her head on his chest.

"You're shaking," he said, rubbing her back.

Tears came, then. She tried to brush them away, but they were too strong. It was helplessness and frustration, too much for her to contain. She stood there and sobbed in Wyatt's arms, as he held her and rubbed her back. He didn't try to fix whatever was wrong. Didn't even ask again. He just held her and gave her a safe space to let out the abject, primal fear that had formed into her tears.

She took a deep breath. "I think I need a tissue," she said, her words swimming, no, drowning, in those tears.

No tissue in sight, Wyatt grabbed the roll of paper towels on the counter. This small gesture brought a chuckle to Tess's lips. "Yeah, I might need all of these after that," she said, peeling one off the roll and blowing her nose.

Tess sighed and sank down into her armchair. Only then did she realize her legs were shaking and might have buckled under her had Wyatt not held her up. He sat on the footstool in front of her.

"Can you tell me what happened? Is everything okay with your parents?" His face was a mask of concern and worry.

She shook her head. "I don't know," she said. "I've been trying to call them off and on today. It always goes to voice mail. I didn't think anything of it, but this phone call just now . . ."

"Who was it?"

"That's the thing," she said. "It sounded like my dad. But it was so strange, like he was calling from another century or something. You know those old radio broadcasts you've heard of something like FDR announcing the only thing we have to fear is fear itself? Which"—she blew her nose again—"I've never understood because we were in the Depression, and people didn't have food to eat or any means and were losing everything—"

Wyatt couldn't stifle his grin at this.

"But, anyway, it sounded like that. Crackly. Thin. First, I heard voices. I couldn't quite make out what they were saying. But it sounded sort of frantic. Tense. Like they were arguing. But then someone else got on the line. Someone louder. It sounded like my dad. He said, 'Let it go, Amethyst.'" She could barely get the words out. "You need to promise me you'll let it go."

She buried her face in her paper towel and let out another sob.

Wyatt was shaking his head. "I don't know what to tell you about that, Tess."

"I do." It was Jane, standing in the doorway. "I hope you don't mind, but you didn't hear me knocking," she said. "I saw you were upset, and I just let myself in."

Tess nodded, slightly dazed. "No, that's perfectly okay. Please—" She motioned to the kitchen table. Jane peeled off the shawl she had wrapped around her shoulders and took a seat.

"I heard what you said about the call," Jane said. "I think you should contact your son and see if he's heard from your parents."

A darkness overcame Tess, then. "Why?" she managed to say.

"From what I heard, I think you received a spirit call."

Tess gave Wyatt the side-eye. "Spirit call?"

Jane nodded. "They're actually quite common," she said. "Spirits— ghosts, if you will—somehow can use and manipulate electricity."

Tess had actually heard of that before. "Okay."

"And your landline is one of those perfect vehicles for communication from the other side," Jane went on. "You said there was static on the call, right?"

"Right," Tess said.

"And it sounded like they were talking from far away, even in a tunnel?"

"Exactly."

"That's a classic call from the other side," Jane said. "Textbook."

"But what are you saying? If it was my dad . . ."

"She's not saying that, Tess," Wyatt interjected. "Are you, Jane?"

"It's possible," she said. "Or it could've been someone else. It was a male, I'm assuming, right? And he knew your name?"

Tess's eyes began filling up with tears. "That was my first thought," she said. "It was my dad. I called my parents just now, and they didn't answer. It went to voice mail."

Nobody said anything for a moment.

Tess stood up and went back to the phone. She picked up the handset and dialed.

"Hi, Mom," Eli said.

Tess took a deep breath, to steady herself. "Hi, sweetie!" she said, a little too brightly. "I'm just wondering if you've heard from Grandma and Papa today at all."

"Uh, no," he said. "Why?"

She looked at Wyatt and shook her head. "Oh, no reason. I've just been trying to call them and haven't been able to get a hold of them all day."

Eli chuckled. "Payback for all of the times they worried about you when you were a teenager," he said.

"I guess you're right," Tess said, pushing her hair behind her ear. "Okay, honey, I'll let you go. If you hear from them, call me. Okay?"

"Wait," Eli said. "Are you actually worried? I mean, should I do something?"

"No, no," Tess said, trying her best to keep her voice from wavering. "They're probably just at a double feature or playing cards with friends or at a museum. There's always something going on in their building."

"Okay," Eli said. "But call or text me when you hear from them, will you?"

"I will," Tess said. "And you do the same. Hey—are you still planning to come up on the weekend?"

"Yeah," he said. "If that's still cool with you."

Tess looked from Wyatt to Jane. "I hope it will be."

She could almost feel her son's confusion wafting through the phone.

"What's that supposed to mean?"

"Nothing, nothing," she said, quickly. "Just the renovations. But there's a winter festival next weekend that you might like. There's an ice bar on the lake!"

"For real?"

"For real. I went there today. It's fun. They have firepits, too."

"Firepits on frozen Lake Superior sound like a recipe for disaster, Mom," Eli said. "What kind of genius thought that up?"

Tess couldn't help but chuckle. "Those are on the shore, smart guy," she said. "I love you, honey."

"Love you, too, Mom."

Just that little moment of normalcy, talking to her funny, adorable boy, calmed Tess from the inside out. She put down the phone and turned to Wyatt and Jane.

"He hasn't heard from them, either," she said. "But I'm not going to panic. We don't know what that phone call was, really, or who was on the other end of the line. And if my parents were in any kind of trouble, if my dad was in the hospital or, God forbid, worse than that, my mom would have called me immediately."

"That's right," Wyatt said.

"I say, let's focus on the task at hand," Tess said. "Eli is coming up here this weekend, and I don't want my boy hearing any disembodied voices. Jane, what is this operation going to entail, and when will the rest of the crew get here?"

CHAPTER THIRTY-FOUR

Just then, there was a knock at the door. Tess opened it to find Grant and Hunter standing there. She was expecting Grant, but Hunter was a surprise addition to the group.

"Hi, guys," she said, opening the door wide. "Welcome back. Come on in."

Tess gave Wyatt a worried glance. They had already determined that Grant and Hunter were the only two other people who might know about the paintings . . . and the only real-world explanation for what had been happening around the house. And now here they were, to help with the ghost hunting? It set off Tess's radar.

The two of them tramped in, taking off their coats and boots. Both had brought shoes to wear inside—they knew the drill. Grant was carrying a heavy black hard-shelled case and set it on the kitchen table with a thud.

"Let it be known I am here under duress," Hunter announced.

Tess couldn't help but smile at his perturbed face. "You're not a regular part of the ghost-hunting crew?"

"I've helped out a few times, and that was plenty for me," Hunter said, pulling out a kitchen chair and sitting down hard.

"We were short a body and needed someone," Jane explained. "Grant volunteered Hunter. He has helped us out before."

"Thank you very much," Hunter said, glowering at his friend.

Grant rubbed his hands together. "Okay, let's get to work," he said.

He opened his case and started unloading their gear—all manner of devices like headlamps, cameras, recorders, and other things Tess couldn't identify.

"What's all this stuff?" she said, picking up a handheld device that looked a bit like a big remote control and turning it over in her hands.

Grant snatched it from her. "Be careful with that," he scolded.

Tess and Wyatt exchanged an amused glance.

All the equipment laid out, Grant began his explanation. Tess got the feeling he had made this same speech many times before.

He pointed to the headlamps. "We'll be doing this in the dark, so we need these, with red bulbs for night vision."

"Wait a minute," Tess interrupted. "Why are we doing this in the dark? Why can't we leave the lights on?"

Grant squinted at her and shot a glance at Jane.

"Ghosts don't like the light," she said. "That's the short answer. Do you want the long answer?"

Tess shrugged. "Not particularly. They don't like the light. I'm okay with not knowing why."

"Don't feel bad, lassie," Hunter piped up. "I asked the same thing. It's all so dramatic, creeping around in the dark when you can bloody well just flip the light switch."

Tess laughed out loud. "That's what I'm saying!"

"May I go on?" Grant asked.

"Please," Tess said.

He held up a small video camera. Tess saw there were several of them in the case. "For recording video, obviously. We'll each have one of these. I'll encourage you to record everything, not just if you see anything."

Tess furrowed her brow. "Why is that?"

"Oftentimes, it's the recordings that show us what was there that we didn't see," Jane explained. "You might go through a place and find nothing, but you'll watch the recording and see a lot of activity floating around you."

Grant held up another small rectangular device. "This is the FLIR. Forward-looking infrared recorder. It records temperature fluctuations."

Tess looked to Jane. "Flir."

"You've certainly heard stories about people who walk into a place and suddenly feel ice cold?" Jane said.

Tess nodded. She had felt that herself, here, in the house. But she wasn't sure if it was the lack of heat those first nights after the storm.

"That's a fairly common way to tell ghosts are present. The FLIR records those temperature fluctuations."

"As if we can't tell if we're suddenly cold," Hunter huffed.

"Of course we can," Grant said. "The important word here is *record*. We'll have a *record* of when and where we felt them, instead of having to rely on our memories. And some of us, whom I shall not name, tend to run squealing like a baby from the room when they hit a cold spot and may forget exactly where and when."

Hunter glowered at him as Tess and Wyatt shared a silent laugh.

"What else do you have?" Tess asked.

Grant held up something Tess recognized, finally. "A voice recorder. Nothing unusual about this. We've all used them. We keep these on at all times, recording everything we're saying and hearing, but especially, not hearing."

Tess furrowed her brow. "What do you mean, not hearing?"

"It's the same principle as using a video recorder. Many is the time that we've investigated a place and not heard anything. But we play back the recordings, and there it is, a voice answering our questions, or otherwise talking to us, plain as day. We didn't hear it at the time, but it got recorded, all the same."

Grant reached into his case and pulled out yet another device that looked like one of those giant television remotes found by beds in the hospital. "This is the pièce de résistance," he said, with a flourish. "The EMF meter."

"Electromagnetic field," Jane said, in a stage whisper.

"This baby is the truth teller. When it goes off, you are in very close proximity to a ghost."

"Or a cell phone," Hunter added.

"Thank you, naysayer. But it's true that we need to leave our cell phones somewhere like the kitchen. It picks up electromagnetic fields—that's what it's for, smart guy—and cell phones can indeed make it go off."

Tess scanned all the various equipment laid out on her kitchen table. "This looks like quite the operation," she said.

Jane smiled. "Some of us do it the old-fashioned way, with sensitive people, psychics, mediums, or people who can otherwise communicate with the dead," she said. "I have a good bit of that in me. I do it that way. But nowadays, there are all these electronic devices that we can use to get proof, solid proof. People today like data, something tangible, rather than trusting the word of a medium. This is really the cutting edge of psychical research."

"Why electronics, though?" Tess asked. "I mean, I get the fact that it records everything, but I'm just wondering how and why. I mean, if we can't hear it or see it, how does an electronic device pick it up?"

"Spirits can communicate through, and use, electricity," Jane said. "You've certainly heard of lights going on and off, televisions doing the same."

"Why, though?"

"It's something to do with the frequency," Jane said. "And their plane. Where they are."

Tess didn't quite understand it, but she supposed she didn't need to. Her stomach was starting to knot up. This was really happening.

She had seen plenty of ghost-hunting programs on television. Much of what she saw on those shows seemed staged and hokey. But some of it? Tess wasn't sure what it was all about, but she knew it sent a chill up her spine. Now it was her haunted house they were investigating.

The idea of really being able to speak to the *undead* . . . If it were true, if they really could communicate with someone who had died, what did that say about the nature of the universe? Of life and death? Was it hopeful, being sure that when life ended, there wasn't just a vast nothingness? Was it naive, thinking a person's being, or spirit, could exist without a brain and a beating heart and a body? Was it foolish, buying into all this in the first place?

Tess didn't know. But she did know she was dealing with something she didn't understand and couldn't possibly live with one more day. After the horrors she had experienced the night before, with the dogs tearing into thin air, she knew she had to do something. And this was the best option she had at the moment.

Wyatt got to his feet and surveyed all the equipment. "I see you have five headlamps," he said. "I guess that means we're all playing."

"I volunteer to sit out and monitor the kitchen for suspicious activity," Hunter offered. "Especially if you have a bottle of Scotch."

"Nice try," Grant said. "We need everyone. I can't use all of these devices myself."

"I guess there is strength in numbers," Tess offered, shrugging. Her heart was beating hard in her chest.

All this banter was taking the tension out of the room. A look of amusement passed between Grant and Hunter, and Tess thought maybe that was the point. If they could joke enough before the group set out, nobody would be tense, nervous, or putting out bad vibes.

"I suppose we should start in the studio," Tess said, grabbing a headlamp and sliding it onto her forehead.

"Not so fast," Jane said. "Grant showed you all of his equipment and doodads. Now it's time for mine."

Jane reached into the macramé tote bag she was carrying and pulled out a box about the size of a shoebox. She opened it to reveal two thick bundles of what looked like dried herbs, each wrapped with white thread.

"Sage," she said, handing a bundle to Tess. "One for you, one for me."

Tess had heard about using sage in haunted places.

"It cleanses the house of any negative energy," Jane said. "And smells good, too. We'll light them after we finish here tonight, paying attention to doorways and thresholds."

She turned to the group. "Huddle up," she said, holding out her hands. The five of them formed a circle, hand in hand.

"I am speaking to the spirits who inhabit this house," Jane said, her eyes closed. "Our intentions are pure; our hearts are open. We come to learn what you want to tell us, and to bring you a semblance of peace. We are here in love and respect. Please tell us what you want us to know."

Tess felt a rush of electricity jolt through her. Wyatt squeezed her hand and nodded. He felt it, too.

Grant handed out the various devices. Wyatt took a voice and sound recorder. Each got an EMF meter and a camera. Grant took the FLIR. The whole group strapped on their headlamps and turned them on.

Jane flipped the lights off, and the headlamps filled the room with an eerie red glow.

"We have a lot of house to cover, so we should split up," Grant said. "Obviously the studio is going to be the hot spot, but we're not sure what else we'll find in other parts of the house. This doesn't have to be anything formal, with room assignments or anything. Let's just start walking around, going where our instincts lead us. Turn on your devices."

Tess took a deep breath. It was time to do this thing.

CHAPTER THIRTY-FIVE

As she stood in the dark kitchen, Tess was glued to her EMF meter. She had half expected it to go crazy the moment it was turned on, but it was so still, she checked several times to see if it was on or off.

"Anybody getting anything?" Grant said, his voice so low it was almost a whisper.

"All quiet," Hunter said.

"Same," Tess whispered.

They made their way, as a group, out of the kitchen and into the hallway. Then they split up, Grant pointing here and there as though he were a general on the battlefield giving orders to soldiers. They veered off into different rooms.

"Call out if you get any readings," Grant said.

Tess had no doubt she would do more than just "call out." Her heart was beating so hard she was sure the whole house could hear it.

Wyatt stayed with her, perhaps sensing her unease, or, perhaps, because of his own.

"Let's go into the drawing room," he whispered to her. "Where the paintings are."

They crept down the dark hall, their headlamps illuminating the way. The minute they stepped into the drawing room, a whoosh of cold air surrounded Tess.

"Do you feel that?" she whispered to Wyatt. He nodded, his eyes as big as saucers.

All at once, Tess's EMF meter started clicking, faintly at first, but as she moved closer to the wall safe, she saw its needle hit the topmost level. She caught Wyatt's eye for just a second and then: "Whoa! Grant! Come quick! I've got something!"

The furious clicking continued as Grant and Hunter rushed into the room.

"The FLIR is going crazy," Grant said. "The temperature dropped by twenty degrees when we entered this room."

Tess just stood there, holding her meter, not knowing what to do.

"Who are you?" Grant said, his voice loud and commanding. "Tell us who you are. What is your name?"

Nothing but the furious clicking of the meter.

"Why are you here in this place?" Grant went on.

He turned to Hunter. "Are you recording this?"

"Aye," he whispered.

"We are here to help you," Grant went on, turning in a circle with his arms wide. "What do you want?"

Tessssss.

Nobody else seemed to hear it. Her blood ran cold. She felt goose bumps on her arms and an icy hand running its way down her spine. She spun around with a shriek.

"Stop it!" she cried. "Stop it right now!"

"What is it?" Wyatt said, his face a combination of confusion, fear, and anger. "What happened?"

And then, just as suddenly as it began, the clicking stopped. The needle on Tess's EMF meter dropped back to zero, and the chill was gone.

"Something touched me," Tess whispered.

Wyatt shot Grant a look. "I think we should just stop—"

"It's okay," Grant interjected. "Calm down. It's really okay. This is what we're here for, remember? To make contact. You just did."

Tess took a few deep breaths. "I guess you're right," she said, a tear escaping from one of her eyes. She brushed it away. "Did anyone else hear my name?"

The men looked at each other.

"No," Grant said. "I didn't hear anything."

Wyatt shook his head. "I didn't, either."

"Somebody rewind your tape," Grant said.

Wyatt pressed the rewind button on his voice recorder. And there it was. As clear as a bell.

"Why are you here in this place?"

"Are you recording this?"

"Aye."

"We are here to help you. What do you want?"

Tesssss.

Tess clutched Wyatt's arm as Grant's eyes grew wide.

"That was definite," he said. "We all heard the same thing, right? Tess's name."

Everyone nodded.

"But what does it mean?" Wyatt asked. "Do they want Tess? Or do they want to talk to Tess? Two very different things."

"We don't know yet," Grant said.

Wyatt turned to her. "I think we should get you out of here," he said.

That sounded like a very good idea to Tess. But Grant broke in to squelch that idea.

"No," Grant said, turning to Tess. "Listen, this is your house and your haunting, and now we know for sure that you're at the center of it. If we want to figure out what is going on and put a stop to it, you're going to have to be here."

Tess's stomach dropped. He was right. "I'll stay, as much as I don't want to," she said.

"I don't think—" Wyatt began. But Tess stopped his words.

"The whole point is to put an end to this so I can get some peace around here and make the place habitable for guests," she said. "I want to run my own inn. That's what I want to do with my life. This is my house. I don't think I have a choice. Without getting some answers, this isn't going to stop on its own."

"It will get worse on its own, guaranteed," Grant said. "Once a haunting progresses to this level . . . it's not going away without some intervention." Turning to Wyatt, he continued. "We're all here. Nothing is going to happen to her."

Tess looked around. They weren't all there. Where was Jane?

"Jane's not here," Tess said. At the thought of it, a darkness seemed to surround Tess, a feeling that something was lurking and waiting, and Jane was with it.

"Oftentimes, she goes off on her own," Hunter said, breaking Tess's train of thought. "I think we should check the rest of the downstairs and then head up to the studio."

They left the drawing room and moved on, splitting into pairs, Grant and Hunter going one way, Tess and Wyatt the other. They walked slowly through the living room, devices in hand. Tess noticed hers was shaking. But the needle on her EMF was still at zero. No activity at all.

"Anybody getting anything?" Grant called out.

"Nothing here," Wyatt called back.

They met at the bottom of the front staircase. Grant nodded to the group, and they started up, each of them holding out their various recording devices in front of them. Tess noticed Hunter stopped midway and pointed his video camera back down the stairs, recording what was behind them. Following them? Tess shivered at the thought of it.

The upstairs hallway was eerily quiet and empty, almost devoid of any sort of human presence, even their own. It was as though whatever was haunting the house had sucked the life completely out of it. As though death reigned there.

A mist seemed to be floating through the air, accumulating in corners, hanging at face height. It was so tangible Tess swished it away with her EMF, and sure enough, the device started clicking.

"There," Grant whispered to Hunter, and the Scot trained his camera on Tess's EMF. Tess felt the temperature drop and caught Grant's eye. He confirmed it with a nod.

"Who are you?" he said. "What do you want from Tess?"

Wyatt held his voice recorder close to her.

The four of them looked at one another—nobody heard anything, except the clicking of the EMF. Tess thought it was deafeningly loud, as though it were coming from inside her own head.

Grant nodded his head toward the studio. Tess's stomach knotted up. She knew, they all knew, the studio would be the epicenter of it all.

And that was where they found Jane.

She had covered the table in the main room with candles, which flickered in the darkness. Tess detected a pungent yet pleasing scent in the air. She guessed it was sage.

Jane was sitting in the middle of the floor, a ring of candles around her. Her eyes were closed, and her lips were moving slightly. It seemed that she was praying. Or whispering to the dead.

As the group walked into the room, Jane opened her eyes and smiled.

"I was just centering myself and the room," she said. "Did you find anything?"

Grant nodded and motioned to Wyatt. "He got something on the recorder." Wyatt rewound it and played the voice for Jane.

"No surprise there," Jane said, reaching over and squeezing Tess's hand. "This is your house. Of course you're the focus of it."

Grant had said as much before, but Tess didn't like it any better now.

All at once, Tess heard a scratching sound. Not like the scratching from the studio. Electronic scratching. Like static.

And then, music wafted through the air, a faraway tune from long ago, from another time, another era.

You are my sunshine, my only sunshine
You make me happy, when skies are gray
You'll never know, dear, how much I love you
Please don't take my sunshine away

She knew this song. Everyone did. Her father had sung it to her when she was a little girl. Most people thought of it as a sweet love song. But, for Tess, it was impossibly sad and even frightening. She had always hated it, even as a child.

But this wasn't the upbeat version she knew . . . It was low and slow and threatening, as if each word were being growled out by a demon.

She looked around wildly at the others—they didn't seem to hear it. Grant was fiddling with his meter. Hunter was saying something to Wyatt. Jane had taken one of the candles and was waving its smoke into the air.

Tess couldn't hear what anyone was saying. And the air in the room seemed to be hazy, almost as if fog had descended around them. It was as though Tess had been pulled elsewhere, while also still remaining in this room.

Only Jane was looking at Tess. She said something, and then her eyes grew wide. Tess watched her mouth move. "Tess," she said, but Tess didn't hear that, either.

It was as though Jane were moving in slow motion. Or underwater. She motioned to the others, and they all turned to Tess, who could see them but could not communicate. She could not break whatever spell had fallen around her, captured her, ensnared her.

And then, the singing became louder. As though it were the only thing in the world, coming from inside Tess and outside of her and all around her. She dropped the devices she was carrying and put her hands over her ears. Wyatt grabbed both of her arms—Tess couldn't feel that, either.

And then the next verse came, which she did not know and had never heard. It had confirmed what she had always thought about that threatening, terrible song.

I'll always love you and make you happy
If you will only say the same
But if you leave me and love another
You'll regret it all someday

Tess was overcome with an intense feeling of being trapped, as though she were in a box. Clawing to get out. She felt herself dropping to the floor. And then everything went black.

CHAPTER THIRTY-SIX

The next thing Tess knew, she was opening her eyes. She was flat on her back on the floor of the studio. Jane had knelt down beside her and was dabbing at her forehead with a cool cloth. Wyatt was on the other side, holding her hand.

"That's right," Jane said. "That's the way. Come back to us now."

Tess moaned. The back of her head was aching. "Did I faint?" she asked.

"Yeah, honey, you did," Jane said, taking her hands and pulling her up to a sitting position. Tess's head swam with vertigo.

"Whoa," she murmured.

It was then she noticed all the lights were on in the room. Grant was blowing out the candles, and everyone had taken their headlamps off.

"Are we done?" Tess asked.

"Hell yes, we're done," Wyatt said.

"For today," Jane added. "The ghost-hunting part, at least. Let's regroup, hook the recorders up to the laptops, and see what we've got. But first, Tess, let's talk about what happened to you."

Tess looked at Wyatt. "My head hurts," she said.

"Can you stand up?" he asked.

"I think so," she said.

Wyatt put his arms around her waist and helped her up. She was shaken, but okay.

"Come on," he said. "Let's go downstairs."

Tess let him lead her out of the room and down the back stairway to her familiar, welcoming kitchen, where a fire burned softly in the fireplace, the AGA was warm, and Tess's favorite armchair was waiting. She sank into it with a groan as the rest of the crew filed in.

Grant and Hunter took seats at the table and assembled all the devices, pulling out two laptops from the case Grant had brought and turning them on. Hunter retrieved a snarl of cords.

Meanwhile Jane checked the kettle on the AGA. "How about some tea, everyone?" she asked, looking around the room. "The kettle's still hot."

"Tea, my arse," Hunter said.

Despite everything, Tess couldn't help but smile. "I have a good single malt if you're interested," she said, her voice wavering a bit.

"Now you're talking," Hunter said. "I thought you might. You others can ferret out ghosts all you like, but I can sense a single malt a mile away. I think that skill is more useful."

Tess caught Wyatt's eye. He couldn't help but grin, either. "Bottom left cabinet," she said.

Wyatt opened it and pulled out the Scotch. "Who wants one? Other than Hunter."

Grant raised his hand. Wyatt raised his.

"I'll take some wine," Tess said. "Jane?"

"Why not?"

Wyatt acted as bartender, pouring drinks for everyone. Tess took hers with shaking hands. But the cold wine felt good slipping down her throat. She tried to breathe in and out to quiet her racing pulse.

"While they're fiddling with the electronics, let's talk about what happened up there," Jane said, pulling out a chair from the table and setting it close to Tess's armchair as Wyatt perched on its footstool.

Tess took another sip. "I don't really know," she said. "I started to hear . . ." But she just shook her head. How could she explain what she heard?

"I know," Jane said. "Sometimes there aren't words for it. What did it feel like?"

Tess thought back. "It felt like I was somewhere else, but also in the room at the same time," she said. "I could see all of you, but it was like I was looking at you from . . . elsewhere."

Jane gave her a knowing smile. "Like from behind a veil?"

This sent a shiver up Tess's spine. That was exactly what it had been like. She nodded.

Now everyone in the room was looking at her, rapt. It was like they were all holding their breath, as though the very room were holding its breath, too, waiting for her to continue.

Jane took her hand. "And what did you see when you were there?"

"I didn't see anything," she said. "I mean, I saw all of you; I was in the room. I don't know quite how to explain it, but it's what I heard."

"What was that?" Wyatt asked. "What did you hear?"

Tess took a deep breath. She was going to say this craziness out loud. Why not? She was in a room full of ghost hunters. Not much would sound crazy to them. Would it?

"I heard a song," she said. "A scratchy, faraway song. 'You Are My Sunshine.'" She winced at the words.

"I know that song," Wyatt said. "My mom used to sing it to me at night."

"Mine too," Grant said.

But Jane was looking into Tess's eyes with a wary look in her own. "I don't think this was the lullaby all of us heard as children, was it, Tess?"

Tess shook her head. "No. This was low, and slow, and . . . almost demonic sounding. Whatever that is. Threatening for sure. A man's voice was singing it. And there was a verse that I had never heard before."

"I know it," Jane said. "Everybody thinks it's a sweet love song. They sing it to their kids, to their lovers. But it's not. It's a song about—"

"Obsession," Tess whispered.

"I don't get it," Wyatt said. "Obsession? What's the second verse?"

Tess looked up at him with tears in her eyes. "It's something about how he will love her forever, but only if she feels the same. And if she loves another . . ." She couldn't get the words out.

"She'll regret it someday," Jane said, her own voice wavering.

"Holy shit," Grant whispered. "That's messed up."

And all of a sudden, the pieces fell into place in Tess's mind, like Legos fitting together. If those obsessive paintings had a soundtrack, that song would be it.

Daisy had loved another. Was it she who would regret it someday?

Grant broke her train of thought. "I'll have all the data pulled together later, or tomorrow, when I can go through it all," he said. "It'll show where the cold spots were, where the activity was, and what time. But right now, I'll get the laptop synced with my video recorder to see if it picked up anything in the studio around the time Tess fainted."

He got busy attaching the USB cable to his device, and then to the computer.

They all gathered around the kitchen table as the grainy night-vision video played.

There was Jane, sitting in the middle of a circle of candles as the four others entered the room. Wisps seemed to be floating in the air around her.

"What is that?" Tess said, pointing to the wisps.

Jane held up her hand to stop Tess's words. "Watch," she whispered.

On the video, Jane opened her eyes and smiled. *"I was just centering myself and the room. Did you find anything?"*

Grant's voice, now. *"He got something on the recorder."*

Tesssss.

The camera panned over to Jane. *"No surprise there. This is your house. Of course you're the focus of it."*

And there it was—the static. The camera caught Tess's reaction, first looking around, and then furrowing her brow and cocking her head to the side, listening.

And then it came.

You are my sunshine, my only sunshine

"Whoa!" Grant said, pushing back his chair from the table, as if to distance himself from the sound.

You make me happy, when skies are gray

"I'll be damned," Hunter whispered. "That's like growling."

You'll never know, dear, how much I love you
Please don't take my sunshine away

"And there we are, oblivious as hell," Hunter went on. "I didn't hear it."

Tess heard Grant's voice, then. *"The EMF has been going crazy."*

"Look," Jane whispered, pointing at the screen. The wisps seemed to be forming into something a little more solid as the camera panned around the room. Three figures, one clearly a woman, although they were just wisps of smoke, or fog, or ether. No faces, no way to tell who they were.

And there was Tess, a vacant look on her face. And Jane, noticing her. *"Tess."* She motioned to the others. *"There's something wrong with Tess."*

Tess dropped her devices and put her hands over her ears. Wyatt grabbed both of her arms, but Tess's head flopped to the side like a rag doll's.

There in the kitchen, Tess gasped at what she saw.
And then the next verse.

I'll always love you and make you happy
If you will only say the same
But if you leave me and love another
You'll regret it all someday

And then, laughter. Horrible, menacing laughter. Tess hadn't heard that before.

Now it was Hunter's turn to jump back in his chair. "Holy mother of God, what is that?"

CHAPTER THIRTY-SEVEN

The crew just looked at each other. No one spoke for a moment. Tension, fear, and confusion hung in the air, as tangible as the fog in the studio. Hunter downed the rest of his Scotch in one gulp and poured another. Grant joined him. Wyatt reached for Tess's hand and squeezed it.

And then, a booming voice broke the silence.

"Tess!"

It was the same voice she had heard earlier. Wasn't it? For a split second, Tess thought she was the only one, again, who could hear it. But everyone jumped. The energy in the house decidedly shifted into— what?—it seemed like a sort of chaos.

"Who's there?" Wyatt shouted.

Everyone stood up from their chairs and tensed, ready for whatever was going to come.

And then Tess saw what it was.

Indigo Bell strode into the kitchen with a flourish, as he always did. The man knew how to make a grand entrance. His stark-white hair was still thick and wavy for a man in his seventies. Behind his modern horn-rimmed glasses, his blue eyes shone. He was dressed in a black coat and fur hat, with a purple paisley scarf wound around his neck.

Tess's mother, Jill, was close behind. She was wearing the magenta cloak Tess had given her the previous Christmas, with skinny black pants and high-heeled black boots. Her salt-and-pepper hair was cut short, showing off her perfect skin and strong jawline. Tess had always wished she had inherited her mother's eternal youth.

Tess blinked at them, not quite comprehending, for just a moment, what she was seeing.

"There you are, honey!" Jill said.

"What is all this?" Indigo wanted to know. "Why are all of the lights off? We thought you weren't here, and then we heard voices."

Tess pushed herself out of her chair as her mother took her into her arms. "It's so good to see you, sweetie," Jill said, smoothing Tess's hair.

"It's good to see you, Mom," she said. "And Dad. But . . . I don't get it. How did you get here?"

Indigo looked amused. "The conventional way," he said. "We hopped on a flight. And we took a shuttle here from the airport in Duluth."

"It was a planes, trains, and automobiles situation," Jill piped up. "Layovers, that sort of thing. We've forgotten how difficult it can be to travel to Wharton from Florida in the winter."

So that was why they hadn't answered the phone when Tess had tried to call, she realized.

"I see you're having a gathering," Indigo said. "Splendid!" He pointed at Wyatt. "You, young man, I know. How are your parents and grandfather?"

The two men shook hands. "Great on all counts, thank you," Wyatt said. "Tess and I took Pop out for lunch yesterday."

"Good for you," Indigo said, patting Wyatt on the arm. Then, he turned to Grant and Hunter. "And you two? I'm sure I've seen you both around town, but we've never been introduced. I'm Indigo Bell."

"Dad, meet Grant and Hunter," Tess said. "They helped open up the studio."

"I see," Indigo said. "Good, good, good." He looked around, smiling slightly. "I see everyone has a drink but me," he said, his eyes twinkling. "Darling, pour your old man a Scotch, will you?"

Wyatt did the honors, handing a glass to Indigo.

Meanwhile, Jill had hugged Jane, and the two were chatting.

"I didn't expect you back until spring," Tess said. "What's going on? Why didn't you call and tell me you were coming?"

A look crept onto Jill's face, then. Guilt, mixed with a bit of chagrin. "You know your father. When he gets something into his head . . ."

Tess noticed Grant and Hunter were quietly putting away the devices and the laptops.

"We really need to be going," Grant said, closing the heavy case with finality. "Don't we, Hunter? But it was a pleasure meeting you both."

"That would probably be best," Indigo said. "We've come a long way to spend time with our daughter. You understand, of course."

"Of course!" Jane piped up. She enveloped Tess in a hug. "Check your text messages," she whispered in her ear. And then louder: "Tess, I'll be in touch tomorrow. You three have a great reunion tonight."

Wyatt, too, was bundling up.

"I'll walk you out," Tess said, under her breath.

"So nice to see you again, Mr. and Mrs. Bell," Wyatt said.

"Nice to see you, son," Indigo said.

Tess stepped out into the cold with Wyatt, not bothering to put on any wrap. The cold felt good on her skin. They walked halfway down the driveway, and Wyatt stopped.

"I really don't like the idea of leaving you here," he said. "I get it, I can't stay here with you, and you can't come home with me, not with your parents bursting in like that. Plus, you probably don't want them here by themselves, after . . . you know."

"I know," Tess said. "But I'm not sure what else I can do. They're here, they're tired from the journey. What, am I going to get them a room at Harrison's House? I mean, I could, but they'd never go. It's just not feasible. We have to stay here."

"Why did they come so abruptly, do you think? Isn't that weird?"

"Very weird," Tess said, looking back up toward the house. "I guess I'll find out."

"I'll keep Storm at my house for the night," Wyatt said. "Unless you want him here with you."

Tess thought about that for a moment. On one hand, she'd love the big wall of protection Storm provided her, given all that had transpired in the house that night. But on the other . . . her parents. It might be too much with the dog, too.

"You keep him for the night," Tess said. "That will give you an excuse to come back here in the morning."

Wyatt put his arms around her and drew her close. "I really hate leaving you."

"I hate it, too."

Wyatt kissed her quickly—like they were teenagers under parental supervision—and sighed. "Will you text me later, when you're in bed? I want to know everything is okay. After what happened here tonight . . ."

"I know. But now that my parents are here, I think it will be okay. I'll shut myself up in my room and hang on until morning."

"Okay," Wyatt said. "I still wish you were coming with me."

"Me too," she said.

Back inside, she found her mother sitting at the kitchen table with a glass of wine. Tess thought she looked so very tired.

Tess poured herself a glass of wine and joined her.

"Mom, what is this all about?" she asked, settling into her chair. "Why would you rush back here without even telling me you were coming?"

Jill had that same guilty look on her face.

"Your father needed to see those paintings for himself," she said. "You know how he gets."

"Is he . . . ?" Tess asked.

"Yes, he went to open the wall safe," Jill said. "I waited here for you."

Tess pushed her chair away from the table and, along with her mother, hurried down the hallway toward the drawing room. She couldn't help but notice it felt so different than it had just an hour earlier. No presence hung in the air. No spirits were floating in the ether. It made Tess wonder if all of it wasn't just a product of the spectacle of it all—the electronic devices, the ghost-o-meters, the recordings stirring up—what? Imagination?

But then, she knew it hadn't been some kind of hysterical reaction. Some kind of trick. She had felt what she'd felt. Seen what she had seen. Heard the ghastly things she had heard. She had fainted, and it was all captured on Grant's various electronic devices.

In the drawing room, she saw her father had the safe open and was taking the paintings out of it, one by one.

He seemed determined, but more than that, almost manic to get them out of the safe.

"Just as I thought, just as I thought," Indigo murmured to himself.

"Dad?" Tess said.

Indigo whipped his head around, startled, as though he didn't imagine she would be there. "Honey, I'm just taking a better look at these."

"But why? Why come all of this way? You and Mom never come back to Wharton in the winter anymore. I sent you the photos, didn't I?"

But Indigo was busy lining up the paintings in order, end to end. When they were all out of the safe, leaning against the wall, he took a deep breath and stepped closer to get a better look.

"Dad, what—"

But Jill's hand on Tess's arm told her to stop talking. Tess got it, then, or thought she did. This was about Indigo, seeing his father's paintings for the first time. If anything could pry him away from his golf clubs, their cabin cruiser, and the swanky country club in Florida, it would be this. She should be quiet and let him experience it.

Jill slipped an arm around Tess's waist and pulled her close. Tess laid her head on her mother's shoulder—a much-needed respite after the day she'd just had—as both of them watched Indigo study his father's paintings.

He turned to them, then. "Now I need to go up into the studio," he said. He started out of the room when Tess took his arm.

"Dad, I've been trying to get ahold of you guys all day," she said. "Before you go upstairs into the studio, we have to talk. There are things you don't know."

This stopped Indigo short. He squinted at her. "What things?"

"Let's go back into the kitchen, and we'll talk. And then, after you know what's going on, we'll go up into the studio."

A flash of anger on Indigo's face just then. But it faded as quickly as it had come.

"Indy," Jill said. "Let's hear Tess out. She's the one who has been here, after all. She's done all the heavy lifting in regard to the paintings and opening up the studio and all of that. Here—" she said, bending down and picking up one of the paintings, "let's put these back in the safe and go on into the kitchen with Tess. Then we'll go up and see the studio before hitting the hay. I'm exhausted, and I'm sure you are, too. Okay?"

Indigo looked from one to the other, a small grin appearing on his face. "A man knows when he is outnumbered," he said. He helped Jill put the paintings back into the wall safe and shut it tight. "I could do with another Scotch anyway."

Back in the kitchen, her parents settled into the armchairs by the fire as Tess perched on the footstool between them.

"Dad, remember the other day when I asked if this house was haunted?" Tess began.

Indigo shooed the comment away with a swipe of his hand. "Not that again," he said. "I grew up in this house."

She looked to her mother for support, but Jill just shrugged. "I'm with your dad on this one, Tess," she said. "All the years we've been coming here for vacations—our whole marriage!—there's never been a single thing that went bump in the night."

"Well, there is now," Tess said, with a note of finality. "It started even before I opened up the studio. And tonight—"

Indigo held up his hand to stop her words. "Tess, forgive me. But your mother and I are exhausted. I'm going up to take my first look into my father's studio in decades, and then we're going to bed."

"But, Dad, there's something you need to know about the studio—"

Again he stopped her words. "Not now, Tess."

He pushed himself up from his chair and held a hand out to Jill. She took it, and they headed up the back stairs. Tess followed.

Indigo hurried down the hall but stopped short before going through the studio doorway. Tess watched as her mother put a hand on her husband's back and he turned to her, enveloping her into a hug. The sweetness of the gesture brought tears to Tess's eyes. She had never seen an ounce of vulnerability in her father. He had always been such a tower of strength, a man who radiated confidence. She wasn't sure if this was a welcome sight or not.

Then he stepped over the threshold. Jill and Tess followed.

Indigo Bell held his breath as he gazed upon his father's studio. To Tess, it seemed as though the room were holding its breath, too. He walked slowly to the table, his footsteps reverberating throughout the space. He ran his hand along the whole length of it.

"He used to let us play under here while he was working," Indigo said. "Grey and me."

But then his eyes strayed to the reddish slash on the wall, and he turned to Tess, his brow furrowed. "What's that?"

"That's what I've been trying to tell you, Dad," Tess said. "I wanted to say this gently, but you're forcing me to blurt it out by stopping me from talking all the time. This studio is a crime scene. Or was."

Indio turned around slowly, his mouth agape. "What do you mean, a crime scene?"

"Come on," Tess said, leading her father to the bathroom. They peered into it. "This is where I found the paintings," she said. "And all of this? The splatters on the walls and the floor and in the tub and even on those rags? That's blood, Dad. Initially, I thought it was paint, but when the police came—"

Indigo whipped his head around. "Police? Why on earth—"

"If you'd just listen to me, I'd tell you," Tess said, the age-old communication problems she had always had with her father bubbling to the surface once again. Some things never changed, even though she was a grown woman with an adult son of her own. "That's the problem. You never listen. But this time, I've got something to say, and you need to hear it."

"Okay, darling. I'm sorry. Go on, please."

"Wyatt and I were out walking the dogs, and as we came up the road, I saw that the lights were on in the studio. I hadn't left them on. I saw, we saw, a figure in the window."

Indigo furrowed his brow and caught his wife's eye. Jill put a protective hand on Tess's arm. "Thank God you weren't in the house."

"Jim saw the person in the window, too. In fact, he called me before we even got to the house to ask if I had a houseguest, because he could clearly see someone moving around in the studio. If I hadn't called the police, he would have."

Indigo ran a hand through his hair. "This is what I was afraid of," he said.

Tess shook her head. "No, Dad. The police came right away but couldn't find any evidence of a break-in. And they didn't find a person, either."

"So, you thought you saw someone," Indigo said. "But it turned out to be nothing?"

"Not exactly nothing. No, they didn't find an intruder, but when the police were searching the house and the studio, they found this."

She waved her hand at the stains. "They did some testing. It's dried blood."

Indigo shook his head, slowly. "No, no, no," he whispered. "It can't be."

"That's what the police believe," Tess said. "I couldn't even spend the night here last night. A forensics team was here."

"I had a bad feeling about this, and I should've listened to it," Indigo said. "You have no idea what you have unearthed."

Tess crossed her arms. "Well, I think I have some idea," she said. "For one thing, the paintings show an obsession with a woman here in Wharton. They're really disturbing, if you didn't notice it. Sebastian was stalking her, or at least that's what the paintings depicted. He stood outside of her house and painted what he saw! He followed her down the street and painted that, too! And then the portrait. Did you notice the look on her face? It was like she was almost afraid. That, coupled with the blood—it looks really bad, Dad. It's like Sebastian Bell was a stalker, obsessed with this woman. We know who she was! Daisy Erickson! And she disappeared, so he might have been the one who killed her. This might be her blood all over this studio. It's like those paintings were his confession."

Indigo Bell's face was ashen, as if his daughter's words had sucked the blood right out of him. Tears welled up in his eyes. He brushed back a strand of his white hair and sighed.

"My father wasn't the one who painted those paintings," he said, his voice soft. Defeated. Deflated. "It was Grey."

CHAPTER THIRTY-EIGHT

Tess just stood there in stunned silence.

"When you told your mom and me that you had found the paintings, I was overjoyed, but at the same time, I had my suspicions," Indigo said.

"You did?" Tess asked.

"Indeed," he said. "You never knew my father, of course, so you couldn't have known how in love he was with his own work. The ego on that man . . ."

Tess knew something about fathers with enormous egos.

"I held open the possibility that he was preparing for an opening where he would display those new works, but the idea that my mother would've shut those paintings away, kept them from the world after he died, just didn't ring true," Indigo said. "Remember, it wasn't just art. It was income for our family."

Tess nodded. "That never occurred to me."

"Oh yes," Indigo continued. "And when she started the foundation, she certainly would've sold those paintings to help fund it. Can you imagine what the last-ever works by Sebastian Bell would be worth?"

"That did occur to me," Tess said.

"I was holding out hope . . . until I got a look at the photos you sent. Then, I knew."

"How did you know?"

"Daisy, for one," Indigo said. "My father didn't like her. She and Grey had been sweethearts since they were children. They were one of those couples. Destined to be together. But when she married that odious Frank Erickson, Sebastian wrote her off. My mother did, too. They were furious. And Grey was heartbroken."

"So, he wouldn't have painted her portrait?"

"Dear God, no," Indigo said. "He never painted portraits, much less of someone he despised. Don't you see—all of his depictions of people are captured from the side, or from the back. He never painted a traditional portrait in his life."

Tess thought back to all the paintings by Sebastian Bell that she had seen—she knew every one. Indigo was right. There were no traditional portraits.

"I never knew Grey was a painter," Tess said.

"He was. Quite a good one, as you saw. His style was much like my father's, but darker. Much darker. But then again, that was Grey. He was always brooding."

Tess thought about the obsession the paintings implied. "Grey was the one obsessed with Daisy?" she said.

And as soon as she got the words out, they made perfect sense to her. Of course he was. She had married another man. That alone could turn love into obsession. But to know she was desperately unhappy? That would stoke the fire even more.

Of course a spurned lover would have been the one peering into her windows and following her down the street. Not his father. The very thought of it being Sebastian Bell sounded ridiculous to Tess now.

"So, what happened here?" she pressed on. "Grandma closed off this studio. There's blood all over the place. Who died, Dad? Was Daisy murdered here? Who did it? And, Grey disappeared. Did they run away together or . . . I mean the blood suggests they didn't, right?"

Indigo let out a great sigh. "The truth is, honey, I don't know. I was away at college. You know Grey was a few years older than me. He went missing around the same time that my dad died. Your grandmother had already closed up the studio by the time I got home, and that was that."

"You didn't even—"

"Tess," her mother interjected. "You need to remember something. When Indy was away at school, his brother disappeared, and his father died. His whole world—our whole world, because I was a part of it by then—had been turned upside down. Serena was inconsolable. You can't imagine the grief in this house. I'm surprised all of that emotion isn't still here, filling up the cracks in the foundation and the holes in the ceiling."

Maybe it was, Tess thought. Maybe it was.

❦

Tess hurried downstairs to retrieve her parents' bags. They were exhausted by everything they had been through that day, the trip, the discovery of the studio, all of it. She wasn't going to press her father for more information before he got a good night's sleep.

While they were getting settled in their guest room, Tess made a tray with two snifters of cognac—her father's traditional nightcap—a pitcher of water and two glasses, and some chocolates. Back in their room, she found them both in bed, propped up against their pillows, a book in her mother's lap. Tess set the tray on their dresser's marble top and brought their glasses to their respective nightstands. Then she lit a fire in their fireplace.

"Darling, you're too good to us," Jill said, taking a sip of her cognac.

"A perfect innkeeper," Indigo said, smiling weakly. "You have found your calling."

Tess smiled at him. What a kind thing for him to say. But, then again, her parents, for all their faults and eccentricities, had always been supportive of anything she had ever wanted to do.

And in a way, she could understand Sebastian and Serena's disdain for Daisy when she had spurned their son, because she knew her own parents felt the same about Matt.

Curled up in bed in his (no doubt, designer) pajamas, Indigo looked small. Vulnerable. Not the giant of a man Tess had grown up with. She thought of Joe in his assisted-living apartment, having to sign in and out, and hoped it would be many years before her own parents needed that kind of care.

After hugging and kissing them both, Tess retreated to her room and started to shut her door, but then decided to leave it open a crack. Just in case her parents woke in the middle of the night and needed anything. She lit a fire, brushed her teeth, washed the day off her face, and put on her pajamas. After slipping into bed, she grabbed her phone, which she had set on her nightstand earlier with the intention of plugging it in for the night. When she glanced down at it, she saw she had two messages.

One was from Wyatt. *Good night. I hope you can get some sleep, considering. If you need anything, if anything happens in the middle of the night, any scratching or . . . whatever, call me. I'm leaving my phone by my bed. Otherwise, I'll see you in the morning with this guy.* He attached a photo of Storm sleeping on Wyatt's bed.

The other was from Jane. *Hey, I didn't want to say this in front of your parents, but did you notice how the energy changed when they came into the house? It all just shifted. I don't think you're going to have any trouble with the spirits tonight. If you do, call me. I'm keeping my phone by the bed.* Tess smiled. Both of them, so concerned. *But those spirits aren't gone. I'll come over tomorrow, and we'll try to get some answers.*

That had to be good enough for now. After everything that had happened that day, she was exhausted. Ghosts or no ghosts, she had to get some sleep. Tess plugged her phone into the charger and turned out the light. She drifted off, watching the flames in the fireplace dance and sway, comforted her parents were right down the hall.

But her dreams were sinister and foreboding. It was as though the world had become one of those paintings, with dark swirls and eddies in the sky. She felt a sort of manic obsession, a frantic need, a hunger. So she walked the streets of Wharton, in search of it.

Tess jolted awake, her sheets damp with sweat. The fire was out. She glanced at the clock—5:00 a.m. She groaned. Just enough sleep to be fully awake hours before she really had to get up.

She lay there for a few moments, eyes closed, trying to will herself back to sleep, when she heard her parents' voices.

"Come back to bed, Indy," her mother said, her voice a harsh whisper. "Before you wake Tess."

"No," her father said, "I have to do this. Now."

Tess pushed back the covers and slipped out of bed. She walked into the hallway, and somehow she just knew she would find them in the studio.

She poked her head in and saw her mother at the door to the little bathroom.

"Mom?" Tess said. "What's going on?"

Jill turned around and pleaded with her daughter with her eyes. "He's in there cleaning."

Tess rushed across the studio and into the bathroom, where she found her father holding a bucket of soapy water and a sponge.

"I need to get this blood off the walls, girls," he said. "We can't have that here."

"Dad? Come on now. You're not going to get it cleaned up after all of this time. We'll have to paint over it."

He held the sponge over the bucket and squeezed it. The soapy water dripped back down into the bucket from where it had come.

"Don't you see? This is a bloodbath. Get it? A bathroom. Covered in blood. A bloodbath." He laughed, then. A terrible laugh. Just like she had heard in this room hours before.

That was when Tess noticed his eyes. They had a wildness behind them, a quality that was definitely not of her cultured father.

Tess flipped on the light. "Dad!" she shouted. "Wake up!" She strode across the room and grabbed him by the arms. The bucket fell to the floor and spilled on its side.

He just kept laughing. It was as though he didn't hear her at all. Or wasn't there.

This was not her father.

Jill had followed Tess into the room and was standing there, wide eyed.

"Indigo!" she said, her voice harsh and low. "Indigo, my love."

Tess shook his arms. "Dad! Wake up!"

Indigo slumped to the floor, moaning. "No," he said, drawing the word out. "No, Daisy, no."

Tess grabbed her mother's hand. She had no idea what else to do.

Indigo cleared his throat and ran a hand through his hair. He shook his head and pushed himself up to a sitting position. Whatever had taken ahold of him was gone. He looked around the room. "What in the devil is going on?" he asked.

Tess helped him to his feet.

"You were sleepwalking," Jill said. "Now, let's get you out of these wet pajamas. Then you can curl back down into bed." She caught Tess's eye as she threaded her arm through his and walked with him out of the room.

"That's the damnedest thing," Indigo muttered.

There would be no more sleep for Tess, she was certain, so she stepped into a hot shower and let the water rush over her for a long time. She didn't know what to make of her father's sleepwalking. Was it the beginning of dementia, like Joe's nightly episodes signified? Or was it something else? Tess's own dreams had been disturbing, to say the least, ever since she had come back to this house. Maybe that was what was going on with her father as well.

Or maybe it was something more sinister. Something inside that room, taking hold of him. Compelling him to clean the mess it had left behind.

❧

Dressed in a comfy sweater and jeans, Tess padded down to the kitchen, lit a fire, and brewed a pot of coffee. She sat at the table with a steaming cup and watched the sun rise over the lake. It was just as spectacular as the sunsets in Wharton, but she couldn't say she had seen it rise very often over the years.

When she heard her parents scuffing about upstairs, she started prepping breakfast. She knew her dad always loved pancakes, but not the traditional fluffy kind. He loved thin pancakes that were more akin to French crepes. She mixed up the simple batter for those—one cup flour, two eggs, one and a half cups milk, a pinch of salt, and a quarter cup of sugar—and let it set. She used that same batter to make oven pancakes in muffin tins—another good breakfast option for her guests, she thought. She hunted for some breakfast sausage in the freezer and put it in a pan to steam, then whisked some eggs.

They were coming down the back stairs as she was frying the first of the pancakes.

"What is all this?" Indigo said, a broad smile on his face.

"I thought you could use a nice hot breakfast after the day you had yesterday," Tess said.

"Honey, you didn't have to do this . . . but I'll take it!" Jill said as she poured cups of coffee for Indigo and herself.

Tess put a platter piled high with pancakes, eggs, and sausage on the table, and they all dug in. As they were chattering away, Tess was biding her time. She hated to break this happy mood, but if she was going to get any more answers out of her father, it was now or never.

"I know you don't believe any of this, but I've been having a problem in this house with, well I know it's going to sound silly to you, but—a haunting," she began.

"Oh, honey, not this again," Indigo said.

"No, Dad. You have to hear me out. I'm not going to be able to open this place until we get it resolved. That's what everyone was doing here last night."

"Ghost hunting?" Jill asked, an amused look on her face. She and Indigo shared a grin.

"You wouldn't laugh if you had been here," Tess said, as she eyed the door. Jane and Wyatt were standing outside of it. "I knew I wouldn't get very far with this without proof, so I called some people over to show you."

Tess ushered them in, "good mornings" were said all around, cups of coffee poured, and Jane slid her laptop out of its case and opened it.

And so, in the bright light of day, as the sun streamed into the kitchen at La Belle Vie, they watched the video of what had happened in the studio the night before.

Tess's parents were stunned into open-mouthed silence.

"There has to be some kind of reasonable explanation . . ." Jill said.

But Indigo was shaking his head.

"That song," he said, his eyes darting back and forth, as if he were searching his memory. "Grey used to sing it all the time. To Daisy."

A shiver shot through Tess, and she and Wyatt exchanged a glance. But Jane just gave a knowing smile.

"That does not surprise me," she said. "You may know I'm a little . . . sensitive. A feeling overtook me last night that I couldn't shake. I've been turning it over in my mind. And I'm pretty sure that whatever happened in the studio all of those years ago happened between Grey and Daisy."

She turned to Indigo. "Can you tell us everything you remember from that time? It would be a great help."

Indigo raised his coffee cup to his lips and eyed his wife over the rim. She nodded. "It's time, Indy."

Time? So, they did know something they weren't sharing.

Tess's father took a deep breath and then began to speak.

"Somewhere, buried down deep, I had the idea that it would turn out this way. That's why I didn't stop you from opening up the studio. I had the feeling the truth might be lurking in there, dormant, silent after year upon year."

He took a sip of his coffee, pausing for effect.

"During the summer of my junior year of college, I had an internship at the Minneapolis Institute of Art. I knew I couldn't be a great artist like my father, but I loved it all the same, and I thought learning the business of art, how to run a museum and a collection, would let me be part of his world in a way that he needed. I was right about that, by the way. In any case, one afternoon, the director of the museum came and found me to tell me I had a phone call.

"It was my mother. The great Sebastian Bell was dead. He died of a heart attack, she said, and I needed to come home quickly. Of course, I dropped everything and rushed to my mother's side. When I got here to La Belle Vie, I found my mother alone and grieving and the studio boarded up. The whole house was shrouded in black cloth.

"My father had already been cremated, per his wishes—or so she told me—and she gave me strict orders to never enter the studio again. It was to remain as it was when he took his last breath, at the easel, forever, throughout time.

"What I didn't know then was, Grey had gone missing. Of course, I asked her where he was, why he wasn't with us, and she said he had been gone for days. Daisy, too. She speculated they had run off together.

"It didn't make any sense to me. So, I asked around. His friends, her friends. Nobody had seen them. Nobody knew anything. I even talked to Frank, whom I had always hated, but I have to admit feeling a little sorry for the man. His wife had apparently run off with my brother, leaving two young children for him to raise alone."

Indigo took another sip of his coffee.

"After my father's funeral—hundreds of people attended from all over the world—I went back to my internship in the Twin Cities. I didn't know what else to do. My mother was grieving, but she pushed me away. She needed time to herself, she said. I should go and finish my education, she said. And then I could come home and take up the business of tending to my father's legacy. It was in my hands now.

"And so, I did. I graduated from school with degrees in art history and business, and you know the rest. We never heard from Grey again, despite looking for him for years. Frank moved from Wharton, and we never saw him or Daisy's children again, either. Your mother and I got married, you came along, and I spent the rest of my life running the foundation. Now Eli is set to take it over."

"But that's not all there is to the story. Isn't that right?" Jane asked.

Indigo let out a dejected, defeated sigh. "No," he said. "That's not the whole story. Because, you see, I couldn't just let it go. I couldn't just accept what my mother had told me. Grey, suddenly disappearing without a trace? It was preposterous. If he and Daisy had run away together, he would've contacted me. Would've told our mother. And more than that. The more I thought about it, the more I realized they didn't even need to run away to be together. My father, with all of his power and influence, could have forced Frank out of the picture. A million dollars to walk away? Frank would've taken it in a heartbeat.

"But the bigger thing that kept nagging at me about the whole thing was—Daisy." Indigo shook his head. "She loved those kids. No matter how much she loved my brother, she loved her children more. She would not have left the kids. Period."

Tess felt a whoosh of cold waft over her, even there, in front of the fire. She caught Jane's eye. Jane felt it, too.

"And, there's something else. Something worse. When Daisy and Grey broke up before she married Frank, it was for a good reason. A very good reason."

Wyatt, Tess, and Jane were all leaning forward, hanging on Indigo's every word.

"What reason?" Tess whispered.

Indigo closed his eyes for a moment. "It was the madness, my dear."

CHAPTER THIRTY-NINE

It was like his words had sucked the oxygen from the room. Nobody said a word. Nobody even breathed. Jill put a hand over her husband's.

"It's okay, honey. It's time they knew."

Indigo turned to his daughter. "When you told me you had found some finished paintings in the studio, as I said last night, I knew they couldn't have been my father's. My mother never would've kept them from the world, and neither would he. I highly suspected they were Grey's, and one look at them told me I was right. You can see the desperation running through them.

"He was born that way, with that undercurrent. Nowadays, we have other names for mental illness, other forms, medication that can help people suffering from it. But . . . to tell you all the truth, I don't think it was about that. I think it was something else. Something deep and primal that ran through Grey. Something evil that slipped through the veil and into him, somehow."

"It was always there?" Tess shook her head. "But from what you've told me, you had an idyllic childhood here in Wharton."

Indigo nodded. "That's right, honey. In a sense we did. But if there was anyone who experienced childhood trauma in this house, it was me."

Tess gasped aloud. Indigo patted her hand. "It's okay. It was a long time ago. But I'm not talking about trauma at the hands of my parents.

They were wonderful, loving as could be. It was Grey. It was always Grey. Some days, he would be my best friend, and we would have endless adventures together on the lakeshore and in the woods around town.

"But other days . . . it was like he was a different person. Angry. Hostile. Cruel, not only to me, but to animals. To other people. He would sneak out of the house at night and roam the streets alone. My parents were beside themselves, wondering what he was doing out there, in the dead of night.

"I started calling him Dr. Jekyll and Mr. Hyde. It was almost as if he would really change into another person. An evil person. Morph, like a werewolf during a full moon. When he was in one of his 'episodes,' as my mother called them, even his voice wasn't his own. It was awful and almost demonic sounding."

Tess and Wyatt exchanged a glance. He took her hand. She knew he was thinking the same thing she was. That was the voice they had heard in the studio the night before.

"I half expected to wake up one morning to hear he had killed someone the night before. It got that bad. He'd fly into these incomprehensible rages. With me, with our parents, even with Daisy. Although, I have to say, when they were together, she had a calming effect on him. She loved him deeply, and when he was with her, he was happy. Himself. His true self. Not the shadow-self he became. Daisy was the antidote to whatever was poisoning his soul.

"But he couldn't sustain it, the happy Grey. Hyde always found a way out. The night she left him, he had come out. It had been a long time since any of us had seen Hyde, but he really frightened Daisy with his rage. He started to strangle her, and I believe he would've killed her if my mother hadn't intervened. Little woman that she was, she dragged him off her so Daisy could get away. She ran from this house and, in a sense, right into the arms of Frank Erickson. And there she stayed."

"What did Grey do then?" Tess asked.

"It wasn't good," Indigo said. "Not good at all. You mentioned the word *obsession*, and that's exactly what it was. He would sneak out at night, and I knew he was going to look for her. I followed him more than once, terrified of what he'd do. It was exhausting for all of us, to tell you the truth. When I got accepted to the university, I was hesitant to go, but my parents, my mother especially, pushed me. They wanted me to get on with a normal life. To find happiness."

Tess looked at her father with new eyes. What a nightmare he had lived through. "You never really believed Grey and Daisy ran away together," she said.

"That was the official story my mother spread around town, the rumor," Indigo said. "But no. I never believed it. I have come to believe he killed her. And then, perhaps, himself."

"Oh, Dad, I'm so sorry," Tess said. "I stirred up all of this stuff. I wish I had never opened that door."

"No, darling," he said. "It's not your fault. Families can try to bury secrets. But in the end, truth scratches its way out of the deepest, darkest of holes. And we may never know what really happened."

"I may know of a way," Jane said, producing a small silver box from her bag.

The box was covered with curlicues and magical symbols, like something the Wizard of Oz would have on his nightstand. She opened it to reveal a large purple crystal on a long silver chain. She held it up, and the crystal caught the sunlight and reflected purple splashes of color all over the room.

"It's a pendulum," she said. "We didn't have a chance to use it last night. It's another way to communicate with the other side. Grant can have his recorders and clicking meters, but this can give us some direct answers without all of that hoopla. I'm fairly certain that the spirits haunting this house are the ones that experienced trauma—and bloodshed—in the studio. They're the only ones who really know what happened there. Why don't we just ask them?"

They made a plan to meet back at La Belle Vie when the sun went down, which was around four o'clock on these December evenings.

In the meantime, Tess and Wyatt went for a long walk with the dogs—they had made the decision to leave Storm at Wyatt's house until this pendulum business was finished—and Indigo and Jill retreated to their room to rest. Tess could sense the whole ordeal had taken a toll on her father. The coming night would only add to it.

As the four-o'clock hour neared, they gathered in the kitchen. Indigo was dressed in a black turtleneck and tan slacks, and looked much refreshed from his afternoon respite. Jill was wearing a deep-purple dress with silver chains wound around her elegant neck.

"We didn't know how to dress for a haunting," she said, shrugging.

"You look great, guys," Tess said, giving them each a kiss on the cheek.

"I still think this is all rubbish," Indigo said, in a huff.

"Oh, Indy, have an open mind," Jill said. "You never know."

He took her hand and kissed it. "For you, anything."

As they settled down at the kitchen table, Jill turned to Tess. "Tell us about Wyatt," she said. "It seems to us that there's more going on than just friendship between you two."

Tess smiled. "There is," she said. "I'm not sure what it is yet, but it's headed somewhere."

"You two seem like an old married couple already," Indigo piped up. Funny, Tess thought. That was just what Jane had said a few days earlier.

"I approve," Indigo went on. "He's a solid person. Kind. Caring. Like his parents. And grandparents."

"We're glad you've found someone, honey," Jill said, taking her daughter's hand in her own. "You deserve all the happiness this world has to offer. Of course, nobody is good enough for our daughter, but he'll do in a pinch." Her eyes twinkled.

Soon enough, Jane was knocking on the door, followed by Wyatt. It was time.

⁂

The group assembled in the studio and stood in a circle. Jane had brought sage packets and candles, and they lit up the room with both the soft glow of their flames and the scent that wafted through the air.

She was holding the pendulum by its chain, which was draped over one outstretched hand.

"We use this to ask yes-or-no questions of the spirits," Jane explained. "I'll give instruction, ask some questions, and we'll see how it goes. No guarantees." She closed her eyes and took a deep breath, held it for a moment, and let it out. "Let's get centered. Breathe in and out, in and out."

Wyatt squeezed one of Tess's hands; her mother squeezed the other.

"Let's begin," Jane said to the group. And then: "To the spirits who are with us. We are here to talk with you. We come with pure intention and love in our hearts. We know you are restless. We can help you go home, if you'll let us."

Tess felt a whoosh of cold waft through the room. She caught Wyatt's eye. He felt it, too.

"You have gone through an awful lot of trouble and fuss to communicate with us," Jane went on. "Why not make it easy? We don't need all of the drama. Neither do you."

Tess was slightly amused by this. Jane was talking to supposed spirits as though they were just people, standing before them. Maybe, in a way, they were.

"I'm going to ask questions. Others may have questions. I want you to swing the pendulum to the left for yes. To the right for no. In between questions, I'll ask you to stop the pendulum from swinging.

That way there won't be momentum, and we won't get your answers wrong." She dangled the pendulum from her hand. It was still.

"My first question is: Do you understand the rules of this game?"

Tess held her breath and watched the pendulum swing to the left. Her mother squeezed her hand.

"Stop," Jane said.

The pendulum stopped. *To swing it is one thing,* Tess thought. Jane could do that almost imperceptibly with her own hand movement. But stopping it midswing like that? Tess didn't see how that could be done by sleight of hand.

"Holy God," Indigo whispered.

"Shh," Jill said.

"Is Daisy here with us tonight?"

It swung left.

"Hello, Daisy," Jane said. "Please stop the pendulum. Is Grey here tonight?"

It stayed still for a moment, then swung left.

Indigo looked around. "Brother?"

"Hello, Grey," Jane said. "Please stop the pendulum."

It stopped.

"Did you paint the paintings Amethyst found?"

Left. Yes.

"Do you want us to know what happened here in the studio?"

The pendulum swung so hard to the left, it flew out of Jane's hand and hit Indigo in the chest. He caught it and handed it back to her. She took another cleansing breath and let the pendulum dangle once again.

"I'm just going to come out and ask the obvious question," Jane said. "No beating around the bush. We all have things to do, and so, I imagine, do you. Did Grey and Daisy die in this room?"

The pendulum swung right. No.

"Did Grey die in this room?"

Right. No.

"Did Daisy die in this room?"

Left. Yes.

"Did Grey kill Daisy?"

The pendulum swung right.

Tess's eyes grew wide. She hadn't been expecting that answer.

Jane looked from one to another of the group, not quite knowing what to ask next. Apparently she hadn't expected that answer, either.

Tess raised a hand. "I have a question," she whispered. Jane nodded. "Was Daisy trapped somewhere, like the bathroom, and trying to get out?" She was thinking of the scratching noise.

Left swing. Stop.

"Was Daisy hiding?"

Left swing. Stop.

"Was Daisy hiding from Grey?"

Right swing. Stop.

Jane looked to the group again. Indigo cleared his voice and spoke up. "Was Daisy hiding from Mr. Hyde?"

The pendulum was still for a moment. And then, left swing. Yes.

Indigo took a deep breath and locked eyes with his wife. "Did Mr. Hyde kill Daisy?"

And with that, the pendulum swung so furiously in a circle that it shot from Jane's hand and hit one of the windows, shattering it. But the pendulum itself did not break.

Indigo buried his face in his hands and let out a sob. Jill put a hand on his back.

"Is this what you wanted us to know?" Jane asked. "Is it the reason for the haunting?"

Left swing, then right swing, then stop.

"Yes and no?" Jane asked.

Left swing. Stop.

"There's more?"

Left swing. Stop.

All at once, Tess knew what it might be. Or at least, a part of it.

"Daisy, do you want us to find your children? Do you want them to know you didn't abandon them?"

All at once, a great wail pierced the quiet of the room, a wail of grief and anguish, of frustration and heartbreak. It was like the wailing of a harpy on a dark night, the very sound of death and destruction and despair. It reverberated through the room and rang in Tess's ears—but nobody else seemed to hear it. Once again, she alone was the recipient.

"I will find your children, Daisy," Tess said. And the wailing stopped.

"I wish we could ask more than yes-or-no questions," Tess whispered to Wyatt.

Jane regrouped, recentered herself, and continued. "Did Mr. Hyde kill himself?"

Right swing. Stop.

"Did Grey kill Mr. Hyde?" Indigo piped up.

Right swing. Stop.

Indigo took a deep breath. "Did Sebastian Bell kill Grey and Mr. Hyde?"

Tess felt decades of pent-up anger and sadness and fury and madness coalesce in the middle of the room, as though it were a living, breathing monster. With that, every window in the studio shattered.

CHAPTER FORTY

Jill enveloped her husband in a hug as Indigo wept softly on her shoulder. Tess didn't know quite what to do.

Indigo produced a handkerchief from his pocket and dabbed at his eyes. "I have long suspected it," he said, his voice torn to shreds. "I knew Grey didn't disappear. It's what we told the world. I have held those words in the darkest part of my heart for decades, not wanting to utter them aloud. The secrecy, the shutting up of the room. It never made sense, but I just went along with my mother. I am all but sure she came upon it and covered it all up somehow."

"You don't have to be 'all but sure' anymore," Jane said, her voice soft and soothing. "They're right here. Let's just ask."

They assembled in their circle once again. This time, Indigo took the lead.

"Grey, my brother, did Father come upon Mr. Hyde in a rage?"

Left swing. Stop.

"Had Mr. Hyde already killed Daisy?"

Left swing. Stop.

"Did he kill Daisy because she wouldn't leave her children?"

Left swing. Stop.

"Did Mr. Hyde attack Father?"

The pendulum was still. And then, left swing. Stop.

Indigo turned his gaze to his wife. "Let's try to work this out," he said to her, and then to the rest of the group: "Sebastian walked in on Grey, who had killed Daisy in a rage. Grey attacked Sebastian. But how . . ."

"I see what you're getting at," Tess said. "How did it go from that to your father killing Grey and Mr. Hyde?"

Jane looked to the group. "Does anyone have any more questions? Can you think of—"

Indigo put up his hand. "God, help me. I have one other question. It is the thing that has kept me up at night, slithered into my brain, and nearly driven me mad all of these years."

Jane nodded and held the pendulum aloft.

"Where are your bodies?"

Tess's heart was racing; the blood drained from her face. Wyatt's hand felt clammy in hers.

"I know it isn't a yes-or-no question, but I don't know how else to say it," Indigo said, his eyes brimming with tears.

The pendulum swung in a circle.

"Are they in the house?"

Right swing. Stop.

"Buried?"

Right swing. Stop.

All at once, a feeling came over Tess. Somehow, she knew. She raised her hand, as if asking for permission to speak. Jane nodded.

"Are they over the cliff on the road leading to Salmon Bay?"

Left swing. Jane dropped the pendulum as though it were on fire.

"Wait a minute," Tess said. "That doesn't make sense. Grey had to have painted at least one of the paintings—the cliff—after the murder."

❧

The next few days were a flurry of activity. Nick reported in with the news that the blood in the studio was from two people, one related to

Tess—she had given a blood sample for comparison—and one who wasn't. Grey and Daisy.

Tess asked Nick to start looking for Daisy's children. She had made a promise, and she intended to keep it. Her own internet searches were turning up nothing, but Nick was confident in his search. Tess asked if she could be the one to tell them the news.

Tess had also told the chief about the ghost hunting, and the pendulum session, and asked if he would do a search of the shoreline beneath the cliff, to see what it might turn up. Accustomed to strange and otherworldly police requests in Wharton, he did just that. The bones he found were being analyzed. But Tess had no doubt who they'd turn out to be.

It didn't tell them how Grey died, what happened in that room, how Serena managed to cover it all up, or anything else about that horrible night. But it did give the Bell family some finality, some closure. And that was going to have to be good enough.

The days were altogether ordinary after that. No more scratching. No more hauntings. No more nightly disturbances. Tess and her mother decorated the house for the holidays, using old family heirlooms plus the new decorations Tess had bought during that ill-fated trip to Salmon Bay the night of the snowstorm, which seemed like a lifetime ago now.

Early in the afternoon on that Saturday, Tess was putting the finishing touches on one of the four Christmas trees they had decorated when a whoosh of cold passed through the room. But it wasn't a haunting this time. It was actual cold, from outside, when Eli came through the front door.

Later that day, the four of them, Tess and Eli, Indigo and Jill, bundled up and walked down to the lake for the Wharton Wonderland tree-lighting festival, Storm leading the way. They got out onto the frozen lake and saw it was filled with people—Simon and Jonathan from Harrison's House, Kate and Nick Stone, Beth St. John, the people from Superior Café, which was closed for the occasion, island families that Tess recognized but didn't quite know.

Grant waved at her from behind the ice bar, where he was pouring mulled wine and other festive drinks. Hunter was standing in front of the fire "bocking" dark beers, the ancient practice of plunging a hot poker into a beer and, for lack of a better term, caramelizing it. Eli noticed that and just had to try it out.

Artists and local merchants had set up tables where they were selling their wares—jewelry, pottery, textiles, macramé, even drawings. A massive grill stood onshore, where Jim was cooking brats and burgers. Someone had brought a huge popcorn machine and was serving up bags of freshly popped corn. A group of madrigal singers, dressed in period costume, sang Renaissance tunes, accompanied by a lute player.

Twinkling lights were everywhere, and a giant Christmas tree and a menorah stood at the center of it all.

The holidays had officially arrived in Wharton.

"This is delightful." Indigo beamed at Jill. "Why have we gone south, again?"

"So you can play golf every day," she said, squeezing his arm.

Wyatt joined them, and they let the three dogs run, playing on the lake together like puppies.

For Tess, these people and this place—life couldn't get any better.

Watching that scene, Tess thought about the morning after the pendulum session, when Wyatt had brought Storm back to the house.

She had opened the kitchen door, and the dog bounded in with a flourish, but not into Tess's waiting arms. He'd run straight for Indigo.

"Oh my!" Indigo said, as the dog jumped up and nuzzled his snout into the man's neck. "Hello there! How are you, my friend!"

As the dog wiggled and barked, Indigo turned to Tess. "We had a dog just like this when I was a child," he said. "A white shepherd. My dad used to walk with him all over town."

Tess's heart did a flip. Joe had said as much during their lunch, which now seemed like a lifetime ago.

"I'll never forget it," Indigo went on. "My mother used to say he was sent to protect me. And he did. He stood between me and Grey . . . and the monster within him . . . more times than I could count."

He scratched behind the dog's ears.

"It was the damnedest thing," Indigo continued. "The dog showed up at our back door during a snowstorm. Local legend had it that a white dog would appear to people in times of great distress. Like a guardian angel of sorts." He chuckled. "But, of course, that's just an old tale."

CHAPTER FORTY-ONE

La Belle Vie, 1970

Sebastian and Serena had been away in New York for an art opening and came home to what he could only describe as carnage. As soon as they walked into the house, he sensed it. So did Serena. Something was off. On instinct, he climbed the stairs to the studio.

And then, his world collapsed.

He saw his son, drenched in blood, smearing a bright-red stain onto the wall. Like a gash. Sebastian looked around in stunned silence for a moment. Utter disarray. Fresh canvases strewn about. He stepped into the bathroom and gasped aloud. It was covered in blood. A knife lay on the floor.

"I tried to wash it off the bathroom walls," Grey murmured. "It wouldn't come off. Permanently stained, I'm afraid."

Sebastian walked back into the main room. "Grey, what in the name of God happened here?"

"I don't know, Father," Grey said, his eyes pleading, imploring his father for answers he could not give. He shook his head. "I woke up and found those." He pointed to the stack of canvases. "And all of this." He gestured wildly around the room.

Sebastian Bell gazed at the canvases, the paintings his son had created. He'd had such hopes for the boy, who displayed a talent even greater than his own. But dread and horror overcame him when he realized what these paintings depicted. The obsession. Fear seemed woven into the images.

Daisy, that poor girl. The father could barely make himself utter the words to the son.

"Did you kill her?" It came out as a harsh whisper.

Grey collapsed onto the floor, overcome by his sobs. "I don't remember," he managed to squeak out.

"Where is her body?" Sebastian hissed.

Grey continued to sob, the wails of the damned.

But he didn't need to ask. The painting of the cliff told him all he needed to know. He grabbed his son by the collar and pulled him to his feet.

"Get yourself together," Sebastian growled at him. "We're going to fix this. As much as can be fixed."

He hurried his son down the stairs, catching his wife's eye as they went. She took a few steps toward them and opened her mouth to speak, but Sebastian shook his head. Their locked eyes spoke volumes to each other. Without even having to say it, somehow she knew. Her hands flew to her mouth as she watched them walk out the door.

As Sebastian drove toward the cliff, Grey seemed to slip into some sort of catatonia. He wouldn't respond to his father's questions. He just stared straight ahead, a slight smile on his face, a tear escaping from his eyes.

And then, they arrived.

Sebastian Bell stood on the cliff, just outside Wharton, his heart racing in his chest. He gazed over the side but saw nothing but the pounding waves. How could it have possibly come to this? That boy, his son, had been evil from the word go. He and Serena had both known that. Early on they didn't want to admit it, but as Grey grew into a young man, it simply became evident. An undercurrent, always thrumming, wanting to get out. Sometimes, horrible times, it did.

But this? A sense of utter dread overcame Sebastian. If his son could kill the one closest to him, his beloved Daisy, what next? Where would he stop? Would he stop?

But it wasn't his son. He saw that now. The boy's eyes were black as night.

"Is this the spot?" Sebastian asked.

A low growl escaped Grey's lips, then laughter. "She knew better than to leave me."

But the voice wasn't Grey's. It was the monster's. The side of Grey Sebastian's other son called Mr. Hyde. The demon that had plagued his family since the day Grey was born.

And all at once, something overcame Sebastian. He saw the years of covering up misdeeds and abuses and hurts. He saw his dear wife, Serena, crying in anguish night after night. He saw poor Indigo, afraid and cowering in the face of his brother's rage. And now this. Nothing was going to make this right again. Nothing was going to make his son right again. Was it even his son? Or was this a demon standing before him?

And so, before he could even think about it or consider the gravity of his actions, Sebastian summoned all the strength he had, ran at the monster as hard as he could, and pushed.

As his son flew over the cliff and hit the rocks below with a sound that pierced a father's heart, Sebastian's chest seized up, a pain worse than he'd ever endured. He turned his eyes toward the star-filled sky. Not the worst place to die. His boy had died there. And so many others.

But no. He didn't die there and then. He managed to drive back to town, back to La Belle Vie. He made it into the entryway before he fell to the ground.

Serena flew to his side. "Call James," he whispered, referring to the Bells' loyal handyman. "The cliff. He needs to hide the bodies."

Serena understood.

And then, he was gone.

After the ambulance arrived and took his shell away, and she had made the call to the handyman, Serena walked up to her husband's studio. A calm had overtaken her. Now it was about Sebastian's legacy and Indigo's future.

So much blood. It was then she noticed the canvases. One look at them told her all she needed to know. She gathered them up and stacked them in the bathroom—maybe she'd burn them at some other time. Maybe she'd keep them. But she knew one thing. They would never see the light of day. It was then she saw the scratch marks on the door, long scratches, deep in the wood—what had happened there? *Grey, what have you done?* It was almost as though he had imprisoned Daisy in this room. Was that what had happened when she and Sebastian were away?

Serena hurried out of the studio and shut the door behind her. She made a mental note to have the handyman seal it up entirely when he was finished with that other business. She didn't want to see the inside of that room ever again.

And the years wrapped themselves around that door, holding it tight, along with the terrible secret, and the demons, it contained. Until the time was right to unleash it.

The End.

ACKNOWLEDGMENTS

This book was written during the teeth of the pandemic, although I didn't set it in this new reality we're all dealing with. My editors and I thought everyone was pandemic weary, and when you're reading a novel for an escape, which many of my readers have told me they do with my books, you all didn't have to curl up with this story and find yourself caught up in this frightening and difficult time again. So I don't make any references to it, and my characters are not dealing with its aftermath. Maybe I'll do so in another book, sometime in the future.

If you're one of those people who reads the acknowledgments first—I have been known to do that—I'm not going to give away any spoilers, but the timeline in this book was a little difficult for me to get my head around. You'll see what I mean when you read it. So the first people I want to thank are my editors Alicia Clancy and Faith Black Ross. Like we laughed about, sometimes it takes a village to get the past and present lined up correctly. Thank you for making this book better, as you always do. I love working with you to make my books the best they can be.

To everyone at Lake Union, the copy editors, author relations manager Gabriella Dumpit, my publicist Ashley Vanicek: You all are the best. The Best. I am so lucky and grateful for you and all you do on my behalf.

And to my dear friend and agent Jennifer Weltz: I love you. I could go on and on, but that covers it.

BOOK CLUB QUESTIONS

1. What is it about Wharton that seems to nurture the otherworldly?

2. What did you think the scratching was when you first read about it?

3. Who, or what, do you believe was scratching at the walls, and why?

4. What was unleashed when Tess opened the door?

5. Why do you believe Serena shut up her husband's studio?

6. What is the significance of the white dog?

7. Do you believe the story about John Wharton? What do you think happened to the village? Was it ever there at all?

8. Indigo called Grey a Dr. Jekyll / Mr. Hyde. What do you believe?

9. What happened to Indigo in the studio?

10. What's going on with the road by the cliff just outside of Wharton?

ABOUT THE AUTHOR

Photo © 2020 Steve Burmeister

Wendy Webb is the #1 Amazon Charts and Indie bestselling, multiple award–winning author of seven novels of gothic suspense, including *The Keepers of Metsan Valo, The Haunting of Brynn Wilder, Daughters of the Lake, The Vanishing, The Fate of Mercy Alban, The Tale of Halcyon Crane,* and *The End of Temperance Dare,* which has been optioned for both film and television. Her books are sold worldwide and have been translated into more than ten languages. Dubbed "Queen of the Northern Gothic" by reviewers, Wendy sets her stories on the windswept, rocky shores of the Great Lakes. She lives in Minneapolis, where she is at work on her next novel when she's not walking a good dog along the parkway and lakes near her home. For more information visit her at www.wendykwebb.com.